the game plan

X's and O's
Book One

allie lasky

one

. . .

Miles

THERE'S a big red A scrawled on the top of my exam paper. *See me*, is written on the top of the page. Scowling, I stuff the booklet into my notebook. I did good. I know I did well. There's no need for the professor to summon me like an obstinate child.

I'm instantly hyperaware of everyone around me. Are they watching me? Did they see the note? I'm used to the stares—after all, I'm a big fucking dude—but they never get easier to deal with. At six-foot-six and well north of three hundred pounds, it's not easy for me to blend into the background. It works to my advantage on the football field when I'm facing down guys my size or even bigger. It's not so great in the rest of my everyday life.

The desk top cuts into my belly, pressing into me no matter how far back I push my chair. It's bad enough that I have to sit at the table and chair at the front of the room, away from the rest of the class. The flimsy little desks everyone else uses can't stand up to someone my size. It's a sad fact that what I'm revered for on the field is a detriment to my life everywhere else.

Professor Cassidy is a weedy, stunted man with thinning

hair and a paunch to his belly that tells me he spends more of his time behind a desk than in the gym. I tower a full head and shoulders above him, and I'm at least double his weight.

"So, how did you do it?" he asks without preamble.

"Excuse me?"

"Was it a crib sheet? Someone give you a copy of the test?"

I rise up to my full height. "Are you saying that I cheated?"

He crosses his arms and stands his ground, unintimidated. A lesser man would cower before me. He must have more of a spine than I thought. "Well, you didn't score ninety-four percent by yourself."

Clenching my hands around my backpack, I take in a slow, rumbly breath to gather myself before I start seeing red —or worse, acting on my frustration. Anger is a tool, one that doesn't serve me well. That wouldn't solve anything, only cause more problems. "Because there's no way I could manage it on my own."

"Come on. I know how it is with you football players. You take a class for an easy math credit. Someone helps you through it. Though usually you pick an Intro to Algebra class and not Statistics."

Anger courses through my veins, straight to the knot in the pit of my stomach. "I'm a math major."

Professor Cassidy snorts. "Right. The point stands, you didn't manage this on your own. Did you have an accomplice? Switch papers with someone else?"

"I'll take the damn test again right now," I tell him, full of bravado, adrenaline, and a fair bit of confidence in my abilities. I'm not usually so bold, and I would typically never speak to a professor in this way; but I know me, and I know what I'm capable of. I'm not a cheater. I'm not a quitter. I don't back down from a fight; I win them. "Give me a blank copy, I'll take it right now."

"I have a class in half an hour."

Steadily, I meet his eye. "Then I have twenty-nine minutes to answer as many questions as I can."

I haven't studied. I don't need to. I know the material backwards and forwards.

At least, I think I do.

Asshole. Pulling my phone out of my pocket, I send a quick message to the group chat.

"Put your phone away."

"I'm texting my teammates, so they know I'll be late for practice." Because a cheating allegation is way more important than being five minutes late to the weight room for an optional lift session. Coach takes academics very seriously.

Professor Cassidy sneers. "Because practice is so important."

"Actually, yeah, it is. It's the same reason we have homework. We work at it so we get better. We can't just walk out onto the field with no preparation. We have to study tape, and review plays, and lift heavy. It's all part of the job."

And it is a job. I'm very well aware of the target on my back. If I don't stay in shape, if I don't perform on the field every Saturday, they can replace me before I can so much as blink. There are a dozen guys on campus who would love to take my job, and hundreds across the country who can do what I do—and do it better. I've come by my starting position through grit and strength and a fair bit of sweat equity. I don't pretend I'm the best—but I'm good.

So I put in the work. I spend my hours in the gym and on the field. I do my homework. I show up to team events and contribute. It's a job, and instead of money, I get bruises and a heavily discounted college education.

Realistically, I'll never make it to the NFL. I won't ever be drafted. I'm good, but I'm nowhere near good enough. I picked Newton as much as they picked me. There's a reason I'm at an amazing university with only a second-tier football program. We're good. We're not great. We're not the kinds of guys who win championships.

But we're going to have fun trying.

The test is… not easy, per se, but not overly complicated. I didn't study nearly hard enough to have memorized every single test question. I make my way through the exam, answering the ones I can right away and coming back to the more complicated ones.

"Time," Professor Cassidy calls when I'm about halfway through the test.

Lumbering to my feet, I walk the paper over to him. He glances through it, flips back to the answer key, and then stares up at me.

"You did this just now?"

I cross my arms over my chest. "You were watching me."

"You have an aptitude for statistics."

Shrugging, I hitch my backpack over my shoulder. "I like math."

"You can go," he says as people start filing into the classroom. He doesn't apologize for the misunderstanding. He doesn't apologize for insulting me.

Seething, I cross campus in a rush. The guys are in the locker room, getting changed for a quick lift session. The good-natured chatter dies when I enter the room.

"Hey, what's with the murder face?" Barrett says, lacing up his shoes.

"Fuck you."

"So the meeting with your professor went well, then," Tucker concludes.

Halfheartedly, I throw my backpack at him. He laughs and catches it, then tosses it into my locker for me.

"Get dressed. We've been waiting for you."

All my life, I've wanted to play for Newton State College. My dad played football, and my mom was a tennis superstar; they met at an athletic department mixer their senior year.

Newton Athletics runs in my blood. I grew up coming to Newton football games and watching Newton tennis matches. Even as a little kid, I knew that one day I'd be walking across this quad and stepping out onto this field and studying in these hallowed halls. It's the only school I've ever wanted to attend.

I'm living my fucking dreams, and I'm making every moment count.

Coach gives us a side-eye for tardiness before he puts us to work. I lose myself in the routine of the workout, warm-ups, and lifting. This is what I'm good at. I can lift more than double my body weight. Today is a quick legs, back, and abs circuit. I know how to put in the work to get stronger, to stand up to the big fucking dudes across the field. This is what I'm good at.

After a quick shower and change, the guys and I head to the Athletic Student Center and the dining hall. We live in Athlete's Village, so while we have a small kitchen at home, it doesn't compare to the splendor of free food courtesy of the university meal plan. It's not particularly good food, but it's plentiful, and considering I need to take in upwards of five thousand calories a day to maintain my size, I'll take what I can get.

We're in that weird lull between afternoon and early evening, so only a few tables are occupied. My eyes narrow in on the group of gymnasts at one table. They're always smiling, always having a good time. One of them is a social media star of some renown. We're not friends, but I like to think we're equals. Athletes. Peers.

There's a bunch of softball players still wearing their muddy practice clothes. They're sitting at our regular table, which isn't a big deal—there aren't any assigned seats. It's first come, first serve, and they were here first. Fine. We move down a table and cluster around it.

As much as I would like a primarily vegetarian diet, that

just isn't feasible with my workout schedule and my nutrition restrictions. I would have to take in so much soy and plant protein to meet my dietary goals, and unfortunately, my body doesn't tolerate soy very well. It doesn't work at this stage in my life. Maybe when I retire after next season.

It's not like I'm downing pizza and double cheeseburgers at every meal. I eat a balanced diet of whole grains, lean proteins, and a shit ton of veggies to get my five thousand calories, topped off with a few chalky protein shakes to get me through the day. Sometimes I get so fucking tired of eating. My teeth get tired of chewing.

My attention snags on the softball player at the end of the table. She's smearing peanut butter on an apple, her hair in a messy blonde knot at the top of her head. Mud is streaked down her cheek. She's gorgeous. She catches my eye and raises her eyebrows pointedly. She looks familiar, but I can't place her. It's a small school; we've probably seen each other before over the years even if we haven't spoken. I don't often talk to people who aren't part of my inner circle of friends, and I don't have that many to begin with.

She's the type of girl who would never look twice at a guy like me. Not many girls do, and the ones that show interest are usually either cleat chasers, pitying me, or both. Nobody is interested in me, Miles Cavanaugh, for who I am. It's some-thing I've gotten used to over the years. Everyone wants a piece of the football player. They don't care about me the person.

Carefully, I focus on my dinner. Barrett and Amir are horsing around. Tucker is ignoring them, as per usual, absorbed in his phone. Wes pulls out the latest John Grisham —he's already halfway through, and I know for a fact he started it this morning after the team meeting. Greg meets my eye, nods, and turns his attention back to his meal.

We're all part of the defensive squad, a mix of outside and inside linebackers and linemen. Collectively, we're six of the biggest guys on the team. We also live in the same house in Athlete's Village. I like living with my teammates. It's a built-in network of friends, peers, guys who work with me on the field every day and are by my side day in and day out. At night, we hang out on the couch and play video games or watch movies because we're friends first, roommates second.

We have a good group of guys in the house this year. Last year we had two of the kickers bunking in with me, Wes, Barrett, and Tuck, and it just wasn't the same. Sure, kickers are usually at least six feet tall and about two hundred pounds, so they're not tiny dudes, but they're so shrimpy compared to us. Dominic and Jimmy also partied far harder than we do. They had girls all over them, and not just the pity fucks girls throw our way. They each had a different girl in their beds nearly every night. The faked moans and creaking bed frames got old fast.

I've been playing football for fifteen years. College is the first time I've been surrounded by a group of guys as big as me or close to it. I've always been the tallest, the heaviest, and while that's worked to my advantage on the field, it gets lonely. Now I'm just one of the guys, no different than any other lineman.

I've finally found my community. The other math majors think I'm a joke. The rest of the department thinks I'm a big dumb jock skating by on my athletic ability. Or they're like Cassidy, thinking I'm cheating my way through life. The guys on my team know me. They know I'm a huge nerd for numbers. They know I'm more likely to be found on a Saturday night playing video games than going out partying. They know my parents come to every home game, and most of the away games, and my sisters are off limits. They're my brothers in everything but blood.

The quarterbacks and the wide receivers don't get it. They're revered for their athleticism in a way the big guys aren't. Girls want to cuddle up next to the football stars and then turn their noses up when our shirts come off. I will never have a six pack of perfect washboard abs. No doctor will ever tell me I'm the picture of health. But I'm strong, I can run fast, and I can hold off guys bigger than me, and for right now, that has to be enough. I am enough.

Even if nobody else sees me that way.

two

. . .

Sam

THERE'S a party going on downstairs, but if I don't get some studying done, I'm going to fail this statistics class.

"Come on, just hang out for a little while," my teammate, roommate, and best friend wheedles.

I love Tamar, she's my ride or die. But she's not skirting the edge of academic ineligibility because of one stupid midterm. I have four weeks until the next exam. If I don't get my grades up, I could be sitting out the entire season.

"Even the football player scored better than I did," I remind her. I've only told her this, like, six or eighty million times. "He destroyed the curve. Nobody else came close to his score."

I saw his test paper before he shoved it into his bag. How the hell did he score an A? I need help, I can admit that. I've asked around at the tutoring center; there aren't any statistics-specific tutors this semester, so either I get a freshman math major to tutor me or I bumble through on my own.

I'll take stumbling in the dark for 100, Alex.

The football player—I don't even know his name—is always sitting at the front of the room in a special chair set aside just for him. I don't think he can fit in the regular desks, he's so massive. His big head is always bent over his note-book, his enormous paws jotting down notes as Professor Cassidy lectures. He doesn't look up. He doesn't talk to anyone. So how the hell is he managing A's? Who is his tutor?

Tamar pouts some more. It's no use. There's no way she's convincing me to go downstairs. One drink will turn into three will turn into me getting shit-faced and losing all of tonight's study time and most of tomorrow's to a gnarly hangover.

The pounding of the music serves as a lullaby, pounding in equal measure in my head as I try to wrap my brain around these foreign concepts. I swear I was paying attention in class yesterday. My notes don't make any sense. The text-book doesn't make any sense.

I'm going to fail this class. And if I fail, I'm out—I can't play next season. I could lose my scholarship. I could lose my housing for the spring semester. I wouldn't be starting at second base, I'd be starting and finishing in the dugout... or worse, on the bleachers.

I've seen the big guy from class around campus a few times. We've never spoken; I don't know his name. He's always wearing Newton Athletics gear, and I've seen him in the student athlete dining hall. He's got to be a football player. Nobody else is that massive. Even the bigger hockey players are weedy little children compared to him.

As a member of the athletic department, we're entitled to certain... benefits. We get priority access at the tutoring center, for one. We also get leniency in taking our tests on different days if needed to accommodate our travel and training schedules. It's early in the football season, but he's only missed one class, and he's always turning in homework on time instead of asking for extensions.

There's a knock on my doorframe. Tamar is back, this time followed by Lex and Aleesha.

"Come party," Leesh says. "We miss you."

"You're wasting your Thursday night," Tamar says.

"There are a few football players and wrestlers downstairs," Lex joins in.

Football players?

I close my books and crack my knuckles. "Okay, let's do this."

They cheer and pull me to my feet. We head downstairs, where the majority of our teammates are hanging out. There are a few guys clustered around. I don't recognize any of them.

The big guy isn't here.

Aleesha pulls me in the direction of the drinks. It's all beer, wine coolers, and alcoholic seltzers on the table tonight, none of the hard stuff. We've got practice tomorrow morning, bright and early. I take a beer and crack the top, licking the foam off my hand like a heathen.

One of the football players—or so I presume, based on the Newton State College Football sweatshirt he's wearing—gives me the nod and goes back to his conversation with the guys. I scope out the situation. None of these guys are even half the size of the big guy. How many guys are there on the team? They have to know him.

"Hey, the big guy on your team—really tall, about this wide, doesn't talk—what's his name?"

The football player on the right laughs. "That describes half of the linebackers, baby. You're going to have to be more specific."

"I don't know his name." I cross my arms over my chest. "And don't call me baby, honey. I'm not your baby."

He snaps off a roguish salute. "Yes, ma'am."

Ugh. Boys playing at being men. Sometimes I really hate guys. Sometimes I really hate everyone.

"What's a peach like you doing up here in the Northeast, sweetheart?" the guy on the left asks with a predatory leer.

"I'm from Mississippi, not Georgia." Not like these idiots know the difference.

"Come on over here and give me some of that Mississippi sugar, angel," the guy in the middle says, giving me what I'm sure he intends to be a winning smile. It just comes off sleazy.

"Y'all are wasting your time," the first guy says. "She wants a linebacker."

"What's your name, baby?" Lefty cuts in.

"None of your fucking business." I turn on my heel and disappear into the throng of people.

More guys have shown up from the football team and the soccer team, as have a few from the gymnastics and tennis teams. It's a party now. I'm not in the partying mood. The idea of playing nice makes my skin crawl.

I take my beer out to the front porch. The street is quiet—cars aren't allowed in Athlete's Village after dark. It's a little Mecca for all of us student athletes, a place where our split focus on academics and athletics is revered, not disparaged. A place for us to be ourselves, not bogged down by judgement.

The leaves are turning colors. It's gorgeous. Back home, our fall is a hot, muggy mess of thunderstorms. Leaves fall from trees overnight. On the rare occasions we get snow, it turns to mud in the blink of an eye.

I've always had this romantic notion of New England in the fall. This is my third year here and that hasn't changed. Winter is hell and spring is a pipe dream, but fall is cozy and picturesque in a way that summer could never compare. It's conditioning season; that means leggings and boots and curling up with my teammates in front of a fire.

There are six athletes to a house. There have to be fifty or sixty guys on a football team. That means there are at least eight houses of football players, maybe more. I can't just go knocking on their doors until I come across tall, wide, and handsome.

I'll have to corner him after class. Make him talk to me. Make him share his tutor or his notes or his study guides with me. Whatever he's doing, he's doing it right.

three

. . .

Sam

I ONLY JOINED a sorority because my mother made me. She's a Kappa legacy. She simply cannot conceive of a world in which I'm not a Kappa, too. So I rushed. And to my surprise, I don't hate it. I found a group of like-minded women who have the same interests as I do. It helps that Tamar rushed with me. It's the two of us against the rest of the world. Neither of us are frilly, frou-frou type girls.

The sisters are throwing a tailgating party in the parking lot of the stadium. It's really just an excuse to get dressed up in a cute sweater and scarf and parade about in front of the fraternity brothers, who are more interested in beer and football than in getting laid at the moment. That'll come later tonight. They won't be deterred for long.

Ostensibly we're here for a canned food drive. Students who donate a can of food get admission for half price, and community members can donate a full bag for free admission.

There's a couple wearing head to toe Newton apparel. Both her beanie and his sweatshirt have #14 on it. Must be his parents, or maybe really big fans.

I'm no stranger to football. I grew up under Friday night lights back home in Dean, Mississippi, a medium-sized suburb of Jackson. My older brother played all four years of high school before he blew out his knee in practice his freshman year at Ole Miss before he ever got to step onto that field. My dad, born and raised in western Washington, watches the Seahawks religiously. My mama throws the best Super Bowl parties in town.

Coach was particularly vindictive today. Our conditioning sessions are getting more and more intense as we get closer to the start of softball season. My ass and thighs are killing me, the muscles are so sore. We've got the better part of five months until preseason starts. There's no need for this bull-shit in the off-season. Standing out here in the cold, collecting cans, and lugging heavy boxes feels like an additional punish-ment after the intensity of the morning's workout. I'm already bruised and battered enough; can't I just have a few hours off to relax?

The game is... decent. We're playing against conference rivals Northeastern, who are adequate. Their quarterback is a seasoned senior with a killer snap and an even better smile if the pictures on the Jumbotron are anything to go by.

Tamar and I huddle under an enormous silver, blue, and black blanket with the school logo. It's early fall, so while the weather is nice for now, it can turn deadly cold in the blink of an eye. We're both layered up, unlike some of our sisters, who are wearing their flannel best and cute NSC-Kappa beanies. They're pink.

I'm not a pink type of girl. My hair is more likely to be in a top knot than it is to be brushed. I'm religious about sunscreen, yes, because skincare is no joke, but I rarely have the time or the inclination to put on a full face of makeup. My wardrobe consists exclusively of workout gear, leggings, and team and sorority apparel, because I have no time to go out and shop for clothes, and because I wouldn't be caught dead in a little black dress.

There's nothing wrong with not being a frilly, frou-frou

kind of girl. I'm happy with who I am. My sisters don't care if I show up in baggy old sweats or in a crop top and heels. They just want me to show up, period, so I do. I have their back like they would have mine.

From the raucous student section, I try to scope out the linebackers. There are a handful of guys who are as big as the guy from my class, the guy who checked me out in the dining hall the other day. Is he Cavanaugh, #14? I don't think he's Zhang or Alkatib.

My eyes keep drifting back to Cavanaugh. He's massive, yes, while still quick on his feet. He throws down with the opposing team's players like they're weightless, inconsequential and ineffectual.

It's a blowout of a second half. Newton wins, 49 to 24. The crowd is loving it. The student section comes alive with school spirit.

"Party at the Delta house," the fraternity brothers yell as they pound the stairs of the stadium.

There's still one player left on the field. I can't make out his number from here. He's holding his helmet, gazing up at the goal posts. From a distance, he almost looks like the big guy. I want to know what he's doing out there, why he hasn't made for the locker room like all the other dudes.

"I'll meet you back at the house," I tell Tamar, gathering my stuff.

"You good? You want me to walk back with you?"

I shake my head. "I have something I need to do. I'll catch up with you later."

She rolls her eyes. "You just want to skip out on the party."

"I am so sore. I want a hot bath," I tell her, which isn't a lie. I have no idea how I'm going to make it up the stairs to the stadium.

Every muscle in my body protests. Once I'm up at the main level, I push through the throng to the tunnels, where the families wait for their athletes to show up. In the path of the harsh wind, I pull out the blanket again and wrap it around me. I don't care how ridiculous I look—it's fucking cold. This is my third year, and I'm still not used to the cold of winter up here in this northern climate. And it's still technically fall.

There are a dozen other family members loitering around. Slowly, the guys start to show up. The ones who have family present greet them, a lot of mothers and grandmothers clucking over their enormous offspring and fathers clapping them on the back, stoic and reserved.

Everyone drifts away, until it's only me and the family of #14. Cavanaugh, reads the dad's jersey. He looks like he could be a player, fit and athletic with a hint of salt and pepper in his full head of hair. If I were into older guys, I might be intrigued enough to take a second look. He's at least twenty-five, maybe thirty years older than me. Too much of an age gap no matter how much age gap erotica I read. And besides, I can see the glint of a wedding ring. He's thoroughly off limits.

A massive guy comes lumbering out of the locker room, wearing an oversized navy Newton hoodie and joggers. It's him, the guy from my statistics class. The guy from the dining hall. His face hardens when he catches sight of me. The one I've been looking for all week.

"Miles! Over here, honey," the woman calls, waving emphatically, as if she's not clearly in his line of sight.

So he's Cavanaugh. Miles Cavanaugh. I commit the name to memory.

"Hey, Mom," he says, his voice a rumbling burr. It makes my insides clench, which is actually ridiculous, because I know nothing about him aside from the fact that he's acing our statistics class and the whole package from where I'm standing is… whew, he's even better looking up close.

"You did great, honey," she tells him. She reaches out and

adjusts the strings of his hoodie, smoothing out an imaginary wrinkle along his shoulder.

"Thanks." He lets her dote on him a bit. It's sweet, seeing a grown man letting his mother cluck over him without letting her coddle him. I get the impression that he has enough of a spine to stand up to her if she ever crosses the line.

"Good job, Miles," the dad says, clapping him on the shoulder. It's clear they're a close-knit family.

He stands at least six inches taller than his dad, maybe twice as wide. There's definitely a resemblance there; the same dark brown hair and dark eyes, the same nose. The dad's nose has definitely been broken once or twice.

His gaze lands on me again, and his eyes narrow. "What do you want?"

"Miles, honey, play nice," the mom chastises.

He waves her away. "Everyone else is gone. There's nobody left. Go home."

This is it. This is my chance. Go time.

"I wanted to talk to you," I say. "Good game, by the way."

Angry slashes of red pop up on his cheeks. "Thanks."

"You're in my statistics class."

He jerks his chin, tugging at the strings to his hoodie. "So?"

"You got an A on the last exam."

The mom clucks. "You did? Honey, I'm so happy for you."

"Who's your tutor?"

His face goes red. "I don't have one."

"Come on. I'm sure the football team found you someone. There's nobody in the tutoring center this semester who's taken stats. The only kid available is some freshman who took AP Stats in high school. We should study together."

"No, thanks," he says lightly. "I'm good on my own."

four

. . .

Miles

WHO THE FUCK does this girl think she is?

Mom touches my shoulder. "Miles, honey…"

"I don't know you. You don't even know my name."

"Miles Cavanaugh," she says, shooting me a victorious grin. "You're number 14. You're a linebacker."

Okay, she's got me there. Maybe if my dad wasn't wearing a jersey with my name on it…

"I don't have a tutor or study guides. I'm doing fine on my own."

She's undeterred. "Come on. I can make it worth your while."

This makes me laugh. "You have nothing to offer me."

"You don't know that."

I look her over again. She's in a sorority, if the teal and silver letters on her navy sweatshirt mean anything. Her dark blonde hair is tied up into a grubby top knot, her makeup light and natural. She's pretty in that effortless way, which means she's bad news for me.

"Trust me, Sister, you've got nothing I want." My stomach rumbles, reminding me I've just spent four hours exerting a tremendous amount of energy on the field. "I'm hungry. Can we go now?"

"Of course, honey," Mom says. "Are you sure your friends don't want to join us?"

They ask every week, and every week, my friends decline. Barrett's family situation is complicated—they all live in Boston or in the surrounding suburbs, but they never show up to the games. Tucker, Greg, and Amir all want to give my parents and me some privacy, considering we never get it when I'm home with my sisters, and Wes is just antisocial as fuck. The guys are cool to hang around for a bit, but they never want to encroach upon my family time.

"Where are Mack and Ash?"

Mom sighs. "Mack tweaked her ankle at practice. She's fine, just resting." She shakes her head. "Ash has a birthday party, some girl from her squad."

My sisters couldn't be more different if they tried. Mackenzie is almost eighteen, a senior in high school and a three sport athlete. Her swim team won state last year, and in her downtime, she plays tennis and basketball, three completely different disciplines. Ashley is fifteen and a high-maintenance drama queen, which is par for the course with cheerleaders. She's not just the captain of the JV team at her school, she also does competitive club cheer year-round. She's the world's cheeriest cheerleader, and I love her for it.

It makes sense. My dad played football in college. My mom was a nationally ranked tennis player. Athleticism is in our blood. Newton is in our blood. It's where they met close to thirty years ago. They lived in Athlete's Village, same as I do. It's our family legacy.

We make idle chit chat during dinner. We come to the pub every week. It's good, it's relatively cheap, and it's packed with people who have been drinking all afternoon. I get a few claps on the back from random strangers as we walk in.

That's what I hate most about being a football player. People think I belong to them, that they deserve a piece of me. At the end of the day, I receive a partially subsidized education in exchange for my performance on the field. I'm an ambassador for the university, whether I like it or not, a semi-public figure. I don't get any true privacy. My height, my weight, even my GPA is public information.

Tomorrow morning, everyone will have forgotten about me and my four sacks. I'll fade back to being a hulking shadow, lurking in the background, a spectacle too big to truly be ignored. But, they will. Ignore me, that is.

I don't know why perfect strangers feel it's appropriate to comment on my size. Maybe they've never seen someone as big as me. That doesn't make me a circus animal, a spectacle to be commented on.

My parents have never treated me as anything but normal. My sisters are brats, yeah, but they don't care about my performance on the football field—they care about me, period.

After dinner, my parents walk me home. Mom offers to come back tomorrow with a pot of chili, which I don't turn down. My roommates will thank me if nothing else. It's better than walking to the dining hall for our three meals a day, or across campus to the football training facility for our grab and go snack stations.

Barrett and Tucker are sprawled on the sofa when I get home, playing Madden. Wes is sitting in the corner chair—his favorite—with a Tom Clancy novel. I know for a fact that it's not the same book he was reading last night when he was sitting in that very same spot. He sits with us so he can pretend he's being social, so he can pretend to be part of the group. We don't mind. Occasionally he'll make a pithy comment or observation and then we'll all go back to normal. He keeps to himself. I respect that.

"You're back early," Greg says, coming out of the kitchen with a banana in one hand and an orange in the other. "Dinner with the parents didn't go so well?"

"It was fine."

Greg grunts. "Are you going to the Delta party?"

"Yeah, right."

He laughs. "Cool. So it's not just me sitting at home on a Saturday night, then."

"And how is that different than any other Saturday night?"

I'm perfectly fine to spend a night on the couch, much like we do every Saturday night. Today's game was a good one. Northeastern's offensive line are big, hulking dudes. There were a couple of plays where I barely managed to get my man. My body is battered and bruised, sore and aching. My knees and hips are killing me. Tomorrow I'll need some time in the team's recovery hot tub for sure.

It drives the rest of the team crazy that the linebackers are content to stay in on a Saturday night. It's what makes this house such a great fit. None of us are all that into partying or dating. Amir has had this on and off thing with his girl for the last two years, but they've been off since the semester started, so I don't know what's going on there. Tucker is celibate by choice. Some kind of trauma none of us has dug too deep into. Wes doesn't talk to people unless they're on the team, and even then, he communicates mostly in grunts. Greg and Barrett are the two most likely to bring a girl back to our place, and on the rare occasion it actually happens, we politely pretend we don't hear any middle of the night bed squeaking.

Other people are assholes. They talk about me behind my back when they think I can't hear. They think I'm as dumb as a bag of bricks because of my size. But I'm rocking a beautiful 3.875 GPA. It would totally be higher if I hadn't bombed my chemistry final two years ago.

But as I sit here, hanging out with my roommates, I can't stop thinking about that sorority girl. Something about her just rubs me the wrong way. Maybe it's her assumption that of course I need help to get a good grade in a difficult class. Or maybe it's the presumption that the football team has access to resources that the rest of the student body doesn't.

We don't get special treatment. Sure, I can take tests on different days if I'll be out of town for a game, but that rarely happens, mainly because I choose to take most of my classes on Mondays and Wednesdays instead of Tuesday and Thursday. The same applies to any other student athlete on campus. We're equals. None of us are better than any other. We're all entitled to the same "perks" and we all receive the same benefits.

Annoyance bubbles in my bloodstream. I want to smash something, crush it beneath my fingers.

"Easy, man," Tucker says, prying the game controller out of my hands. "Hulk no smash."

"Fuck you." I crack my knuckles. It doesn't soothe that itch inside of me. I can't sit still. "I'm going for a walk."

"Don't get into trouble," Wes says, not looking up from his book.

"Thanks, Mom."

He turns the page, responding without ever looking up. "You're welcome, sweetheart."

It's chilly outside, refreshing at the same time. The cold permeates through the fabric of my hoodie to settle deep within my bones.

Athlete's Village is nearly deserted. There are no cars—they aren't allowed in the Village after dark—and barely any people. Everyone's probably at the Delta house. The fraternity throws a party nearly every weekend. It's not a surprise.

There are two girls in Newton Athletics gear walking towards me. I recognize them as being from the cheerleading team, though I don't know either of them by name. I nod, and they cross to the other side of the street.

I try not to be offended. I'm a big fucking dude, and they're a lot smaller than me, walking alone in the dark. Mackenzie explained it to me once. It's not that they're afraid of me, the person, it's what I represent. I could easily overpower them. I could easily be bad news. They don't know me. It doesn't matter that I would never do that. I've never laid a hand on anyone, never been in a fistfight outside of friendly tussles with my cousins or the neighborhood guys. That's not me. I'm not violent, and I'm certainly not a predator.

But they don't know me. All they see is a massive guy lumbering towards them in the dark.

The closer I get to campus, the more people I see. Clusters of student athletes in team apparel are replaced by clusters of students in going-out clothes: short skirts and crop tops or clean jeans and button-downs, the college student partying uniform.

The quad is an idyllic paradise, a square of green and trees surrounded by tall buildings. We're a weird suburban college town on the outskirts of the city, just close enough that we can take the metro twenty minutes into the heart of Boston.

Somehow I find myself walking through Greek Row. This isn't where I meant to go. I have no business being here.

It's not hard to identify the Delta house. Even if it weren't for the letters on the front of the house, the people spilling out onto the lawn would be clue enough.

A couple guys clap me on the back as I walk past. My feet turn in the direction of the house almost without me noticing.

Sullivan, one of the safeties, meets me on the front porch.

"Cavvy! Didn't think I'd see you at one of these things."

I grunt. When in doubt, let people think I'm a caveman.

"Come on, man. Let's get you a beer."

I've done scientific tests. It takes at least five beers before I start to feel the slightest bit tipsy. A quarter of a handle of vodka will get me decently drunk. My roommates and I experimented shortly after Barrett turned twenty-one and could stock up our fridge last spring. We didn't even go out to celebrate my twenty-first during summer training; we stayed in and played a video game tournament.

I don't see the fun in drinking. It's extra calories that don't fit into my macros, empty carbs that leave me hungry. I would much rather drink a nasty, chalky protein shake than waste my time on beer. No judgement against anyone who likes to drink. It's just not for me.

We're at the keg when I see her. The sorority girl from earlier. She's wearing the same distressed jeans and navy sweatshirt with the Greek letters on it. Her comfortable sneakers have been traded in for cognac colored wedge sandals. She's wearing a little more makeup, drawing attention to her rich brown eyes. A deep eggplant-colored lipstick has stained the rim of her cup. She isn't petite by any stretch of the imagination; her body is a glorious hourglass of muscular legs, thick thighs, and generous chest wrapped up in fabric and denim.

Annoyance and attraction war within me. She's effortlessly gorgeous even with all that goop on her face.

"Who's she?" I nod towards her.

Sullivan isn't shy about checking her out. "Samantha Burke. Softball player and Kappa member." He laughs, shakes his head. "Man, she is so out of your league."

I grunt again.

She's standing in a cluster of women. They're talking and laughing, having a good time. She's relaxed and in her element. Because other people like this shit. They like parties. They like drinking. They like the dancing to bad music and overpowering B.O. and the stale smell of pot. They like socializing.

My hands clench around my flimsy plastic cup, sending beer sloshing over the side.

I shouldn't be here. This isn't for me.

Setting my beer down on a nearby table—no coasters, of course—I exit the party. Sullivan calls after me. I don't respond. I don't belong here. I don't belong anywhere.

five

. . .

Miles

THE FAMILIAR SOUNDS of the weight room are as soothing as a lullaby. I'm not sleepy, though; I'm pumped up, energized, ready to tackle whatever gets thrown at me, whether it be a three hundred pound grown man ready to rip my head off or a new personal best on Romanian split squats.

Today is a deloading day, which means lifting decreased weights in shorter repetitions in favor of recovery. After my hour or so of lifting, I do a quick thirty minutes of cardio before I head to the hot tub for a rejuvenating soak. My bruised and battered muscles will thank me for it later.

There's a routine to Sunday. It's my day off, my day to be on my own. The guys all have their own things to do, so unless we cross paths in the gym or in the dining hall, I might not see them until our house dinner and weekly Wheel of Fortune and Jeopardy! binge.

After being around people all week, after the game and dealing with my family the day before, sometimes I need time to myself to mentally recuperate before doing it all again. I'm not what most people would consider to be a social person, and the day-to-day onslaught of life is hard enough to manage without the demands the university places on me and my time.

I play football because I love it, because I'm good at it. It brings me joy. Being in school doesn't exactly bring me joy, but I like the majority of my classes; I like learning about math and the practical applications of it, so I'm not about to complain. And I need the degree for a career after college and football—though I'm not exactly sure what I want to do, just that I want it to involve math. Numbers make sense to me in a way that people don't.

Sometimes I feel like I don't fit in anywhere. I get along with my teammates, sure. My roommates and I are on friendly terms. Outside of that... I'm not the guy with a roaring social life. I would rather hang out on the couch and play video games with a few guys than go to some party. I would rather have quality one-on-one time with someone I care about than get drunk off my face. That's how I've always been.

I don't have a lot to say. My thoughts aren't interesting. My life revolves around football and school. Outside of my roommates and my sisters, I have virtually no friends. Are my sisters even my friends, or do they only tolerate me because we're related? Sometimes I really don't know.

At the same time... sometimes it's a little bit lonely. I've never had a best friend. I've never dated anyone. I've never had a close personal relationship with anyone that isn't related to me. Guys don't want to hang out with me outside of the gym. Girls aren't interested in me as anything more than—

As anything, really.

Samantha is the first person who has ever wanted to study with me. And all she wants is whoever is helping me pass this class to tutor her, too. I don't know how to tell her that I'm the one who taught myself everything I know about statistics. It's none of her business. Even if I had a tutor, even if the athletic department found me someone to help pass this class, I don't know that I would share that resource with her. She has the nerve to show up to the player tunnels and *demand*—

No. The player tunnels are sacred. It's for friends and family only, not for random strangers to come up and accost us and place demands upon us. It's the one place we can be ourselves.

And for her to come in and… and…

I blow out a breath. She's a stranger. It was literally the first time we've ever spoken. She's gorgeous, and she's popular, and she's exactly the type of woman who has absolutely no interest in a guy like me. Of course she only wants my study guides or access to my tutor.

She would never want me to tutor her. She would never want to study with me. She would never be interested in me. And why should she? She exists in an entirely different social realm than I do. She's not just out of my league—she's out of my stratosphere.

I'm lonely. I can admit it. College was supposed to be this amazing experience. I was supposed to make lifelong friends. I was supposed to find the love of my life. My parents did. My dad still keeps in touch with his buddies from the football team, and my mom has been best friends with my Aunt Carol since they were on the tennis team together. I don't know that my roommates and I will stick together after this year is over. This is the end of the road for me. I'm going nowhere.

This is the peak: life will only go downhill for me. I'll get a job somewhere doing something with math, and I'll live out the rest of my life. If I can't meet anyone now, when I'm theoretically in the prime of my career and desirable, I don't know how I will ever find someone that likes me for me. Women don't even like me now. *I* barely like me now.

How can I make myself be more interesting without sacrificing who I am? At the end of the day, I'm a math nerd who plays football, and outside of those two things, I don't have many other interests. Video games? Boring. Superhero movies? Boring. Lifting heavy weights? Boring.

Let's face it: I'm a boring dude. Even my own family only spends time with me because they have to, not because they actually want to. My life revolves around football and math and that's about it.

Football makes me happy. Math makes me happy. I don't want to become someone I'm not just to convince a woman to be interested in me. I don't want to change who I am to make other people like me. A square peg doesn't have to fit into a round hole.

I am who I am, and I don't have any desire to force myself to fit into a box in which I don't fit. I'm a big fucking dude—I don't fit everywhere. And that's okay. I've come to terms with it. Now I just have to get my head and my heart on the same page.

six

. . .

Miles

ON MONDAY, Samantha is standing in front of my usual desk at the front of the room, holding a bottle of purple Gatorade. That's my favorite flavor. Immediately my annoyance with her ebbs just a tiny bit.

"I think we got off on the wrong foot," she blurts. She thrusts the bottle towards me. "For you."

"You don't have to bribe me." I'm still not going to change my mind.

"I need a statistics tutor," she says. "You got an A on the midterm, so clearly you're doing something right. We should study together."

"What's in it for me?"

For the first time, she looks stumped. She's had an answer for everything, and I've finally got her defensive. This is where I thrive. "What do you want?"

"Nothing. I want to be left alone."

"I can pay you." She winces. "Not a lot, I don't have a job, but I—"

"I don't want your money. I don't want your anything."

Grape Gatorade is only available at one of the student athlete fueling stations on the far side of campus. I have to walk across the entire quad, through the science building, and into the science library to get my daily stock. It helps me get in my 20,000 steps a day, that's for sure. That she walked all the way over there...

She squares her shoulders. "Look, I need this. I really need this."

"And how is that my problem?"

"It's not, and I realize that," she assures me quickly. "If I don't pass this class, I can't play next season. I could lose my scholarship, my housing, everything. Please. You understand this stuff and I don't."

Well, when she puts it that way... My resolve weakens. I couldn't live with myself if I lost football. I couldn't live with myself if I was the reason another athlete lost their scholarship.

Pulling out my notebook, I scribble my number on a piece of paper and hand it to her. "Meet me at the ASC at seven."

She doesn't balk at the mention of the Athletic Student Center. "In the dining hall?"

"No, I'll reserve a study room." I'll eat dinner with my teammates before I meet her, and if I play my cards right, I can grab a late evening snack before I head back to Athlete's Village.

She pushes the Gatorade towards me again. "This is for you." Her cheeks tint red. "I, um, I noticed you drink the purple flavor every class."

"Thank you." I take the bottle from her, and her tiny, calloused fingers brush against mine. Electricity sparks along my veins, coiling deep in my gut.

"Oh. My name is Sam."

"I know."

Her eyes go wide. "You do?"

I might have gone home and researched her on Saturday night after the party. She's a junior like me, originally from Mississippi, though there's only the faintest hint of an accent in her voice. The softball team is middle of the pack in the conference, not particularly amazing and not terrible. She plays second base and is one of the best batters on the team.

She's also hot as fuck.

She's wearing black form-fitting leggings and an over-sized Newton long sleeve shirt that does nothing to hide her shape, the sleeves pushed up her muscular forearms. I want to map the luscious curves of her body with my hands. And then my tongue.

How the fuck am I supposed to tutor her?

I'm on edge the rest of the day. At practice, I barely manage to eke out my normal reps; I can't add any weight, not today. Coach isn't pleased, but there's nothing I can do about it right now. My body isn't cooperating with me. I eat dinner with the guys like nothing is wrong, and they're cool enough (or oblivious enough) not to call me on it. It's turkey meatloaf night, one of my favorites, but my food tastes like sawdust in my mouth. Even my salad tastes dull and limp. I move the food around on my plate without eating it.

At six fifty-five, I get up with my half-full tray and start to walk away.

"Heading back to the house?" Barrett asks.

"Study group."

He makes a face. "Good luck."

I'm going to need it.

The second floor of the ASC is devoted to study rooms of varying size. I booked one of the larger rooms, intended for groups of six or more people. We're going to need the space to spread out. I don't think I can be close to her right now.

She knocks on the open door at six fifty-nine. She's changed out of her outfit from earlier, wearing a different pair of navy and silver Newton Wolfpack leggings and another oversized shirt, this one with Greek letters on it. Sullivan said she was a Kappa; I guess that's what the K on her chest signifies.

"Hey."

"Hi." I pull my textbook out of my backpack.

She hesitates in the entrance to the room. "Thank you for agreeing to help me."

I grunt out something that could be "no problem" if you squint a bit.

"What are you having trouble with?"

She worries her bottom lip with her teeth. "Um. All of it?"

This is going to be… awful. Terrible. The fresh scent of her cherry vanilla perfume washes over me. My cock is stirring just sitting near her. Arousal is a lukewarm and frankly alien feeling deep in my bones. Girls don't like me, so I've learned not to show any interest in them, either.

"Do you have your midterm with you?"

She finds the packet of papers and passes them over. Her fingertips brush against mine, sending shocks of electricity down my spine and straight to my cock. Pressing my lips into a firm line, I look over her test.

She's got the math part down. That's the easy part. It's the concepts she's struggling with. Probability is a whole other can of worms.

I don't know how to explain this in a way that will make sense to her. I'm not a teacher. Probability makes sense to me in the same intrinsic way that football does. As I start to explain things, I try to relate the concepts to football plays. She seems to follow along. I don't know that I make much sense.

Sam chews on her bottom lip, and my cock instantly reacts. She's so close, only the width of the table separating us.

It's been two years since I last had sex, and that only lasted about three thrusts before she was calling it quits. My libido is healthy; I just take care of it on my own. I've never had a girlfriend. There are a few girls I fooled around with, girls who "took care of" the football team my freshman year of college, but it was clear they were only interested in the jersey on my back, not the person wearing it. I try not to take it personally. I'm not always successful. I don't want a pity fuck.

Around eight-thirty, I'm distracted by a low groaning noise. Sam goes pink and wraps her arm around her stomach.

"I skipped dinner."

I check my watch. "The dining hall is still open for another hour. We can go over this downstairs." I clear my throat. "If you're willing to be seen with me, that is."

She blinks. "Why wouldn't I be?"

"I don't know. You might not want people to see us together."

"I don't care what people think about me," she declares, tossing back her shoulders. "Come on. It's turkey meatloaf night."

My stomach churns, reminding me I didn't really eat my dinner earlier. "I could eat."

seven

. . .

Sam

THE DINING HALL is nearly empty when we arrive, which is just how I like it. I pull out my phone and the school nutrition program's app, surprised to find him doing the same. Taking a tray, I have to scan the barcode of each item I take, and it automatically loads in the nutrition information for me, sending it directly to my school-assigned dietician.

"You have to log your food? I thought you could eat, like, anything you want to."

Miles goes a bit pink. "Within reason. We still have to log everything and follow our macros. I didn't really eat dinner."

We both take a portion of meatloaf. It's not something my mama ever made, but since entering college, I've developed a taste for it. Where I take a portion of mashed potatoes, he takes two of mashed cauliflower, and fills the rest of his plate with a mixed greens salad with cranberries and goat cheese. I opt for a double portion of the roasted veggies. Green beans with almonds, my favorite. I still have enough room left in my day for some soft serve ice cream. Ooh, or maybe a protein brownie.

Without speaking, Miles heads towards a table at the back of the dining hall. There's nobody around. At the other end of the room are a trio of basketball players lingering over empty plates. There's a cluster of women from the swim team enjoying ice cream sundaes.

His movements are stiff as he sits down across from me. I don't know how to read him. Is he ignoring me? Is he just lost in his own world?

He's a surprise in every respect, a far cry from the grunting rock I initially took him to be. His explanations of probability as it relates to football make sense. I don't think one session is going to magically cure me; we're going to need more tutoring sessions.

"What are you doing on Wednesday night?"

He freezes. Slowly, impossibly slowly, his rich brown eyes rise to meet mine, wide and unblinking. He's not unintelligent. I don't know why he lets everyone think he is.

"Why do you ask?"

"Maybe we can get together again. Study some more."

There's a cough behind me, like a stifled snicker. It happens again. I turn to look over my shoulder. There's a table of men's volleyball players a few feet away. None of them are paying attention to us.

Miles's face goes beet red. "I, um, I don't know."

I hear it again. It's more distinct now. Someone is laughing. What I don't know is why.

"Come on. It really helped."

They're outright laughing now. I spin around to the volleyball players two tables away and catch them in the act.

"Can I help you?"

I recognize the guy on the right, Josh Sinclair; we had two classes together last year. Everyone knows Tony O'Rourke is an asshole. I've never met the guy on the end, but considering he's chuckling away at a joke that isn't funny, I'm not sure I want to.

"You and Tubby over there on a date, Burke?" O'Rourke

says, sitting back in his chair with a sleazy smirk. "Didn't think you would stoop that low."

"I didn't think you were that stupid, O'Rourke. I guess we're both disappointed," I fire back. Turning back to Miles, it's to find he's hunched in on himself, as if that will make him disappear.

"What's the matter, Tubby?" O'Rourke calls. "You get enough to eat today, big boy? Getting your five squares a day?"

"Don't listen to them," I tell Miles. "They're assholes."

He grunts, his eyes focused on his plate.

I paste a bright smile on my face. It probably looks a bit manic. "So, Wednesday?"

He jerks his chin, once, a curt nod. "Same place."

"Perfect."

Miles pushes his chair back. "I've got to go."

"Are you heading back to Athlete's Village? I'll walk with you."

He grunts.

"I need a yes or a no, dude. I don't read minds."

His face is still red. "I'll walk you back to your place."

He's not done yet; his plate is mostly full. He takes my tray, stacking our plates together and neatly organizing the silverware. Without asking, he carries both trays over to the repository.

The volleyball assholes are still snickering. I flip them off as we leave the dining hall. #no-regrets

eight

. . .

Sam

WE WALK IN UNEASY SILENCE. He doesn't mention the jerks from the dining hall, so neither do I. I wish I could say this was brand new, but every time I so much as talk to a guy, suddenly O'Rourke is all up in my face. I don't know why. It's not like he likes me. He's sleazy and scummy. He doesn't have a nice word to say about anyone.

"I'm on State Street," I tell him as we approach the corner of State and Third.

He turns, ready to head down the street. Before I can think about it, my hand catches in the sleeve of his hoodie.

"Listen, about what those guys were saying…"

He grunts.

"They're assholes."

"Forget about it," he says roughly. "O'Rourke is a piece of shit."

"You know him?"

He grunts again. I take that as a confirmation.

Everyone knows everyone in some roundabout way. Miles knew who I was. The athletic department is small but tightly knit. I knew enough about him to recognize him as a football player, to pick him out of the lineup. I wonder why he didn't show up to the party last week. He was at the frat party over the weekend. I caught a glimpse of him, and before I could work up the nerve to go talk to him, he was gone.

He's cute. Like, insanely cute. His dark hair is a touch too long, his unshaven face stubbly with a few days of growth. His brown eyes are kind. He might pretend to be an oblivious rock, but I know deep down he has a kind soul. Something about him calls to me.

Still, I need a study buddy. And he understands statistics. He explains it so well, I actually almost understand what we went over tonight. He didn't get upset when it took a few explanations for something to make sense. He didn't get condescending when I asked followup questions. He just... he was kind, and he was sweet, and even if he didn't *want* to help me, he still did it. Out of the goodness of his heart, for another reason, I don't know.

And then O'Rourke had to go and stomp all over his good spirit. I have half a mind to run back to the dining hall and punch his face in. There was no need for him to make fun of Miles.

We were having such a nice time.

"I learned a lot during our study session."

He grunts. I don't know what happened to the communicative (albeit quiet) guy I was with an hour ago. It's like when O'Rourke descended upon us, he lost the ability to speak in complete sentences.

I understand that. Sometimes O'Rourke makes me so angry that I'm speechless, too.

"I really do want to meet up again." Regardless of whatever that asshole has to say about it.

"Maybe," he says.

"Miles. Please." I stop in my tracks. "I'll fail without your help."

An expression I can't identify wars on his face. He's hesitant. Is it because of O'Rourke, or was he already going to turn me down before that jerk got involved?

He squeezes his eyes shut and swallows. When he opens them, his rich brown eyes are soulful, wounded.

"You're willing to be seen with me? Have rumors spread about you?"

Who does he think he is that people will automatically start gossiping about us? We're both nobodies. There isn't anyone that cares about the intimate details of what we get up to.

"I don't care what people say," I roll my eyes. "They don't know me, and they don't know you."

He's silent as we make our way down the street.

"Well, this is me." I hook my thumb towards the softball house.

He nods towards the green and grey house two doors down and across the street. "I'm right there."

"We've been neighbors all this time and we've never known it," I smile kindly. I kind of like that the big guy is my neighbor. He makes me feel safe. Protected.

Which is ridiculous, because all we've done is study and walk home together. We're not friends.

He tucks his hands into the pocket of his hoodie. "Yep."

"I should get inside. Homework. And we have weights early tomorrow." I make a face. I'm not a fan of early wake ups.

And for some reason, I don't want this simple interaction to end. It's so nice being in his company. I had such a good time tonight, even with the statistics and the volleyball assholes interrupting us.

Miles shrugs into his hoodie. "Well, good night."

I don't want him to go. I manage a faint smile.

"Good night."

nine

. . .

Miles

"SINCE WHEN ARE you hooking up with Sam Burke?" Greg says the instant I close the door.

My roommates are sprawled across the living room, a superhero movie on the big screen. Amir pauses the movie to get the good gossip.

Bitterly, I laugh. "I'm not."

"That's not what everyone is saying."

"We literally had dinner together less than half an hour ago. How is the news out already?"

"O'Rourke," he says, at the same time I do.

"He's such an asshole," Tucker says. "Do you know he called me *fatso* last week? Like that's supposed to be an insult."

"I hate him." My blood boils all over again. "He can't ever fucking leave us alone. I don't get it."

"He likes to feel powerful," Wes says, turning a page in his ever present book. "It's because he has weak moral character."

"Yeah, well, he's a pretty great volleyball player, so the school isn't going to do anything but slap him on the wrist," I remind him. There's no use in complaining to administration.

Technically he isn't breaking the code of conduct, just skirting the line of what's allowed. He's slimy, but he'll get away with it.

"Sam Burke is stupid hot," Amir tells me, as if I'm not well aware. "What's your game plan there?"

"We're in the same statistics class. We were studying."

The guys nod, accepting this. They know I care about my grades. They know I'm not the idiot everyone else on campus seems to think I am. I'm not sure why everyone thinks I can barely tie my own shoes. I didn't get into college purely because of my athletic capabilities. I am a perfectly functional human being. I can balance my checking account and drive a car and sort my laundry like a real grown up.

Still, when I go up to my room and collapse onto my bed, that interaction replays in my head over and over again. *Tubby.* It's nothing new. People have been finding new and creative ways to call me fat for years. I've heard it all before.

I just wish it didn't bother me as much as it does.

I don't fit in. Even with the football team, I'm bigger and stronger than half the guys on the field. That's my job. I need to be big. It's a shame that what gets me revered on the football field gets me reviled everywhere else. I'm too big, too tall, too wide. I can't sit in the front of the classroom because then the people behind me can't see the whiteboard. I can't sit in the middle seat on an airplane because then my limbs touch the people on either side of me. I can't fit in the backseat of a cab. Bicycles aren't built for people my height and weight. Even the special order treadmills in the football gym groan beneath my weight.

I have to make myself small in order for other people to accept me. Nothing about me is small, not my personality and not my heart and not my brain. I can't control my physical size and shape. Most of the time, I don't even want to.

When guys like O'Rourke start in on me… I just want to be invisible. Maybe then they will go away. Maybe then it will all stop. I don't ever want to be the center of attention. Nothing good ever happens to me, only bad.

Like the masochist I am, I pull up my social media profile. My name has already been tagged in vicious rumors involving me and Sam doing nefarious things. Or rather, me existing and she doing nefarious things to me. There's a photo of us leaving the study room upstairs at the ASC, my face red and hers satisfied. There's a series of pictures of us eating in the dining hall. From the angle of the photo, it looks like… it almost looks like it's coming from where the volleyball players were sitting.

Except the profile that tagged us is anonymous.

I don't wish this on anyone. The comments are spewing hateful, hurting things. Degrading me, fine, I can deal with that. Degrading her?

Rolling over, I clutch my favorite pillow to my chest and force back my emotions. They will not control me. They will not define me.

Once I have everything under control, I pick up my phone again. The comments are downright nasty. Speculative and malicious lies. Why are people so interested in this? Is it because I'm that terrible of a person? I know Sam is popular, but I didn't think she was so much so that people take pictures of her everywhere she goes.

She's a fucking catch. She's an eleven out of ten, hot and nice and smart and a good athlete if the stats in her bio are anything to go off of. She was perfectly kind to me, and even if we got off on the wrong foot, since then, it's been smooth sailing. As a person, I like her.

As a woman… yeah, I can't deny that I *like* her, too. She's gorgeous. More than that, she has a beautiful soul. She's smart and funny and confident. She knows what she wants and goes after it. Look at how deftly she pursued me—she got me to tutor her with a purple Gatorade and a pretty smile.

And, yeah, the sob story contributed to it. I would hate to

be the reason another athlete was kicked off their team. I would hate to see another athlete prevented from playing their sport because of academic ineligibility. Especially when it's because of statistics. Math is easy. Statistics are a piece of cake. Nothing should stand in the way between Sam and playing softball. If I can help her pass this class… yeah, that will feel good. That will almost be as good as getting another A+ myself.

She's not interested in me as anything other than a study partner, so I'm going to be the best damn study buddy she's ever had. I'll make sure she knows the principles behind probability so damn well, she can recite them backwards and forwards.

In my head… yeah, privately I can admire her from afar. It won't go anywhere beyond private admiration, though. I would never in a million years have a chance with her. I know better than to get my heart involved in this situation. Girls like her don't go for guys like me, and if they do, it's only at the expense of an unfunny joke.

I refuse to be the butt of any more jokes. O'Rourke thinks he pulled one over on me; he's about to find out what happens when he messes with the wrong guy. He's not going to like it, not one bit.

ten

. . .

Sam

PEOPLE STOP TALKING the minute I walk into the weight room, so obviously they're talking about me.

"What?" I say, glaring at the closest baseball player. I hate sharing a weight room with these losers. They think they're so much better than softball because they get all of the funding and upward career mobility, whereas ours dies with graduation.

"What? I didn't say anything," he says.

The rest of the guys go mum. My teammates won't meet my eye.

"What's going on?"

Tamar tugs at my sleeve. "Maybe we should talk in the locker room..."

"Come on, just tell me."

"There's a rumor going around."

She pulls out her phone. I can see she's commented LOL on the photo—the same picture I was sent anonymously this morning.

I roll my eyes. "What is it this time?"

"They say you're..." She glances around, lowers her voice. "That you're fucking Miles Cavanaugh."

46

"I'm not. But why would it be a big deal?"

"Because he's... you know..."

"What?"

"He's huge."

"So?"

"Like, how would that even work?" she says. "Wouldn't his belly just get in the way of all the thrusting?" She does a few wild hip thrusts.

My jaw literally drops. "Wow. I can't believe you right now."

"What? It's a serious question." Her voice goes high-pitched like it does when she knows she's done wrong. "So if you're not fucking him, why are you hanging out?"

"Once. We hung out once, last night. He's in my stats class. We were studying."

"But aren't you, like, failing?" My so-called best friend says. "How would studying with him help?"

Flabbergasted, I shake my head and walk away. "I can't even with you right now."

Tamar runs up behind me. "Sam, come on. It's an honest question."

"You think he's an idiot just because he's a football player. He's fucking brilliant," I tell her. "He understands statistics and is able to explain them in a way I actually understand. I learned more from him in an hour and a half than I've learned in the last six weeks."

Her cheeks go pink. "So are you, like, into him or something?"

I don't bother to answer her. Our workout is written on the whiteboard: a circuit of arms, chest, shoulders, and abs. Normally we work out in twos and threes, partners who can help spot us if we need it. I don't want it today. I'm not in the mood for any more of this patronizing bullshit.

Putting in my headphones, I crank up the music and eke out the first set of bicep curls. I wasn't lying last night. I hate weightlifting days. I would much rather do cardio or batting practice or infield drills than lift weights. My mind drifts, and I can't focus.

I wonder how Miles is doing in his workouts. I bet he lifts a lot more than a measly sixty pounds.

He was pleasant company last night. Up until those assholes had to ruin it, I enjoyed our time together. He doesn't speak much. I don't know if he's naturally reticent or if he's somehow afraid of me. I'm nobody to be scared of.

My bad mood continues through the rest of my workout. My teammates give me a wide berth, and I don't make any attempts to laugh and joke with them like I normally would. Everything is pissing me off right now. Those clowns last night, these idiots this morning… Why are people so stupid?

Rushing through a shower, I get dressed in leggings and an oversized Kappa sweatshirt. I wasn't even planning on wearing it. I brought a Newton Softball shirt for today. But I can't stand the idea of supporting these bitches right now. Maybe it's anti-feminist of me, but I can't understand how women can cut each other down over who they may or may not be fucking. It's none of their business. As long as everything is healthy and consensual, what business is it of theirs? As if there's something shameful about being interested in a guy like Miles. There's absolutely nothing wrong with him.

I have an hour before my first class, so I hit up the dining hall for a quick breakfast. My teammates clamor around me, talking and laughing like nothing is wrong. I don't join in. Filling my tray, I check out and eye the cafeteria carefully. This is so much worse than high school.

At the back of the room are three tables of football players. I notice Miles right away, sitting with a group of guys all equally as enormous as he is. One of the guys is on his phone; another one is reading a book.

There's a table of people from the swim teams and some

of the men from the gymnastics team. Across the way are two tables of basketball players. The tennis players are clearing up their trays.

My mind made up, I make my way over to Miles and his teammates. He looks up as I approach, his fork clattering to the table.

"Is anyone sitting here?" I point to one of the three empty seats at the end of the table.

"Um, yes," he says, his face going red.

So he doesn't want me to sit with him. Got it. It's bad enough that people are talking about us; now they're going to see the rejection, too, plain as day. I turn away, my cheeks flaming.

Miles coughs and kicks out the seat in front of him. "This one is open."

The other guys stop eating and turn to stare at me. I pull back the heavy chair and drop into it.

"Thanks."

Nobody reacts. Nobody does anything except watch me, the lone female in their very masculine midst. All of these guys are massive, well over two hundred and seventy-five pounds of muscle and strength. They could snap me like a twig.

I don't think they will. Considering Miles wouldn't hurt a fly, I don't think I have much to fear from his friends.

"I'm Sam," I tell them, when they still don't return to their meals.

"Nice to meet you," says the guy closest to me in a rumbly burr, a dark-haired and tan-skinned man with two or three days' of growth to his beard. "I'm Amir."

"Barrett," grunts the Asian guy.

"Tucker," says the lone black guy. He hooks a thumb at the guy across from him, fair haired and light-eyed. He hasn't looked up from his book. "This is Wes."

A shadow falls over me. The guy is tall, yes, same as the rest of them—maybe six-four, six-five. He sits shoulder to shoulder with the rest of the guys. He has a full caveman style beard and thick hair pulled back into a bun at the crown of his head. I half expect him to bust out a flannel shirt and ironic black plastic glasses.

"That's Greg," Tucker says for the guy, as he takes the seat I had originally picked out.

So there is someone sitting there after all. It wasn't all an elaborate ruse to humiliate me in front of the crowded dining hall.

"Nice to meet you all," I say, offering a lame wave.

Barrett coughs. Wes doesn't look up from his book. Amir grunts something that might possibly be construed as a pleasantry.

"Why're you sitting with us?" Greg asks, not unkindly.

"Do I need a reason?"

He grunts, like that's an answer. I blink expectantly at him, not letting him off the hook.

"Nobody sits with us," Miles finally says. "Nobody wants to sit with us."

"Well, I want to."

"Haven't you…" His face goes red, and he looks down at his half-full plate. "Haven't you heard the rumors?"

"That we're sleeping together?" I roll my eyes again. "These people need a hobby."

"You're just going to feed the fire," Greg says.

"I don't care what people say about me, especially when I know it's not true." I'm not fussed about rumors. I care even less about strangers' opinions of me.

Miles won't meet my eye. "I'm sorry."

"About what? Being seen with me?" So people are talking about us online. Whatever. Some people have too much time on their hands.

He shakes his head but refuses to elaborate.

"You're going to get so much shit for hanging out with us," Greg explains. "They're going to call you awful names."

"Like what? Trust me, I've heard worse."

"They'll say you're fucking all of us, because you dared to be seen with us," Tucker says, rolling his eyes. "Just you wait, within two days there will be a rumor that we gang-banged you in front of the entire dining hall."

Miles grimaces. "You don't deserve to be dragged down with me."

"You say that like there's something shameful about dating you," I tell him. "There isn't. There's absolutely no reason at all a girl should be ashamed of being with you."

He drags his fork along his plate, not eating. "Wish other people felt that way."

"People are idiots."

He coughs out a laugh, some of the color returning to his cheeks. "Yeah, they are."

"So, Wes, what are you reading?"

Without looking at me, he raises the book so I can see the cover.

"David Baldacci. Nice."

He grunts, taking a bite of his eggs.

"And you're all on the football team?"

Amir nods. "Defense."

"Nice. I went to the game on Saturday. You all played well."

"Thanks. Always glad to have other athletes in the crowd."

"Right? It's so much more meaningful than regular fans in attendance," I agree. "Not that we have nearly as many people in the stands as you guys do. People will show up for baseball, sure, but they tend to forget softball exists. We're kind of an afterthought."

"That's bullshit," Tucker says. "Y'all are badass."

"Thank you! I like to think so." I beam at him, and he quirks his lips into half a smile.

Barrett is politely curious. "When does your season start?"

"Not until February. We're still in conditioning season."

"Oh, gross," Amir says. "I hate conditioning."

"Same!"

This is going way better than I thought. The guys aren't exactly verbose, but they're hardly kicking me out. And Miles is warming up to me the longer we sit here. He's wearing a navy Newton Football sweatshirt, his dark hair styled neatly to the side. There's about three days' growth of beard lining his cheeks, but it looks purposeful rather than lazy. He was clean-shaven after the game on Saturday. On Mondays in class, he has a hint of scruff, and it develops into most of a beard by Wednesdays.

He's cute. I don't know why I didn't notice it before. He is good-looking already, but when he smiles that tentative half-smile, he shoots right up to a perfect 10. I don't care that he's on the bigger side. He's solid muscle beneath his bulk, strong. It adds to his charm. There's absolutely nothing wrong with him, and I hate that other people think he's somehow less than because of his size.

I hate that *he* thinks he's less than because of his size. I've heard the comments before. I'm what could politely be called curvy and less kindly called fat. I'm that in-between size between plus size and large. Sure, I work out all the time. I have muscles on muscles. But I also have bulk. I have a butt and hips and boobs. I'll never be stick-thin. That's just not me.

Eventually, I have to get to class. As much as I'm enjoying hanging out with the football guys, political science waits for nobody.

"Have a good day," I say to the guys, lingering over their empty plates.

Barrett grunts. Tucker waves. Wes turns a page in his book.

"You, too," Miles says, his cheeks going pink.

"Nice to meet you," Greg says, standing when I do. He escorts me as far as the tray return receptacle before he turns back and returns to the table.

eleven

. . .

Sam

THE SORORITY HOUSE is teeming with people by the time I arrive after classes. That's not unusual. What I'm not expecting are the half dozen guys loitering about the living room. They're all wearing Gamma shirts and sweatshirts, representing our brother fraternity.

"You're late," Wendy, our president, tells me when I walk in.

"I brought donuts," I say, holding up the box.

"Okay, you're forgiven," she says. "What flavor?"

Laughing, I pop the top. I know she's going to take the buttercream filled donut. That's one of the reasons I got extras of that flavor. It always goes quick, as do the maple bacon logs and the red velvet cake donuts. Every week, a different sister is in charge of supplying snacks, and I know donuts are always a hit.

The meeting starts out normally enough. Tamar is sitting on the opposite side of the room with Kiersten, Haleigh, and the other girls in our class. So far, nobody has commented on our abnormal distance. Normally we're attached at the hip. Right now I can't even look at her without my blood boiling all over again.

"Don't forget, formal is coming up, we're only five weeks away," Wendy says. "The guys are here to help. Elijah will pass around the committee sign-up lists. We'll have Jake and Dylan on bartending duty. Sarita has already agreed to check dates' IDs. There's still room on the decorating committee and on cleanup duty."

Shit. Formal. Also known as my least favorite event of the year. I hate every minute of dressing up, putting on a formal dress and heels, and finding a date for an interminably long evening of partying. Because it's not only the formal dance. It's the getting ready, the pictures before, the bus ride there, the dinner and dancing, and then the unofficial afterparty. It's an ordeal.

Freshman year I took a baseball player I was kind of talking to at the time. He tried to feel me up during pictures before the bus even left, then pouted the rest of the night because I didn't want to sleep with him. He might be the reason I'm so disdainful of baseball players now. Last year I went with one of the Gamma brothers, Jake, who had recently broken up with his long term girlfriend and wasn't ready to commit to anyone else yet. We had a decent time, drinking and dancing, and at the end of the night, we went our separate ways. Okay, so maybe formal isn't always so bad.

Across the room, Jake meets my eye and winks. It's not flirty, more friendly. I'm not opposed to asking him to accompany me again, though last I heard, he and Stacey are back together.

I have no idea who I'm going to ask this year. Going dateless is simply not an option, but there is nobody even close to being on my radar. I don't date much, preferring anonymous hookups I meet at a party and take home for a night or two. It doesn't last much beyond that, and that suits me just fine. Not every girl is cut out for a serious relationship, and right now, I don't think I could handle it. I have enough going on between school, softball, and my sorority obligations. I don't have the bandwidth to devote any real attention to a guy on top of that, too. Right now, I have to prioritize myself and my existing commitments before I even think about adding anything—or anyone—else into the mix.

Immediately my mind flashes to Miles and his shy smile. Which is ridiculous, because I hardly know the guy. We've talked two, three times now. We're not even friends. Although I could see it turning out that way... The faint bead of arousal rears its head again. Yeah, he's cute. Yeah, I could see myself going out with him. That doesn't mean he's interested—and if he is, if he's interested in what I have to offer. I'm not cut out for long term. Once or twice and then I'm done. I can't do much more than that.

After the meeting, I stay for dinner with my sisters. I try to spend as much time with them as I can. I'm already disconnected from them by living in Athlete's Village and spending every waking moment in the softball house. I'm stuck in that awkward liminal place between being part of the crowd and an outsider.

On his way out the door with the rest of the brothers, Jake comes up to me and gives me a half hug. "Hey, girl," he says, tugging on my ponytail, and I laugh and bat his hand away.

"Hey. You looking forward to this formal?"

He makes a face. "Not really."

"If we can't find any other dates, you cool with going together again?" I hold my breath, half hoping.

Jake raises his pinky finger, and I lift mine. Together we shake on it, a pinky promise.

"It's a deal," he says. "Stace and I are… well, I don't know. TBD, basically."

"I get that."

"When you going to get a boyfriend?"

It's my turn to make a face. "Um, never."

"You're not interested in dating?"

"Meaningless sex? Yeah. Dating, a boyfriend? No, thanks,"

I tell him. "I have too much on my plate to worry about that. Softball season will be here before I know it and then I'll have even less time."

"So that story I heard about you and that football player…"

I roll my eyes. "We were studying."

This rumor must be gaining traction if people outside of the athletic department are hearing about it. Not that there's anything wrong with Miles. He's great. I just wish other people believed me.

"Uh-huh."

"Seriously. He's brilliant," I say. "People are trying to make it into something that it's not."

"People? Or Tamar?"

I say nothing. So the distance between me and my best friend did not go entirely unnoticed.

"It's been awhile since you've gone out with someone for more than a date or two. Do you want me to hook you up with one of the brothers? Chase has mentioned you once or twice…"

"Which one is Chase? Is he the tattooed beefcake or the guy who taps the kegs?"

Jake looks like he's tasted something bitter. "Beefcake."

For a moment, I consider it. Only for a moment.

"No, thanks. I'm good on my own. I just need a date for this stupid formal."

Wendy, the sorority president, scowls at me. "Did I hear you say the formal is stupid?"

My face heats. "Um…"

"Sam, the formal is about celebrating our sisterhood."

"Yeah, by getting dressed up, taking lots of pictures, and drinking."

She shakes her head. "It's so much more than that. It saddens me that you think that lowly of us."

"I don't—"

"You do. We know why you rushed. You put in the bare minimum of effort. You don't want to be here."

"I do. Really, I do."

Now.

Back then, I didn't. Over time, my opinions have changed.

"Pull your weight, show up with a smile on your face, and stop being such a goddamn bitch all the time," Wendy snaps. "Nobody is forcing you to be here. You aren't being held hostage. You got in. You were a legacy. You can tell your mommy you did her proud. If you want to be here, great. If you don't, there's the door. It's up to you, babe."

I don't know how to react to that. People are staring, whispers floating across the room. I'm not used to being the center of attention, not like this.

"I want to be here," I mumble.

"What was that? I didn't hear you?" Theatrically she cups her ear.

"I want to be here," I state definitively. "I want to be part of the sisterhood."

"Then fucking act like it," Wendy snipes.

Nobody talks to me at dinner. It's like they've decided I'm persona non grata, too, so I'm shunned by both my sisters and my teammates in the same day. Okay, maybe the thing with the team wasn't on me. They were content to pretend like nothing was wrong; I was the one who refused to sweep their poor treatment of Miles under the rug.

Normally, Tamar and I walk home together and gossip about who said what and who wore what. Tonight I walk home alone. She doesn't even wait for me—she just leaves. My roommates are hanging out in the living room, watching HGTV. I don't join them. I would rather be on my own.

In my room, I pull out my phone and sigh. Devoid of messages, as per usual. My brother's busy with his life, and anyway, we're not that close. My parents are busy with work. I miss them, don't get me wrong, but it's a little easier to deal with them from a distance. They won't be able to make it for Parents' Weekend next month, though they try to come out for a long weekend in the spring when we're playing games.

My finger hovers over the button for Miles' contact. I want to call him. I want to hear his voice. I don't know why exactly I want it so badly. It's this inexplicable need bubbling up inside of me. He'll make everything better. He'll make me feel better. I don't know how I know that. I just do.

But we're not that type of friends. We're not friends, period. Two meals together doesn't create a strong and solid friendship out of nowhere. It will take time to develop. Maybe after another couple tutoring sessions, I can broach the idea of us hanging out sans books sometime. He has to do something with his other than play football and study plays and work out.

That half-smile drifts into my mind again. I roll over and scream into a pillow. It helps a little bit.

Everything is wrong. I feel off-balance, off-kilter. My whole world has tilted sharply to the left and I'm not sure how to get it back to normal. If I even want it to go back to normal.

twelve

. . .

Miles

SAM IS ALREADY in class by the time I arrive. Instead of sitting in the back of the room like she usually does, she's right up front, in the chair directly next to the fat guy desk. There's another bottle of purple Gatorade on my desk.

"Hey," she says, giving me a mega-watt smile. My heart skips a beat.

"You don't have to keep bribing me. I already said I'd study with you."

Her cheeks go a bit pink, but she meets my eye and doesn't flinch at the unintended harshness in my voice. "I know. I wanted to."

"Thank you." I twist off the top of the bottle and take a sip, letting the artificial grape flavor dance over my tongue. "Purple is my favorite flavor."

She grins. She doesn't try to fight me, try to tell me a color isn't a flavor. Today she's wearing another pair of leggings and an oversized sherpa jacket over a Newton shirt.

"You ready for this?" I ask, nodding to the board at the front of the room. The professor is organizing his notes, shuffling papers around.

"Never. But it's going to happen whether I'm ready or not."

Almost against my will, a smile pops out. She's pragmatic and I like that.

"How was your weight lifting session?" she asks.

I grunt. "Good. Hit a new PR."

My entire body aches, a bone weary exhaustion that comes with heavy weightlifting. At the same time, I feel impossibly energized. I wonder if this is why people do drugs. The natural endorphin high is amazing; I can only imagine how good artificially created endorphins would feel. I want to feel like this all the time.

She beams at me. "That's fantastic!"

A warm glowing feeling spreads deep in my chest. I scratch idly at my clavicle. Nope, it's not going away. Shit. This isn't good. This isn't good at all.

I like her. I really don't want to like her, but I do. Every time she smiles at me, my stupid traitorous heart skips a beat. My blood rushes in my ears and my pulse goes thready. I hate this. I don't want to like her. I'm only setting myself up for disappointment. There's no way she would ever feel the same about me. Nobody has ever has before.

"Thanks."

There are people whispering about us. It's a small class, only about fifty students. They're all watching us. Watching me. The big guy who couldn't possibly ever be normal.

I just want to be normal, to disappear into the shadows. Instead I stick out like a sore thumb.

I duck my head and pull out my notebook. Sam says something. I don't hear her over the sound of the blood rushing in my ears.

She seems to get the hint that I don't want to chat. She turns to her own notebook, drumming her pen against the spiral as she waits for Professor Cassidy to start the lecture. I can smell the cherry vanilla of her perfume, fresh and comforting.

I want her to want me. I'd settle for friendship at this point, though of course I'd be thrilled if she wanted more than that. I'm not the kind of guy that girls want to go out with. I've never been that guy. I went to my high school homecoming only because I played in the football game. I didn't go to any of the formals or dances. I skipped my senior prom because no girl would ever want to go with me and it was easier to pretend I didn't want to go than to face the disgust on their faces. It was difficult enough talking to girls in a non-romantic setting, much less trying to ask them out.

The good thing about college is there aren't any stupid formal dances with required attendance. The closest thing is our annual end of season football banquet, and even then, nobody blinks twice if we show up without a date.

Am I only interested in her because she defended me? I really don't know.

I don't think so. I was attracted to her from the get go, from that awkward interaction after the football game and at the frat party, way before I even knew who she was. Still, I know it won't go any farther than us studying together. There's simply no way someone like her would ever be interested in someone like me.

And isn't that a kick in the pants. I can't sacrifice my education in hopes it will make girls like me. I have to put myself first. Even if I'm only setting myself up for disappointment in the meantime.

thirteen

. . .

Miles

WE MEET in the same study room. Sam is fresh from a shower, her wet hair pulled back into a sloppy top knot. Her cheeks go pink when she sees me in the small room.

"Sorry I'm late," she says.

I glance at my watch. It's 7:01.

"You're not."

She slumps into the chair across from mine. "I came straight from practice. Fuck. I hate conditioning days. I can't wait until we can get back out on the field."

"I know what you mean." Offseason training is the worst. My fingers itch to just get out there and do it.

"Do you have any fun plans for your weekend?" She pulls out her notebook and textbook, her eyes conveniently not meeting mine.

It's only Wednesday, but for most college students, the weekend starts on Thursday, if not earlier. Some people have week-long weekends.

"Football game."

Sam nods. "Yes, but aside from the game? It won't take up your entire weekend."

"Dinner with my parents." We meet every Saturday after

the game. It's our little tradition. They used to take me out after games all through high school, too. It was our special time together, away from the craziness of day to day life.

"That's great that they live close enough that they can come visit you," she says, a bit wistfully. "My parents only make it out once or twice a year. It's hard. I miss them."

I cough. "What about you?" My cheeks are flaming red. "Your weekend?"

She sighs. "Not sure yet. There's a frat party on Saturday I'm supposed to be at. I don't know. I haven't been in the partying mood lately. My friends and I aren't really talking right now."

My stomach drops. "Because of me? The other night?"

She nods, a quick jerk of her chin. "They're being assholes, and I don't really want to be around them right now."

"I'm sorry."

"It's not your fault." She offers me a tentative smile. "They're the jerks. I don't want to associate with people that stupid."

"They shouldn't be giving you shit for hanging out with me."

"They know nothing about you. They shouldn't make assumptions and believe rumors," she counters. She sighs again. "I don't want to talk about them. I have to deal with them enough at home."

I crack open my textbook and, after a moment, she follows suit. We go over today's lecture until she has a good grasp on the material, and she feels confident enough to complete this week's homework.

"How do you feel about dinner?" she asks around eight-thirty.

"I already ate." No loss of appetite today, thank goodness. "I'll sit with you. I have enough room in my budget for a snack."

Her smile makes my heart skitter to a stop. "Great."

We pack up and head downstairs to the dining hall. It's pretty sparsely populated, which is good. Ideal. Not as many people here to make fun of me this time.

It's chicken souvlaki night. Sam loads up her plate, and I grab a protein shake and a peanut butter sandwich for my last meal of the day. I'm not even hungry, but according to my nutrition app, I haven't eaten enough today. If I don't keep my calories up, I'll start to lose weight, and with it, I could lose my starting line position.

"How was your day?" We take seats across from each other at an out of the way table for two, far away from everyone else.

"Fine." I take a bite out of my sandwich, letting the rich peanut butter flavor linger on my tongue.

She rolls her eyes. "You can talk to me."

"Isn't that what we're doing?"

"Come on. We should be friends. Real friends," she says. "I don't have enough of those."

I grunt. I know what she means. I have the guys in the house. That's about it. I don't hang out with the rest of my teammates when we're not on the field or the weight room. My social circle is limited. That's the way I like it. Less risk of people being nice to my face and then stabbing me in the back.

So, maybe my attitude isn't the healthiest. I'm working on it.

"Sure," I finally tell her. "We can be friends."

Her smile makes my stomach twist. My sandwich turns to paste in my mouth.

I don't think we can be friends. I want more than that.

Except that's all we can ever be. There's no way she would ever be interested in me. I need to forget about her and move on. I'll get used to the disappointment. I've lived through worse. I can handle this.

fourteen

. . .

Sam

THE NEXT DAY, Tamar is waiting in the locker room with a cookie bouquet from my favorite bakery.

"I'm sorry," she says.

"Okay." I push past her and head to my stall, pulling out my practice gear.

"I miss you."

"Well, bully for you."

"I'm sorry I was mean about your new friend."

"Yeah, you were a real piece of work."

"I just… I don't understand."

"Well, now you do."

"I don't, though. I don't get it," Tamar admits. "What do you guys even have in common?"

"Statistics. And he's sweet," I tell her. "Being around him puts me in a good mood. I can't explain it. He's going to be my friend. The only question is if you're going to be my friend, too."

"I miss you," she says again, which is still not a real apology.

"I haven't gone anywhere."

"Except you have. There's this distance between us now. You've barely been able to look at me all week."

"I wonder why." I pull my shirt over my head and tug on my sports bra to avoid looking at her.

"I've been a bitch."

"Yeah, you have."

Tamar is quiet for a few moments. "I don't get it, I really don't, but I'm going to try to be a better friend and support you. It's not about me, it's about you."

"I don't think I'm asking for a lot," I point out. "Basic human decency."

She winces. "I deserve that. I deserve a lot worse than that."

We finish getting dressed in silence and head to the gym. It's another fun day of cardio drills. I'd rather do suicide sprints all day, every day, than relive that conversation over again. The other girls seem to have picked up on Tamar's and my reconciliation and are all over me again.

"Are you joining us for dinner tonight?" Aleesha asks. "We haven't seen you in forever."

"I'm right here. I haven't gone anywhere."

She rolls her eyes. "You sit at the table and don't talk to anyone. You come home and go straight to your room. You're here, yeah, but you're not with us. What happened? What did we do?"

"It's nothing you guys did. It's me. I needed some space."

A strategic retreat. I needed to hole up and lick my wounds in private. To stew in my own anger without letting it bubble over and impact other people, too. My ire was mainly aimed at Tamar and her stupid comments. I don't care that the rest of the team is gossiping about me behind my back. It's what they said to my face that got to me.

It's been a fucking *week*, and it's only Thursday.

I want to talk to Miles. It's an ache deep inside me. I don't know why. We barely know each other. We've studied together twice. We've talked a handful of times. I'm not saying we're best friends or anything like that. I don't even know if we're regular friends yet.

But being with him is peaceful. Restful. Something about him soothes my soul in a way I didn't know I needed. He makes my whole day better.

I want to see him again. Now. And not just to study.

I wonder what he's doing. Does he have class? Practice? There's another home game this weekend. Is he getting ready, studying plays, watching tape? I want to know. I want to know everything about him.

After practice, I head to the dining hall with the girls like nothing is wrong, and for the first time, I think everything might be okay. I'm still a little too much in my head. I'm not purposefully withdrawing this time, though I have withdrawn. I wonder if he's going to be there.

Following the girls to a table, I take a seat facing the back of the room. Miles has sat at the same table every time I've seen him. He's a creature of habit.

We're halfway through our meal when I spot him. He's wearing a Newton Football windbreaker and a dark green hoodie. It's a good look on him. I've only ever seen him wearing school hoodies—a new one every day, sure, but always sweatshirts. I don't blame him. It's fall. The chill in the air has a way of seeping into your bones if you're not careful.

He takes his usual seat at the back of the room. Miles unrolls his silverware and looks up. We make eye contact, and he blinks. Then he breaks into a brilliant smile.

My heart skips a beat.

"Hi," I mouth from across the room.

His cheeks go red, and he dips his head.

Beside him, Barrett looks over in my direction and nudges him. He waggles his fingers at me and snickers.

I roll my eyes. Miles doesn't look up again. He toys with his food.

As I watch, Tucker and Greg join them, Amir not far behind. Wes pulls another book out of his backpack and proceeds to ignore everyone.

It's always the six of them. They don't hang out with anyone else that I've seen. Wes always has a new book. Tucker is always on his phone. Amir, Greg, and Barrett are usually laughing and joking. Sometimes Miles joins in.

He's still not eating, just pushing the food around on his plate. His head comes up, and his eyes dart over to mine. We make eye contact for a brief second, and he looks away again, his cheeks flaming red. I wonder what that's about.

"How do you feel about movie night?" Lex asks. "We were thinking either Legally Blonde or Grease."

"That sounds fine," I tell her, not really paying attention.

I pull out my phone and bring up Miles' contact. I added his number on Monday and haven't used it yet. I don't know what to say. I just know I want to talk to him.

"… Sam?"

I drag my focus back to the conversation. "What?"

Aleesha smiles at me, not unkindly. "We're all done. Are you still eating?"

I glance down at my half-finished plate. "Yeah, I'm still working on it. You guys go ahead. I'll catch up to you."

"You don't want us to wait?"

"I'll be fine. I'm going to grab dessert. I'll meet you back at the house."

They pack up and go. I wait about five minutes, and then I'm up out of my seat, walking across the dining hall with my tray. It's more crowded now. There are more people lingering over their meals.

"Hey," I say, hovering at the seat across from Miles. "This seat taken?"

He looks up at me and drops his fork. "All—all yours," he manages. He swallows loudly, so loud I can hear it. "You want to sit with us?"

"I like you guys."

Greg, beside me, laughs. "Why wouldn't you like us? We're fucking fantastic."

I grin at him and pat his arm. "See? We're all going to be best friends."

Barrett grunts. "You want to hang out with us?"

"All of y'all need an attitude adjustment," I tell them. "It's like you can't believe someone would actually want to be friends with you."

"Because they don't," Wes says, not looking up from his book. His voice is deep and rich with a hint of Midwestern twang. He turns a page. "You'll change your mind."

The guys look shocked. I'm not exactly sure why.

"I won't."

"You will."

"Dude…" Amir says, trailing off.

Wes doesn't respond to him. He takes a bite of his chicken and acts like we're not in the middle of a conversation.

"People don't like us," Barrett finally says. "We don't fit in."

I laugh. "I'm a tomboy from the Deep South and an athlete in a sorority house. My mama wanted me to be a good ol' Southern belle. Trust me, I know what it's like not to fit in. It wasn't until college that I found other women like me."

Even the girls on my softball team back home were frilly, froo-froo girls. Not that there's anything wrong with it. That's just not me.

"You're all right to me," Greg says, and it might be the best compliment anyone's ever given me. He steals an apple slice off my plate, and I let him. "You can sit with us any time."

fifteen

· · ·

Sam

I CAN'T KEEP my eyes off of him. No matter where he is on the field, I can find number 14. I don't pretend he can see me in the crush of people in the student section.

Tamar, Lex, and Aleesha all wanted to come to the game. Fine by me. I have no issues with going to events or parties alone, though it's always nicer to have my friends at my side. Because they are my friends. Little hiccups don't mean I'm suddenly going to drop them. We simply work harder to iron out our differences.

The center hikes the ball to the quarterback, and Miles launches into action, clashing with a massive guy opposite him. He gets the tackle as the ball is thrown twenty-three feet to the nearest receiver.

I cheer with the rest of the crowd. I'm not cheering for the play. No, my eyes are directly on Miles Cavanaugh and his broad form. His tight ass is on display as he bends over on the ten yard line.

I've never been a bigger fan of football pants than in this moment.

He's nothing like my usual type. Sure, I usually go after other athletes—not baseball players, never baseball players—

or frat guys. But they're typically fit guys with great bodies and self-confidence up to wazoo. Maybe too much confidence.

But Miles... that endearing smile, the way he's gone out of his way to help me with statistics, that bashful look on his face whenever I compliment him...

There's no doubting his strength. He works hard. And he's kind. He's so nice. I just want to curl up and bask in his warmth. He makes me want to smile, like, all the time. He makes me feel good about myself.

Shit. I like Miles Cavanaugh.

I track him through the game. When he's on the sidelines, his eyes are focused on the field, tracking the plays. When it's his turn to take the field, he claps his teammates on the shoulder before he takes his place across from guys equally as massive as he is.

"Look, it's your boyfriend," Tamar says, pointing out number 73 on the sidelines. Sawyer.

"Greg isn't my boyfriend," I tell her, rolling my eyes. "He's just a friend."

"You had dinner with him yesterday."

How do they know about that? I waited until after my friends left to change tables. Or is it already on social media?

"Trust me. There is absolutely nothing going on between me and Greg. I didn't even know who he was until four days ago."

She hums. "Four days? Isn't that all it takes?"

I ignore her, cheering when Miles manages to pin the offensive player opposite him. He does a quick spin and is able to tackle the receiver, too. I'm on my feet, clapping and cheering. The rest of the crowd is enthusiastic, sure, but nobody else seems to have noticed the amazing double tackle.

Newton wins, 42 to 14, in no small part due to Miles's excellent game play.

Tamar nudges me. "You going to visit the player tunnel again?"

How does she know about that?

I hadn't even thought about visiting him. Immediately an itch burns deep inside of me. I want to see him. No, I *need* to see him. Right now. Right this very minute.

"You want to come with me?" I ask, an olive branch.

"Sure."

There are clusters of friends and family waiting outside of the player tunnels. Tamar and I huddle together in the brisk chilly wind.

Ahead of us are a group of people decked out in gear for number 14. Miles's family. I recognize the mom and dad from last week. There are two girls with them now, both wearing Miles's number. One girl is tall, nearly six feet, and even her bulky coat can't hide her lithe, athletic form. The other girl is younger, shorter, with a more curvy shape and her long blonde hair expertly curled. I'm instantly jealous of her hair. It would take me two hours to do that, and my hair still wouldn't look half as good.

Greg and Wes lumber out of the tunnel, both of them holding a protein shake.

"Hey, boo," Greg says when he gets close enough to be heard without shouting. "What are you doing here?"

"Had to come out and support my favorite guys," I say, injecting some enthusiasm into my voice. "Good game."

Wes salutes me with his protein shake.

"You know, I think this is the first time I've seen you without a book."

His mouth turns down into a sour frown.

"Don't worry, he'll pick one up as soon as we get home," Greg says, clapping him on the back. Wes scowls at him.

"Miles!" the girl with curly blonde hair squeals, jumping up and down.

Craning my neck, I just barely spot him before the girl

throws herself at him in a flying tackle hug. He catches her easily, wrapping his arms around her.

"Hey," he says, his voice deep and rumbly.

Greg snorts. "I'll leave you to it."

"To what?"

He rolls his eyes. "Come off it. I know why you're really here."

"You're the worst," I tell him, and he laughs.

Miles catches my eye over the head of the other girl. His face goes red.

His mom follows his eye over to me. "Oh, Miles. Is that your little friend from last week?"

I don't know whether I should be offended by that or not. I'm hardly little. Thick, they call me. Muscular, maybe. I'm not little.

He sidesteps his family and comes over to me. Like the other guys, he's carrying a protein shake in a clear plastic cup.

"Hey," he says, his eyes bright. "You're here."

"Had to come out and say hi to the guy with the three sacks," I tell him. "Great game."

Behind him, Greg sniggers. Wes elbows him in the ribs.

"Thanks," he says, lifting one of his massive hands to rub the back of his neck.

"Have you met Tamar?"

"Hi," he says, looking none too pleased.

"That's your family?" I nod over to them.

He looks back at where they're clustered, not five feet away. All four of them are blatantly eavesdropping.

"Yeah. Would you…" His voice drops to a whisper. "Do you want to meet them?"

"Come introduce us to your little friends, Miles," his mom says.

His face flames red. "I'm so sorry about them."

I pat his strong arm. "There's nothing to be sorry about. They're cool."

"You say that now…" He shakes his head.

We close the gap, Tamar and the other guys not far behind us.

"Sam, this is my family. Everyone, this is my friend Sam. We have statistics together."

The taller girl giggles. The shorter one—she looks way younger up close—looks me over with interest.

"My mom, Nancy, and my dad Steve," he says, introducing us. "My sisters, Mackenzie and Ashley."

"Nice to meet you, honey," his mom says. She has a broad smile on her face. Her eyes are warm. "I'm always so happy to meet Miles's friends."

"Nice to meet you, too," I manage.

"So you're the girl keeping my boy on his toes," his dad booms, clapping Miles on the back. "Good for you."

"Oh, I don't know about that…"

"We're just friends," Miles says, and I don't know why, but there's a rock in the pit of my stomach.

Friends. We're friends. We study together. We've had dinner together a few times. We barely know each other.

I don't want to be his friend. I want more than that. And he is so completely not interested, he's introducing me to his family. He would never do that if he saw me as anything but a friend.

"We're on our way out to McRory's Pub," his mom says. "Would you like to join us for dinner?"

"Oh, I wouldn't want to impose on your family time," I manage.

"Maybe another time," his dad says. "We'll see you next week?"

"Next week is an away game," Miles cuts in. "We're playing Harvard."

"If I can get a group of girls together, we'll be there," I promise him. "I've never gone to an away game before."

"Oh, it's really cool," the younger sister—Ashley—says.

"There's a whole group of us that go to all of the regional games. And the Harvard stadium is really pretty."

"I'll think about it. Hopefully I'll see you guys there."

The older sister giggles again. His mom—Nancy—smiles kindly at me.

"Will you be at the Delta house later?" Tamar asks.

Miles goes pink. "Oh, I don't know. I'm not a big fan of parties."

"Well, we'll miss you," Tamar says. I elbow her, and she smirks at me. "Sam will be there."

It's a Delta party. Of course I'll be there. I'm there every week, whether I want to be or not. It's not like there's much else to do in our sleepy college town. On Saturdays we go to frat parties. Attendance is basically mandatory for sorority members.

"I'll think about it," he finally says. He clears his throat, glancing back at his family. "You all about ready to head out?"

"It was nice meeting you, honey," Nancy says, clasping my hand briefly.

"See you next week," Steve says.

Greg sniggers and throws his arm over my shoulder. He's remarkably demonstrative.

"Just friends, eh," he murmurs into my ear.

I elbow him in the ribs, and he lets out a soft *oof* of surprise.

"I hate you," I tell him casually, and he laughs.

"You love me, baby."

sixteen

. . .

Miles

I CAN'T BELIEVE I'm here. I'm not the kind of guy who goes to frat parties. Most of my Saturday nights are spent at home on the couch, recovering from a brutal game with a superhero movie and a bowl of ice cream. It might not be cool, but it works for me.

Sam. It's because of Sam that I'm even at this party, and she's nowhere to be found.

With Amir and Greg flanking me, we head towards the keg, more for something to do than any real desire to drink. Tucker opted to stay home, and Wes wouldn't be caught dead at a frat party. Barrett had a few rough tackles this afternoon. We don't all need to hang out together all the time. We just like it. It's nice finally having a group of people that look like, think like me, like the same things I do. We come from all different places, have vastly different life experiences, but there's a thread of commonality there that simply existing in the same space for so many months has made us friends. No, not friends. Brothers.

Drinks in hand, we meander through the party. People cut a wide berth to allow us to pass. Greg heads towards the back patio so we follow him. The Greek houses are built differently than the ones in Athlete's Village. There are twenty-five bedrooms, enough for fifty or more brothers to live here, plus a media room with an enormous flatscreen and squishy recliners. The kitchen is huge. There's a formal dining room with seats for—I count quickly—thirty people, currently being used for beer pong at one end and what looks like strip poker at the other.

There are a few guys on the team who are in fraternities. I never once considered joining. It's different with the football team. We've poured our blood, sweat, and tears onto that field, into that weight room. We battle together every week. That's forged the fire that binds us together, whether we like it or not.

"Boys!" Sullivan, our best safety, cries out at the sight of us. He's flanked by a girl on each side, both wearing tight jeans and crop tops, both pawing at him like he's NFL caliber and not mediocre on a middle of the pack team. "Glad you could make it."

I don't think Sullivan is part of the fraternity, so I'm not sure why he's acting like this is his party. He missed a pretty fucking important tackle at the end of the third quarter. I wouldn't be partying like this if it were me.

But it's not me. Sullivan and I are two completely different people. Where he goes high, I go low. The only thing we have in common is we play for the same team, and even then, sometimes it's iffy.

The back patio is packed with people. Fraternity guys wearing their letters, girls all over them. There's a cluster of Kappa girls by the heat lamp, dancing in a circle. Sam isn't part of them.

I wonder where she is.

I'm glad she came to see me after the game, even if it was the most awkward interaction in the history of the universe. My mom kept asking me about that nice blonde girl all through dinner. My dad clapped me on the back and said it was good I'm making friends.

Yes, I'm grateful to count Sam amongst my limited group of friends, but that's not what I want from her.

The crowd parts and I spot her. She's with her friend again, the bitchy one. Her hair is tied back in a braid. It's longer than I thought, falling to the middle of her back. She's wearing tight black jeans and a baggy grey top and I—

I can't think straight. My cock reacts against my will. She's across the room. She doesn't even know I'm here. She's not giving me the slightest hint she's interested.

I don't care. I want her. I want her so bad my hands shake and my palms itch and my stomach churns with anxiety over never getting a chance to be with her.

She turns and I catch sight of the berry color staining her lips. Her eyes are done up with dark shadow and thick, black lashes. Shit. Lust fogs my brain. My blood pounds in my ears. I feel dizzy.

From across the room, she catches my eye and grins. She tips her cup up to me in silent greeting.

I down half my beer in one hurried gulp. It doesn't taste very good. I don't care.

Sam says something to her friends and then she's making her way through the party. Making her way to me. She stops about a foot in front of me, giving me some breathing room while still being close enough we don't have to shout to be heard over the pounding, pulsating blast of music.

"Hey. I didn't think I'd see you here."

I take a hefty gulp of my beer, more for something to do than any real desire to drink it.

"Didn't know I was coming."

She smiles at me. "Are you having a good time?"

"Not my scene."

Sam laughs. "Yeah, me neither. I can't wait to get out of here."

"Why're you here? If you don't want to be?"

She shrugs. "I kind of need to be. It's a sorority thing."

People jostle into us and she takes a step closer to me. I can smell the sweet cherry and vanilla of her perfume, rich and innocent.

"Do you want to dance?" She looks up at me guilelessly.

My face heats up. "I don't dance."

I'm too big. I get in the way. There's no way I can do the grinding that's going on in the living room.

Her cheeks are pink. "Oh. Okay then."

"I think I'm going to head out." I hook a thumb over my shoulder.

Her smile falls. "Oh."

"This isn't really my thing."

"Mine, neither," she admits again.

"Do you… do you want to come back to my place?"

She gulps down half of her drink, her eyes wide. "Wow."

"The guys are probably playing video games or watching a movie. It's super chill. No pressure."

Her sigh of relief is like a punch to the gut. She doesn't want to hang out with me. With us.

"Yeah, okay," she says, and my heart skitters to a stop. "Video games or a movie sound fun."

My beer is half full. I don't want to drink it. I took it more for something to do with my hands than anything else. Setting it down on the nearest flat surface, I turn to Sam, who's draining her cup.

People move out of the way for me to pass. Sam follows in my wake. There's a tug on the back of my hoodie.

Looking back, she has her hands on my sweatshirt, holding on. She's so close I can smell her sweet perfume through the stink of stale B.O. and pot clouding the room.

Without thinking about it, I offer her my hand. To my eternal surprise, she takes it, her small, calloused palm sliding against mine.

Sparks dance along my arm, coalescing into a ball of fury deep in my gut. My cock jerks to life again at the innocent contact.

She squeezes my hand and I take a deep breath, turning towards the front of the room and the hazardous path to the exit.

Are people talking about us? Is anyone going to see this and comment? I'll just die if they start giving her shit for leaving with me. It's bad enough people are being assholes because we ate dinner together a few times. Her best friends are giving her a hard enough time for deigning to spend time with us. I don't pretend to think this will be any better for her.

In the gym the guys on the football team clapped me on the back. They all think I'm sleeping with her. She's hot, there's no doubt about that. She's a fucking catch.

She just won't be caught by me.

Finally out of the house, I breathe in fresh air for the first time in way too long. Beside me, Sam's still holding my hand. We're side by side now, walking at a more sedate pace than my frantic escape from the frat house of hell.

"Thanks for getting me out of there," she says, squeezing my hand. "I was starting to go crazy in there."

"Me, too."

She doesn't seem to be in any hurry to let go of my hand, so I don't prompt her. If this is all I get from her, I'll go to sleep tonight happy I got this much.

The first drop of snow takes me by surprise. It's cold, yes, but not nearly cold enough for that. The flurries start in earnest as we cross the quad to head back to our part of campus.

Sam lets go of my hand, and I mourn the loss of contact. She spins in a circle, her arms outstretched, her head thrown back.

"What are you doing?"

"It's snowing," she says, like I'm crazy for not under-standing.

"We live in Boston. It snows three quarters of the year here."

"It's the first snow of the season. Isn't it beautiful?"

It's October.

She's beautiful. Her cheeks are flushed, her hair is pulling out of her braid, and she's never looked more gorgeous in her life.

But I can't say that to her. We're friends, and tentatively so. We're still learning about each other. Something clenches deep in my gut. I don't want to be her friend. I want more.

After a few minutes of admiring the snowfall, Sam seems to gather herself. She skips over to me, wrapping her arm around mine and taking my hand again. It's all innocent, inci-dental contact. It still sends my pulse pounding like a ten piece brass band.

seventeen

. . .

Miles

LIKE I PREDICTED, my roommates are on the couch. Tonight they're playing Jeopardy! on the big screen TV, Wes against Barrett and Tucker combined. They don't bother to look up when we enter.

"Hey, y'all," Sam says. "Whatcha playing?"

Wes pauses the game. All three guys turn to look at her, eyes wide.

"What're you doing here?" Barrett grunts.

She offers him a brilliant smile that sends my heart into overdrive. Not fair. She shouldn't give her smiles out to just anyone. I want them all to myself.

"Miles said something about video games and a movie tonight. Much more fun than a frat party."

"The more, the merrier," Tucker says.

"You can join our team," Barrett adds. "Wes is kicking our asses tonight."

The bookworm grunts. He never talks in front of people he doesn't know very, very well. He barely talks to the coaching staff or any of our teammates. It took him six months to say more than "pass the salt" at dinner freshman year.

The couch is full, so Sam settles in the giant armchair in the corner. It dwarfs her, making her look impossibly tiny. I take the other armchair.

"Turkey," Sam calls out, and I turn my attention back to the screen.

Tucker presses the right button and wins the question. The next answer comes up, and she knows that question, too. Between Tucker and Barrett, our "team" gets the chance to solve six out of ten answers, and Sam knows the right question every single time.

She's brilliant.

Final Jeopardy! time. Wes has about a $100,000 lead over us. He bets very strategically, and he got all three Daily Doubles right.

Even combining our scores, Wes still beats us in a landslide.

"I think I'm done," Tucker says, throwing down the game controller. "How do you feel about a movie?"

"I'm down for whatever," Sam says, giving him her beautiful smile again. Unease rumbles in the pit of my stomach.

"I'll make popcorn," I announce. I need something to do with my hands.

"I'll help." She springs to her feet and follows me into the small galley kitchen. There's barely enough room for one person to move around in here, much less two.

I pull three bags of popcorn out of the cabinet. She takes them from me, her delicately calloused fingers brushing against mine, as she tears off the plastic wrap. Getting down the bowls is a stretch, even for me, and my hoodie rides up a bit, exposing my stomach. My face heats up when I notice her eyes glued to the strip of skin revealed by the errant fabric.

Sam swallows. "Do you need any help?"

"Got it."

Tossing the first bag into the microwave, we wait in silence as the clock winds down.

"Do you want anything to drink? We've got water, vodka, juice, hot chocolate…"

Her eyes light up. "You have hot cocoa?"

I nod, showing her the canister.

"It's perfect. Popcorn and cocoa and a movie," she says.

I grab two mugs and fill the kettle. Wes takes his tea very seriously. He has about fifteen different varieties of tea in stock at all times. When he saw Greg make tea one time by microwaving his mug, he freaked out. Two days later, the kettle arrived.

Glancing carefully at the main room, I make sure the guys aren't paying attention before I pull out my secret stash of marshmallows from inside the box of cereal. If I'm not careful, the guys will eat all of them in one night. I always have to buy two bags, one for them and one for me.

"Oooh!"

"Shh!"

Sam presses her lips together, trying to hide her smile. She lowers her voice. "Are these secret marshmallows?"

My face heats up, but I nod.

"It'll be our little secret," she whispers, grinning up at me.

My heart slams into my chest with the force of a freight train.

The kettle sings, and I pour hot water into two mugs. She mixes in the hot chocolate powder. I top the mugs with a small handful of the mini marshmallows.

When we get back to the main room, the couch is conspicuously clear. Wes has his book again. Barrett and Tucker have relocated to the armchairs.

"You guys moved," Sam says, pouting.

"I need the back support," Tucker lies.

"I didn't want to sit on the couch by myself," Barrett lies.

Idiots. I know what they're trying to do. It's not going to work.

Sam settles on the couch, and I gingerly sit beside her. She scoots over until our thighs are nearly touching.

"So what are we watching?"

Barrett names the latest superhero movie. "That's okay with you?"

"Sounds perfect," she says. She tucks her feet under her legs and takes a sip of her cocoa, letting out a contented sigh.

"This really is turning into the perfect night," she says. "Thank you for inviting me. I'm glad you did."

I clear my throat. "Thanks for joining us."

Tucker turns on the movie, and Barrett dims the lights, so we're immersed in the brightness of the TV.

Ever so casually, I rest my arm on the back of the sofa. Sam scoots closer to me, her hand on her thigh brushing against my leg. Arousal jolts down the backs of my legs and settles deep in the pit of my stomach.

Her braid brushes against my arm, tickling me even through the thick fabric of my sweatshirt. She shifts, her head falling against my shoulder.

I don't hate it. I don't hate it one bit.

She adjusts again.

"You okay?" I murmur quietly, as to not distract the guys. Or to not attract their attention.

She swallows. "Do you have, like, a throw blanket? I'm a little cold."

We normally keep a blanket on the back of the couch. Wes's sister bought it when she visited last spring, to make the place more "homey," whatever that means. It went in the laundry last month and never made it out. It's probably still in the dryer.

"I'll go grab one."

"No, I'll be fine."

"Sam, it's not a big deal. We have plenty of blankets."

We disentangle, and I head for the stairs. Swiping the soft blanket off the top of my bed, I retake my place on the couch.

She tucks the blanket around her legs and immediately scoots in next to me. I move to put my arm on the back of the couch again and she shifts, pulling my arm down around her so my hand rests on her hip.

Okay, then.

"Thank you," she whispers quietly in my ear, so the other guys can't hear. "This helps a lot."

I'm basically hugging her. Her hand settles on my knee. I can't think, can't breathe.

"You doing okay?"

The smile she sends me is radiant. "Never better."

She rests her head on my shoulder again.

I wish I could say I know what's going on in the movie. I spend most of the evening watching her instead. She has a small mole beneath her left eyebrow. There are clusters of freckles dotting her cheeks, no doubt from spending so much time in the sun. She's fully made up. I've never seen her this done up before. I like it, yes, but I like her just as much when she's fresh-faced straight from practice.

I just like her, period.

She falls asleep about halfway through the movie. I shift, letting her fall against my chest, so I'm carrying more of her weight. The better to support her, I rationalize. I'm pathetic. I give up pretending to watch the movie. I'd rather watch her.

As the credits roll, I come back to myself to find the other guys whispering. No doubt about us, I roll my eyes, and then shame rolls through me. There is no "us."

"You guys look cozy," Barrett says, his eyes bright with amusement.

"Fuck you."

She stirs and then settles again. Her arm comes up to hug my leg. I go stock still, even as another piece of my anatomy reacts instinctively.

I shake her shoulder. She lets out a low whine deep in her throat that goes straight to my cock.

"Sam. It's time to wake up."

"No." She snuggles into me further. "I don't want to get up."

"Sam."

She groans, slowly blinking open her eyes. "It's not morning yet."

A laugh bubbles up in my throat. "No, it's still night time."

She burrows into the blanket. Into me. "I'm so warm and cozy. I don't want to get up."

"You can stay here tonight," Barrett offers. "In case you don't want to make the trek back home."

I glare at him. What's he playing at?

"No, I should go home. It's only two houses down."

"You can stay as long as you like," Tucker adds.

She stretches and yawns. "Maybe next time we can have a slumber party," she says, grinning.

My cock likes that idea a little too much. I choke at the sudden burst of arousal flooding my veins and she turns to look at me.

"What? You're not a fan of sleepovers?"

"It's getting late," I say instead. "Let me walk you home."

She gets her shoes on, and I fold up the blanket. It smells like her perfume now. I'm never washing it again.

It's wet and slick outside. The snow is coming down harder now. Sam skids and grabs onto my arm for balance. It feels so natural to wrap my arm around her, bringing her into me as we make the treacherous walk all one hundred and fifty feet to her house.

"I had a lot of fun tonight," she says when we reach her front porch.

"Me, too."

"I'm glad you invited me over. We should do it again sometime."

She's smiling up at me, standing much too close. Do I kiss her? I want to kiss her.

We're friends. We've barely established whatever this is. She doesn't need one of her so-called friends slobbering over her.

"Good night."

Her face falls. "Have a good night. Thank you for walking me home."

"Any time."

eighteen

. . .

Sam

LAYING in my bed all day on Sunday, warm and cozy, I can't keep from replaying our evening in my head. We snuggled! He let me snuggle with him! He held my hand on the walk home and didn't complain when I made such a big deal out of the snow. He made me cocoa and gave me his super secret stash of marshmallows and then he let me cuddle him and—

I could die happy now. Except, no, I couldn't, because he just thinks we're friends. The dreaded friend-zone.

Eventually, I pull myself out of bed and head downstairs. Most of my roommates are out of the house, watching a men's swim meet. Lex has a crush on one of the swimmers. We all support one another, so when there's an event or a meet or a game on campus, we all bundle up and go.

He held my hand!

Bundling up, I trek all the way across campus in the snow to the science center grab-and-go field station just to acquire a bottle of grape Gatorade. All I want is to see the smile on Miles's face when he sees it. That'll keep me going.

There's a knock on the front door around five. Aleesha came home about an hour ago—she wasn't feeling very well, period cramps from hell—and she's locked away in her room.

Athlete's Village is a restricted community; people need a student athlete ID card to get in. Not even parents are allowed to drop by without written permission and being signed in. Nobody comes to visit, so I wonder who's here.

Miles is standing on the front porch, his coat and strong shoulders dusted with snow.

"Hey," he says, tucking his hands into his pockets.

"Hi." A giddy burst of excitement wells up deep within me. He came to see me! He sought me out!

"I'm heading over to the dining hall in a bit. With the guys," he adds quickly. "Do you want to walk over with us?"

"Sure! That sounds great!"

Shit. Was that too enthusiastic? I'm showing all my cards here. "I just need to get dressed."

His eyes scrub over me. I feel naked under his gaze in the best possible way. "You look great."

I'm wearing fuzzy lounge pants and a Dean High School Football shirt I stole from an ex boyfriend I don't miss one bit. My feet are covered with cozy socks. I haven't brushed my hair today. I—shit, I haven't brushed my hair today. I don't know if I even took off my makeup last night. Shit, shit, shit.

"You're a liar, but thank you," I say, because my mama taught me manners, and I only sometimes remember to pull them out.

He goes pink. He scrubs the back of his head with his enormous hand. I wonder what I would be like to have those enormous hands all over me, touching me, those thick, blunt fingers pressing inside of me…

"Are you okay? You look flushed," he says, a furrow appearing between his eyes.

"I'm fine."

Miles coughs. "So, um, we'll pick you up in about fifteen minutes?"

"I'll be ready," I promise.

"Well, um, bye?"

He turns away, making his way slowly down the porch stairs. I close the door behind him and scurry into action. In fourteen minutes, I scrub my face, brush my teeth, tie my hair up into a messy top knot, and change into actual clothes, a pair of leggings and a flowing tunic top. There's no time to worry about makeup or looking cute. If he doesn't like me as I am, I'm not going to become someone else just to please him.

There's a knock on my door sixteen and a half minutes later. Miles is on my front porch again, the rest of the guys clustered together at the end of the walk.

"You ready?"

Grabbing my coat off the hook, I shrug it on and follow him down the porch steps. I want to hold his hand again. Can I? Maybe he doesn't want his friends to know.

"What did you guys do today?"

The back of my hand brushes against Miles's as we walk. He makes no attempt to take hold of it, so I try to relax and enjoy the incidental contact for what it is.

"Went to the gym, had a deloading day," he says, as his hand brushes mine again. "Did some laundry. Caught up on homework. Not much, really. How about you?"

"Not much for me, either." I don't want to tell him about the grape Gatorade. I want it to be a surprise tomorrow morning in class.

"Sometimes that's what you need, a day to do nothing," he says, and then he goes red. He flushes so easily.

Fuck it. I grab hold of his hand. He startles beside me and goes tense before he relaxes with a blustery sigh. He tightens his grip on my hand.

If the other guys notice, I don't know about it. We're lost in our own little world, the two of us against everyone else.

We walk in silence for a bit. The guys are chatting—well, everyone except Wes, who occasionally nods. It's peaceful. Being with them is relaxing. Being with Miles is—it's like fireworks on New Year's Eve. Bright and magnificent against a clear black sky, filling the world with hope and wonder. He lights up my whole world.

And I've only known him for a week and a half. I wonder what will happen once we know each other better, once we've had time to settle into… whatever we are. Friends, not friends, it doesn't matter. I just know I want him in my life. I'll take whatever I can get.

We get to the ASC and Miles opens the door, ushering me in first. It means I have to let go of his hand. I feel the loss acutely.

The dining hall is sparsely populated. They seem to like eating at times when there aren't a lot of people here. Thinking back to O'Rourke and the way he seemed to deliberately target us, I can't blame them. Bullies like O'Rourke are the absolute worst.

The guys like the table at the very back of the room. Wes makes a beeline for it and the other guys follow more sedately in his wake. He takes the seat on the end—the same one he usually sits in—and pulls out his book before he even sits down.

Shaking my head, I take what's become my usual seat, beside Greg and across from Miles.

"Hey, stranger," Greg says as he sits down, bumping my tray with his. "So you decided to slum it with us again."

"Always," I joke, but I'm not joking. As long as they'll have me, I'll be here. "You getting sick of me yet?"

"Never," he says, giving me a half-grin. "We missed you at the Delta party last night."

"I was there." For a little while.

"So I heard," he says blandly. Across from me, Miles goes red. "How was the movie?"

"I fell asleep."

He tsks. "Such an exciting Saturday night."

"I had fun," I tell him self-consciously. "Every weekend doesn't need to be a raging party."

"I'm just teasing, babe," Greg says seriously. "You do you. If you want a night in, there's no shame in that. Same if you want to go out and drink until your face falls off."

"Is that what you did last night?"

He laughs. "I had two beers, and then I got annoyed with all of the drunk people. Ended up in the back room playing video games with a few of the guys."

"Sounds like a good night," I say, cutting into my chicken. For mass-produced dining hall food, it's pretty damn good. I have no complaints.

Miles is quiet, methodically eating his food. If he has any complaints about me chatting so much with Greg when he's the one who invited me, I don't know about it. He hunkers over his plate and keeps his head down.

He's a man of very few words. On rare occasions he'll say two full sentences in one go. Most of the time getting anything more out of him is like pulling teeth. I started to take it personally until I realized he's reticent with everyone, not just me. When he does speak, I listen.

It felt right being in his arms last night, like I belonged there. I'm already trying to think up ways that we can make that happen again.

My phone buzzes. It's Wendy, my sorority president. I didn't sign up for any committees for the formal. Surely that's a misunderstanding, because she knows I want to support the sorority in all of its endeavors. I roll my eyes.

"What's wrong?" Miles asks.

"I'm being manipulated into doing something I don't want to do."

"So don't do it," he says, like it's that easy.

"She's going to guilt me into it for the good of the sorori-ty," I try to explain.

"If you're not interested, tell her. She'll respect your decision." He considers. "Or maybe she won't, in which case she doesn't deserve your respect."

I sigh. "I want to *want* to participate. I'm just not good at any of the tasks she has available. I suck at decorating. My hand lettering is terrible. I don't want to deal with a bunch of drunk freshmen. It's all just… not my idea of a good time."

"There's nothing you can do?"

"I barely want to go to this stupid formal to begin with. I hate everything about it."

He swallows loudly. "You have a formal coming up?"

"Yep." I rest my cheek on my fist. "And I don't particularly want to go. Last year wasn't bad, I went with a friend, but freshman year was awful. It's not the way I like to spend my time. Getting dressed up to go to a stuffy formal dance… count me out."

"I wouldn't know," he says. "I've never been to one of those."

"A sorority event?"

"A formal dance. I went to the homecoming dance my freshman year of high school," he says. "It was in the school multipurpose room. It was terrible. I left after the first hour."

"Exactly. And this is even worse, because everyone will pre-game and then drink at the event, and girls will be puking by, like, ten o'clock." If my experience last year is any indication, I'll be the one taking care of Tamar and the girls when they get too in their cups to function.

Miles winces. "Yeah, that doesn't sound fun."

I sigh again. "I have to attend, whether I want to or not."

I'm not looking forward to finding a date. I have no problems with asking a guy out—that's not the problem. It's just that the guy I would want to go with is completely oblivious to my feelings for him. He let me hang all over him last night. When he walked me home, I was this close to grabbing him and kissing him.

And then he said goodnight. And then he walked away.

I lost my chance. I know I won't get another one. I'm going to have to make the best of it and find some random guy to go with. Maybe Greg would—

No. I don't want to go with Greg or any of the other guys. I don't even want to go with Jake. I want to go with Miles. I want to spend the night in a pretty dress with a nice, cute guy on my arm, dancing and having a good time. I want Miles. I don't want anyone else.

nineteen

. . .

Miles

THERE'S another bottle of grape Gatorade sitting on my desk. I cut my eyes over to Sam, who smiles weakly in my direction.

"So you should probably know," she says, and then bites her lip.

"What's wrong?"

"Some people posted photos of us. Leaving the party Saturday," she says.

It's like there's a rock in the pit of my stomach. "Oh?"

"I don't care, but the comment section is… not nice. Don't waste your time with them."

I pull out my phone. I'm not into social media, but the athletic department requires us to have accounts on all the major platforms. The team usually tags me in highlight reels or clips from the game, so I'm not surprised to see several hundred unread comments. I never check them unless I'm in the mood to torture myself. Today, though… I need to.

There's a photo of us leaving the party hand in hand. It's grainy, zoomed in and cropped, trying to fabricate gossip. There is no denying that we're leaving together.

Looks like tubby found a butterface.

She's thick, he's huge. Wonder how that works?
Uglies bumping uglies. How fitting.
Why is she slumming it with him?

My vision goes red and then black. I hate them. I hate this. I want to reach through my phone and shake the people on the other end of the screen. I want to punch them. I want to punch everyone. And then I want to curl up in a ball and dwell in the misery. Sometimes it's worse that they're all anonymous comments. There's nobody I can challenge outright.

And Sam… they're talking about me, which is bad enough, but now they're bringing her into it. My hands clench so hard around my phone my knuckles go numb. I want to call out every single one of these fuckers. I want to punch them all until they're bleeding in the brain. I want to—

"I told you not to look," she says sadly.

"How are you? How has it been?"

Does she have as many comments on her own handle? The ones on mine are equally disparaging and clapping me on the back for scoring such a catch.

"It's not great," she finally says, worrying her lip with her teeth. My gaze focuses on her mouth and that rock in the pit of my stomach sinks heavier. I tear my eyes away. Now is not the time to get distracted.

"I'm sorry."

I'm sorry she's getting hateful comments online. I'm sorry she's getting lumped in with me. I'm sorry people are dicks. I'm sorry that her private life is being exposed online like it's some sort of game. I'm sorry that associating with me is dragging her down.

But mainly I'm sorry that I'm not sorry. She left with me. She went home with *me*. She wanted to hang out with me. I'm not sorry that we spent the evening together.

I just wish she wasn't getting shit from idiots who don't know when to keep their mouths shut.

"There's nothing to be sorry about," Sam says quietly, earnestly. She touches my arm and sparks shoot up my veins and directly to my heart. "I have no regrets about Saturday night."

There's a lump in my throat. "But—"

"They're assholes. They don't know me. They don't know you. They don't know anything." Her eyes flash with muted anger. "I don't care what they think."

"Fuck 'em," I tell her. "Fuck 'em all."

Her smile is still too sad. She can say it, but it's clear she doesn't believe it, not really.

"Exactly."

Professor Cassidy breezes into the room. She takes her seat—she still wants to sit beside me?—and pulls out her notebook.

"We're still on for tonight?" she murmurs quietly as he gets set up.

She wants to study with me? She still wants to be seen with me in public?

"The guys and I meet for dinner at six, if you want to join us," I finally say.

She bites her lip. "I'll be coming straight from a sorority meeting. My schedule is pretty packed today."

"Oh. Okay."

"Tomorrow my day is wide open, if you want to meet up."

YES! Yes, I want to hang out. Yes, I want to spend all my free time with her. How could I not? She's perfect.

"Sounds cool," I tell her, totally chill.

The smile she sends me is radiant. It buoys me all through class, through my workout, and through dinner with the guys. Nothing can bring me down when she's smiling at me, not even stupid internet comments. She wants to spend time with me. She wants to hang out with me.

So what if she doesn't want to be anything other than friends? I can be her friend. I can be there for her. I'll take whatever scraps of her affection I can get. Because anything is better than nothing. Now that I know her, I don't think I can go back to not having her in my life again.

I'm not the guy with a big group of friends. I don't hang out with most of my teammates; we just don't have much in common. The friends I do have, I keep close. Usually I keep to myself. I don't talk a lot. I don't have a lot to say. These aren't bad things; they're just facts.

Sam makes me want to be different. She makes me want to be better, to be more social. I wish I could make friends as effortlessly as she does. I wish I could be as open and honest with my thoughts as she is. I wish I could let the insults roll off my back. I wish—

There are a lot of things I want, and a lot more I can't have. There are things I have the power to change. I can talk more to the other guys on the team, try to forge a friendship outside of us playing the same sport. I can tell people what I'm thinking instead of keeping my thoughts to myself. I can join in on conversations happening around me instead of letting them fly over my head. I can ignore the idiots online.

twenty

. . .

Sam

MY ACADEMIC ADVISOR, River, is a pretty chill person. Their whole job is to make sure I'm taking the right classes for my double majors—communications and marketing—and that I'm passing my classes. They aren't afraid to sign me up for tutoring or encourage me to go to office hours for a particularly confusing professor. Basically, they're on my side... except when they're on the school administration's side.

"I'm sorry, Sam," River says, which makes me frown as they look over my midterm progress report. "One more grade like this and you'll be academically ineligible for next season."

"I'm doing my best."

"I know you are," they say soothingly.

"I found a tutor!"

"Good. Through the student resource center?"

"A classmate. He got an A on the last exam, though."

River sighs. "Okay. That's a start."

They aren't a fan—they want me to utilize the university's free and available resources, the options available to all students.

"I went to the SRC. They don't have any math majors who

have taken statistics already," I tell them. "I've tried to go to the professor's office hours when they don't conflict with practice, but he's rude and condescending."

"Well, he *is* a math professor," River says with a small smile. "It kind of goes with the territory."

"He doesn't respond to emails, and when I ask questions in class, he doesn't actually explain anything in a way that I can understand."

"So you found yourself a tutor," they say encouragingly. They make a note on my progress report.

"Yeah. And he's smart, he's brilliant, and he explains things in a way that makes sense to me. When he starts talking about football or baseball or softball, it clicks in my brain."

"That's great, Sam," River says. "I'm glad you found someone that helps you."

"He does."

Miles is helping me so much, maybe more than he knows. For all the drama that's come up in my life in the last week or so—the rumors online, the tension with Tamar, the confrontation with Wendy—he's not actually at fault for any of it. He's just living his best life, studying, eating dinner, going to frat parties, and it's like he doesn't care what anyone says about him. It all rolls off his back like an ineffectual lineman trying to get past him. Like on the football field, he excels at not letting it bother him.

River's eyes glimmer. "Do I want to know? No, I don't. Okay, yes, tell me. Tell me everything."

I laugh. "There's nothing to tell."

"He's cute?"

My face heats, and I look away.

"Oh boy."

"Yeah, he's cute," I allow.

"And you'll be okay studying with him?"

I blow out a breath. "Well, yeah, since he's not interested in me, there's no reason we wouldn't be able to."

"I wouldn't be so sure about that. You're a catch, honey. I'm sure plenty of people are—"

"I don't want plenty of people. I want him."

Now that I'm admitting it out loud… yeah, I want Miles. I have no idea how to make something happen when, A, he's not interested, and B, I don't have the headspace for an actual relationship, but I do want something to develop here. I don't want a fling or a fun night or two. I want something real.

I want Miles.

And he doesn't want me. Sure, he might want a friend. Yeah, he's cool to study with me or watch a movie on a Saturday night. He doesn't want more. I was practically laying on top of him on the couch and he didn't even react. He didn't try to make a move despite ALL THE SIGNALS telling him I was inviting him.

"So, back to my grades," I say, and River sighs.

"If you don't pass this class, or if your grades dip in your other classes, I'm sorry, honey, but you'll be on the bench all next season," they say.

I swallow the bitter truth. Shit's about to get real.

"Okay."

"This isn't my choice. It's the university's rules."

"I know."

"If you have to miss the season…" River sighs. "Okay, so you can stay enrolled, and you can stay in your housing. Your tuition waiver for next season wouldn't be issued, nor would your housing allowance. You'd have to come up with about forty thousand dollars for tuition, housing, and a meal plan."

"For a year?"

They shake their head. "For one semester."

"Shit."

"You're being charged out of state rates, plus you're taking more than fifteen units per semester. Student housing on campus is expensive. Add in the meal plan… everything has a cost. The gear bag alone is fifteen hundred dollars, and without the waiver… It all adds up."

My stomach rolls. "Forty thousand dollars?"

There's no way I'll be able to afford this. I won't be able to take out a loan without a cosigner. I have no income, no job, no assets. Nothing. My parents are so obsessed with Dave Ramsey, they refuse to let me take on student loan debt, even though they can't afford to take on the cost of tuition.

"I can give you financial aid pamphlets, but from what we talked about last spring, your parents earn just enough that you don't qualify for any grants, and if they refuse to cosign on a loan…"

"Rock, meet hard place."

"Yep," River says sadly. "So your best bet is getting this statistics grade up. You can do it, I know you're capable of it. And it sounds like you're on the right track with this hot new tutor of yours."

"I didn't say he was hot."

"You're right," they agree. "You said cute. I'm the one that said hot."

Biting my lip, I look away. Miles is pretty hot…

"Just promise me one thing, Sam," River says. "Don't fall for this guy."

I blink. "What?"

"Don't jeopardize your grades for a guy. Don't sacrifice your season or your financial future over a guy. You're better than that, girl. No guy is worth that. Study hard, make the grades, and you can go after him next semester, once you don't need him to tutor you."

I leave River's office feeling like I've just been through a therapy session instead of an academic counseling appointment. I'm conflicted over their advice. How am I supposed to avoid falling for Miles when he's so cute and nice and interesting? He's right there. As we spend more and more time together, it's getting easier to imagine something happening.

Except for that whole bit where he isn't interested in me. Right. That part isn't so fun to admit.

I have to focus on myself: passing this statistics class; maintaining my athletic eligibility; making things right with my sorority sisters; and maybe making things right with Tamar, too.

I don't want to throw away my future, my season. I don't want to fail this class. I don't want to end my commitment to the sorority, and I don't want to let down my teammates. I'm being pulled in a million different directions, all at once.

One thing at a time. One step at a time.

Tonight we have our meeting, so I'll show up and wear my Kappa letters and try to convince the girls that I want to be there. Because I do. Really, I do. I just don't always know the best way to express that.

I'm not used to being the girl with a big group of friends. Teammates, yeah. Acquaintances, sure. Friends?

Tamar is my best friend. Lex and Aleesha are great. And then there's my sisters. Kiersten and Haleigh are amazing. Sarita and Jun are so cool. I've found myself a nice group of kind, supportive friends and built myself a community of people.

I should be leaning on my friends. I want to hang out with them. They're trying their best. It's just that their best isn't quite good enough.

Wendy looks me up and down and turns away, her expression carefully blank as she gavels the meeting to order. Haleigh gives me a small smile.

Sisterhood is new and confusing. At home I only have my one brother, and he doesn't like me half the time. Now I have this new community of women. We all have different backgrounds, different majors, different interests. The one thing we all have in common is that we choose to be here, choose to be part of the sisterhood. Nobody is required to be here, even the legacies like me. We all have to choose this of our own volition.

And most of the time… well, I like the events we go to, even if the never-ending frat parties get a little boring. We do philanthropy in the community. We celebrate women and lift each other up. And, yes, there's a lot of social events. We have girls' night basically every night. There's always a sister around if I want to watch a movie or go out to the bar or need a good cheering up. I know that all I have to do is say the word, and I'd have half a dozen girls at my side.

Sisterhood is about more than fraternity parties. I hope that five or ten or fifteen years down the line, I can count on these girls to still be there for me. Because I'd be there for them. They're my friends, and that means something to me.

Glancing across the room to where Tamar is sitting with Sarita and Jun, a glimmer of sadness takes over. She's supposed to be my best friend, my ride or die. I hate that she showed her ass and showed me who she really is. Am I the person I thought I was? I really don't know. Mostly I don't know how to get over my disappointment that she's not the person I thought she was.

I can't talk to her about what happens if I don't pass this class. She wouldn't understand. Her parents are supporting her; she only got a partial athletic scholarship, so her parents somehow found a way to make it work. She's lucky. *I'm* lucky. Just not lucky enough.

twenty-one

. . .

Sam

AS MUCH AS I'd like to stay with my sisters and have dinner, tonight I've got plans—with Miles. Just the thought of his endearing smile and the way he looks at me like I'm the only person in the world have me giddy. He treats me like a human being, like I'm capable. He doesn't coddle me. He doesn't treat me like a child. We're equals, even if he's the one teaching me.

And it doesn't hurt that he's gorgeous and kind and so charming. He's a genuinely good guy. I didn't think they still existed. Nice guys typically aren't as nice as they'd like everyone to believe. I don't think Miles has a single mean bone in his body. It's not in his nature to be cruel. He's kind and polite and caring, if a bit distant. I don't doubt his intentions like I might with other guys.

Most of the time, I'm surrounded by estrogen. My teammates are all female, and my sorority sisters are all female. Occasionally we hang out with our brother fraternity, so I might spend time with Jake and his brothers, or we go to a fraternity party on a Saturday night, and I'm exposed to other people there. For the most part, my circle is female. I don't really hang out with athletes from other sports—they're too busy, and I'm too busy. We might throw a low key party one night after practice, but it doesn't devolve into a rager like some other houses do.

I wish I had more male friends. It's hard. They tend to want things to be different than what they are: I'm looking for friendship, and they want a friend that will warm their bed for a few hours. I'm not opposed to a good few hours' romp beneath the sheets, but for the most part, I try to keep my friends separate from my *male friends*.

With Miles, though... I wouldn't be opposed if he wanted something to happen. I doubt he does, though. I basically threw myself at him last week and he barely even blinked. He must not be interested in pursuing a relationship right now, because he could have any girl in school he wanted. I've never seen him so much as talk to another person who isn't on the football team. He keeps to himself. I can respect that. He isn't distracted by interpersonal problems: he's focused on himself, on his performance and improving. We should all be so focused. It would stop a lot of the unnecessary drama.

He's already waiting in our study room by the time I get there. His dark hair is pushed back from his face, like he's been running his hands through the short strands. I want to be the one that rakes my hands through his hair. I want to touch him, and not only in a sexual way. I want to discover who he is, what makes him tick, what makes him the way that he is. I want to know all about him.

But he holds me at arm's length.

"Sorry I'm late," I announce as I walk in. "Thanks for waiting for me."

He checks his watch and mumbles something. It doesn't sound accusatory; it almost sounds apologetic, which is ridiculous, because I'm the one that's late.

Shucking my rain jacket, I settle into the seat across from him. His body language is making it clear that he doesn't want me to sit close, and it's not like we're in a playing footsie beneath the table kind of friendship. I like him, I *like* him, but I'm not blind to his complete apathy for me as anything other than a study buddy.

We study together. We aren't friends. Maybe one day we can be, but we're not there yet.

He opens his textbook, and so I do the same, trying to understand yesterday's lecture. Professor Cassidy might be a brilliant mathematician, but as a lecturer, he leaves a little to be desired. Okay, a lot to be desired. His classes jump too much for me to follow, and he goes off on tangents that don't seem to have anything to do with statistics until finally he pronounces the problem solved—without any explanation of how he got there.

When my brain has ceased the ability to learn new information, I push my books away. "How do you feel about dinner? Or a snack?"

Miles swallows carefully. "You want to eat with me?"

"Yeah. I mean, we're here, I'm hungry." I shrug. It's not rocket science.

"I mean... you want to be seen with me?"

"Why do you act like you're some kind of outcast? You aren't some kind of social leper."

He blushes. "The rumors..."

"Are rumors. People are always going to say hurtful shit on the internet. I can't control that. The only thing I can control is how I react to it."

"It's not that easy," he says, shaking his head.

"I never said it was easy," I warn him. "All I know is, social media and their lies are not going to go away, so all I can do is modulate my response."

O'Rourke is an asshole. I know he's the one behind all of this drama online. I know it deep in my bones. There's something in the way he looks at me that makes my skin crawl. I'm hypersensitive when he's around, and I don't like it.

Miles sits across the table from me, drinking a protein

shake and eating a peanut butter sandwich as I eat my dinner. He doesn't hurry me, he doesn't try to rush me. He's probably tired. He has early morning weight-lifting sessions every day, plus classes and practice and homework and a full life. He doesn't have time to waste tutoring me.

Still, I'm glad that he does. I like spending time with him. He's restful company. He lets me talk his ear off, occasionally jumping into the conversation with a quiet question or thoughtful observation. He speaks in more than grunts and monosyllables now, though rarely does he contribute more than a full sentence or two at a time.

He makes me feel good about myself. He treats me like a person worthy of respect. He doesn't care that I'm a little thick or that I'm not a frilly frou-frou type of girl. He doesn't care that the softball team hasn't won a conference championship ever, in the history of the program, or that I'm not the chatty, bubbly type of sorority girl everyone expects me to be. He gives me the space to just be me.

O'Rourke and his volleyball teammates are lounging at a table across the dining hall. At this late hour, there aren't a lot of other people still eating. That just means there are fewer people around to hear the pathetic vitriol he constantly spews.

In the middle of our conversation, Miles goes from verbose—for him—to monosyllabic. I have a feeling he caught sight of O'Rourke, too.

"Just ignore him," I tell him, and his face creases before it goes carefully blank. "He's a jerk. He's always going to be a jerk. There's no truth to anything he says."

He frowns. "Logically, I know that. He's trash."

I sigh. "It's just not always that easy."

"Right." He pokes at the crusts of his sandwich. "I think I'm done. You ready to head out?"

Leaving means passing by O'Rourke's table to get to the

tray return. I know he's going to make some pithy comment at my expense like he always does. At *our* expense.

"I'll take your tray," Miles says, pushing back his chair. "Be right back."

He's going to take the brunt of O'Rourke's commentary. He's drawing his attention away from me and onto him. I should be thankful. I should be happy he's protecting me. Instead I just feel dirty. I can't allow him to be the target of O'Rourke's hate.

But dread keeps me rooted to my seat. I have to sit there and watch as Miles takes both trays to the return carrel, passing by O'Rourke as he goes. I can see O'Rourke's mouth moving. The volleyball player beside him sniggers.

Miles squares his shoulders, lifting up his chin. His face goes red. He drops off the trays and plates. Now he just has to make his way back unscathed.

He's halfway back across the room when I hear O'Rourke running his mouth.

"Looks like Tubby finally found a girlfriend," the asshole says, his voice pitched loud enough to carry. "Wonder how much she charges. Is it by the hour or by the minute?"

Before I can so much as blink, Miles has O'Rourke by the collar, his enormous fist colliding into the bastard's face. O'Rourke lets out a shrill shriek. Blood pours out of his face.

"You shut the fuck up!" Miles roars, his voice deep and rumbly. His face is red, creased with concentration, as he shakes O'Rourke like a rag doll. "You don't talk about her like that."

The two volleyball guys spur into action, grabbing ineffectually at Miles's arms. He shakes them off like they're nothing. He shakes O'Rourke one last time before he tosses him back into his seat.

He's breathing hard, his chest rising and swelling. Miles clenches his fists and stalks back over to me. His eyes are bright. Wild.

"Miles…"

"Let's go," he says gruffly, scooping up his backpack and practically throwing it over his shoulder. "Now, Sam. Let's go."

I scramble out of my chair and onto my feet. He waits for me to be vertical before he's striding away.

"Miles!"

I catch up to him in the vestibule of the ASC. He shoves open the door, and we're hit by the icy cold blast of the night air.

"What?!"

"Um, what the hell was that?" I dodge in front of him and stand my ground. I won't let him push past me. "What happened to ignoring him?"

He's still breathing hard, his face now a dull pink. "I couldn't…" He flounders. "I couldn't let it go by. The shit he was saying… I had to let him know. It's not right."

"I don't care about him. Nothing he says has any power over me."

"It's not right," he repeats firmly. "I couldn't just stand there and let him spew his bullshit. He needed to be put in his place."

There are three feet between us. I cross the distance in two steps, tugging at the front of his hoodie.

"What?" His voice softens now. He swallows thickly.

I tug on his sweatshirt again. "You're too tall."

He towers over me, at least a foot taller. He bends his knees a little, and I pull him into range. My hand closes around the strong expanse of his shoulder.

His stubbly cheek is scratchy beneath my lips.

"Thank you. You didn't have to, but I'm glad you did. Thank you."

His hands settle tentatively on my hips. I slide my arm around him, bringing us chest to chest in a hug. We're hugging. It takes him a second to react, and then he's wrapping his arms around me. He tucks my head under his chin, one hand cupping the back of my head. He's shaking. I tighten my grip on him.

"You're okay," I tell him quietly. "Everything will be okay."

"I'm not that guy." His voice breaks. "I don't fight. I'm not that guy."

"I know."

"I couldn't let him—" His voice hitches. "I *couldn't*."

"I know, honey, I know."

It takes a few minutes for his shaking to stop. I release him, taking a step back and adjusting the weight of my backpack over my shoulder. I don't think he would hurt me. He'd die before he ever hurt me. The safest place in the world is for me to be by his side.

"Let's go home," I tell him quietly. I offer my hand and he takes it, squeezing. "It's been a long day."

Miles lets out a blustery sigh. "Yeah."

We walk home in silence. His tight grip on my hand is an anchor to this world, grounding me. Grounding him, too.

Reaching my house, he tugs on my hand before I can climb the porch steps.

"Sam…"

My heart is in my throat.

"Yeah?"

He swallows thickly. "Thank you." He darts down and kisses my cheek, his lips warm and soft against my skin. "For being you."

I offer him a nervous smile. "There isn't anyone else I'd rather be."

twenty-two

. . .

Miles

I CAN'T WASH the blood off my hands. When I close my eyes, I remember the crush of cartilage as O'Rourke's nose broke beneath my fist. I hear the slurs he baited me with, the trash he said about me. About *her*.

I couldn't stand by and let him ruin her reputation. She deserves more than to be lumped in with me.

And then afterwards… when she kissed my cheek, when she hugged me, when she thanked me for defending her… I roll over in my bed and pull my blanket up over my ears. I want to relive that moment forever and ever.

She's not afraid of me. She's not disgusted by me. She still wants to spend time with me. I didn't just destroy the best thing that's ever happened to me with an impulsive, ill-timed punch.

She approaches our table the next morning like absolutely nothing is wrong. Her gaze falls to my bruised knuckles before she offers me a brilliant smile.

"Good morning," she chirps, settling in across from me and next to Greg.

"Morning," he grunts, his attention on his coffee.

From the broad smile on her face, she isn't offended.

"Good morning," I manage, clenching my sore hand around my fork.

"How was your workout?"

"Good." We did legs today. I love leg day. I'm fucking strong, and seeing the amount of weight I can lift increase week after week strokes my ego like nothing else. "You have weights too?"

"Chest, shoulders, and back," she says, and my eyes fall immediately to her chest. She's wearing a boxy sweater that only serves to highlight her... assets. My face flames red. It takes me a minute to meet her eyes. When I do, she's grinning, her lips twitching. "It was a good morning."

"You're not sitting with your friends."

"I spend enough time with them," she says. "I live with them and we train together. Sometimes it's nice to have a little space to miss them."

Wes grunts, his contribution to our otherwise private conversation in the middle of the dining hall.

Sam is smiling at him. No fair. I want all of her smiles for myself.

"Exactly, Wes," she says, like he said something worthwhile.

"So things are better?" I gesture with my fork. "With your friend?"

She sighs, worrying her bottom lip with her teeth. I want to kiss that lip. I want to do a whole lot of things to her mouth, none of them appropriate for people I call friends.

"I think so. She's been on her best behavior." She swallows. "She didn't say anything about Saturday night or the photos, so I guess that's a good thing."

"Nothing happened," I remind her. It was all innocent. We left a party to go play video games and watch a movie. We didn't hook up.

No matter how much I wish we did.

"No, I know. But if something... of note were to happen,"

she says, her face tinting pink, "we would have already talked about it by now. We don't have a lot of secrets."

I don't think I like the idea of her talking to her girlfriends about the private stuff we do together. I don't go blabbing to Greg and Tucker that she let me hold her hand. Mainly because then they would know the truth, that I'm a pathetic loser whose sexual experience is so limited it's almost nonexistent. Who am I kidding? We've lived together for a year and a half. They probably already know.

I'm not interested in pity fucks. Freshman year, living in the athlete's dorm, there used to be certain girls who would hang around and… *hang out with* players. They did all the work. And they seemed to enjoy it enough to keep doing it. Cleat chasers. Jersey chasers. Some girls were exclusively interested in football players. Some girls went for all athletes, regardless of the sport they played.

But they weren't actually interested in me, the person.

It sounded like a good idea at the time. Meaningless, no strings attached sex for a poor touch-starved virgin with virtually no self-esteem, where I didn't even have to do any of the work, emotional or physical. They climbed right on top of me and did everything.

It didn't feel good. In the moment, sure, it was fantastic. But as soon as they was done, they pulled their clothes back on and left without a word. It was nothing like they show in movies. There was no emotional satisfaction. I just felt empty. Used.

It's easier to lock that part of me away. I keep to myself. Eventually, one day, some woman might want to be with me. Until then, I'm going to work on being the best version of myself I can be.

Sam makes me feel like it might actually happen for me, like it's a possibility I might one day find someone who likes me for me. She hangs out with me enough, at times that don't include our study sessions, that it's not inconceivable that she enjoys my company. She's the one seeking me out.

And I like *her*. I like the way she bites her lip when she's concentrating. I like the little furrow in her brow as she works to understand the lecture. I like the way she treats each of my teammates with respect, like they're actually people instead of faceless blobs. I like the way she curls her hand under her chin when she watches movies, and I like the way she leans on me when she gets tired. I like that she's trying to work out her issues with her friend, that she isn't abandoning her or sweeping everything under the rug when things get difficult. And I like that she's devoted to her teammates and her sorority sisters, that she has a group of friends to fall back on, but she isn't afraid of standing on her own two feet.

Mainly, I just like *her*.

And, sure, the outside is quite nice too. She has gorgeous eyes and the kind of smile that could stop traffic. The curves of her body makes me lose all rational thought.

Sam meets my eyes, and I realize that I've been staring at her like an idiot. Drooling over her in the middle of the dining hall.

"You all right there, big guy?"

Big guy. From other people, it's an insult. From her, though, it feels more like a term of endearment. Yeah, I'm big. I can't change that. Most of the time, I don't even want to.

"Fine," I tell her, focusing my attention back onto my plate. It's nearly empty. I can't remember eating any of it.

She gives me one of her brilliant smiles, and my stomach flips. "I have to get to class in a few minutes. What do you have planned for the day?"

"Library." I have a paper due next week for my linear algebra class. I thought it would be an easy course, but it's surprisingly challenging. I kind of dig it.

She beams at me. "Great. I'll walk with you."

"Are you done?" I take her empty tray and stack it with

mine before making my way over to the tray return. She's talking with Greg, saying something I don't catch, though I hear him grunt at her like a mannerless caveman. "Ready?"

She pops up, slinging her backpack over her shoulder. "Ready!" She waves back at the guys. "See you later."

We cross the dining hall in silence. Making our way through the lobby, she tugs on her coat and gloves. She waits for me to do the same before she reaches over and takes my hand.

"What?"

"Nothing," she says, dropping it. Her cheeks flame red.

I take her hand in mine. "I didn't say I didn't want to."

Her smile is like a punch to the face. "Okay, then."

We're friends. We're friends that hold hands. She chatters on the way to the political science building about the paper she's working on and the test she has coming up in her kine-siology class. She fills the distance between us so effortlessly, I almost don't notice until we've reached her classroom.

"I'll see you later," she says, tugging at the hem of her coat.

I let go of her hand. "Right."

"Miles?" Turning to leave, I stop at the sound of my name. "Yeah?"

She shakes her head. "Nothing. I just… it's nothing."

"If it's nothing, that means there is something."

Sam crosses the three feet between us. Her hands fist in my coat, and she tugs. I let her pull me down.

Her lips land on my cheek. "Thanks for walking me," she says, her face bright red.

I go dumb. "Um…"

She releases me at once, taking a step back. "See you later," she says again.

"Right. Dinner?"

She nods, worrying that bottom lip with her teeth. "I'll be there."

twenty-three

. . .

Sam

THE NEXT FEW days settle into a routine. Wake up, jerk off, go to the weight room. Try desperately not to think about Sam. Have breakfast with her. Walk her to class, usually holding her hand. She lets me hold her hand! Sometimes she kisses me on the cheek when we get to her destination. On Wednesday, there's another grape Gatorade waiting on my desk. Spend most of class trying not to think about her. Dinner with the guys. Study room, trying not to think about how close she is. Second dinner with her. Walk her home, hand in hand.

I don't see her at all on Friday. My day feels oddly bereft without her. I don't like it.

Saturday morning, I get my first ever text from her.

Have a great game today. I'll be rooting for you!

I don't know what to say back. I'm not good at texting. The only people I ever talk to are my sisters or my teammates, and that usually consists of sending memes and gifs back and forth. I don't know how to put my thoughts into words without blurting out my feelings for her.

It's an away game today, across town in Cambridge. It's close to where I grew up in Charleston so I have a few aunts and uncles coming to the game along with my parents and sisters.

The game gets off to a rocky start. From the get go, Harvard has our number. I miss my first three tackles. On the fourth, I completely trip over my feet and get a knee to the shoulder for my trouble. It hurts like a bitch.

Harvard scores first, and then they score again. By the end of the first quarter, we're down 0-21, and it just gets worse from there. Our sophomore quarterback gets sacked twice in a row, despite Coach reconfiguring the line to protect him. Nothing we do is good enough.

At half time, Coach yells. There's no pep talk, no pumping up. Even Sullivan, who's usually joking around and goofing off, is unnaturally reserved.

Coach tugs me aside before I can join the rest of the team heading out of the tunnel. "We need to talk."

"Yes, sir."

He pulls out his phone. "Why don't you tell me what this is about?"

He presses play. It's a video. I'm clearly in the center of the screen, wailing on O'Rourke. He is very clearly bleeding from his face. I'm very clearly wearing a Newton Football sweatshirt. There's a banner behind him with posters for Newton Athletics.

"I'm sorry, son, you're riding the bench the rest of the game. There will be an investigation into the matter beginning on Monday."

"But he—"

"I don't want to hear it. You signed the honor code. Fighting goes against that code of conduct," Coach says. "You have the choice to sit in the locker room for the rest of the game, or you can sit on the field. Either way, you're sitting out until your case is investigated. Not my call."

I'm benched. My day is over. My *life* might be over. He's right: I agreed to the code of conduct. Fighting isn't allowed.

Fighting with other athletes is really not a good look for the department. Beating on a seemingly defenseless dude for no foreseeable cause really doesn't look good.

I could lose my scholarship. I could lose football. I could lose everything.

I wish I could say it was worth it. Defending Sam… I'd do that any day. Does that mean I'd sacrifice my education for her? No. I don't think so. I don't know. I like her. I like her a lot. But I've only known her for a few weeks, and we've been friends for even less time. I don't wade into battles that aren't mine to fight.

"I'll sit on the field," I finally say through clenched teeth, and Coach nods.

"Good lad. You'll get through this," he tells me, clapping me on the shoulder.

The stands are raucous with energized Crimson fans. The Newton contingent is quiet. By the end of the third quarter, the visitor's stands are nearly empty. Only a brave few remain.

I wish I could say I blame them. I don't. I wish I could say I played my best. I didn't. It's a shitshow of epic proportions.

Barrett tries to talk to me between plays. I shrug him off. I don't want to get into it. I don't want to tell everyone the reason I'm benched. Let them think Coach is unhappy with me.

I like to think I'm an honorable man. I mind my manners. I open doors for people. I don't lie, cheat, or steal. I stand by my word. I look out for other people and I donate to those less fortunate than me. I try to be kind to everyone I meet. I'm not a violent person.

It rankles that I've broken the code of conduct, that not only I did, but I got caught and filmed breaking the rules. That's not me. I'm not the kind of guy who gets into fights. I'm not the type of person who takes things personally. I don't use my fists; I use my words.

But O'Rourke had me seeing red. And it pisses me the fuck off that he's going to get away with spewing his poisonous vitriol at everyone else and get away with it scot clean.

There has to be consequences for what I did. I recognize that I shouldn't have broken his nose with one punch. I just wish it didn't mean potentially losing everything that's important to me.

It's a miserable game. Every single second of it sucks. Even when we score two touchdowns in four minutes isn't great, because we're trailing 14-42 with less than two minutes to go. It's bitterly cold. And I can't do a fucking thing about it, because I'm sitting on the sidelines instead of playing out there with my brothers.

There are clusters of Newton fans in the crowds, huddled under warm blankets and so many layers, their features too fuzzy to make out. I know my family is out there somewhere. I wonder if she's here, if she made it to the game. If she stayed.

We lose, 17-49. It's a somber group that troops back to the locker room. Greg claps me on the shoulder.

"You okay, man?"

I never told him about O'Rourke. I haven't told anyone. As far as I'm concerned, what happened stays between me and O'Rourke and his buddies. And now, whoever took that video and sent it to Coach.

"Just great," I tell him, heading to my locker. Taking off my jersey and pads, I head towards the shower. Maybe the warm spray will help.

It doesn't.

There's a routine to game day. Whether we win or lose, we still need to shower, we still get our protein shakes. We get dressed with decidedly less enthusiasm than we do after an epic win.

My phone vibrates on the locker shelf, and I swallow the lump in my throat. I don't want to put on a smile and play nice for my family right now. I don't want to stand there and listen to my aunts tell me how much I've grown and my uncles pick apart all the things I did wrong.

It's not my family, though.

It's Sam.

I'm sorry it didn't go your way, the text says. *You'll get them next time. I'll be cheering for you every step of the way.*

Jogging out of the tunnel, I take in the sparse collection of friends and family gathered to commiserate with us. There are a half dozen people I recognize, teammates' parents and girlfriends who come to every game.

She's there.

I hardly notice my family and friends gathered in a circle a few feet away. Sam's here. She came.

"Hey, big guy," she says, tucking her hands into her coat pockets. "Fancy meeting you here."

I swallow back the emotions threatening to burst out of me. "You're here."

"I told you I would be."

"Your friends?"

"They're around here somewhere. We're meeting at the diner across the street in ten minutes."

"You didn't go with them?"

She worries her bottom lip with her teeth. "I, um, I wanted to see you. After your game."

"Why?"

"Because I—um, well—" She swallows, throws back her shoulders. "There's a video going around. And I have a feeling it has to do with why you weren't playing in the second half."

Surging forward, I close the distance between us. My hand cups her cheek, and she leans into the contact.

"Miles..."

I cover her mouth with mine. I don't know what I'm doing. This is all instinctive.

Her lips part on an exhale, and she melts into me. Her hand slides from my chest to the back of my neck, anchoring me to her. I couldn't let her go if I wanted to.

Sam deepens the kiss, her tongue coming out to tangle with mine. My hand moves from her cheek to her hair, my fingers tangling in her loose braid. She lets out a whine against my lips.

"I don't care about the video," I lie.

"I do. You could—"

"We'll worry about that later," I tell her. "Right now I just... I want..."

Her hands fist in my coat. "Yeah?"

I want to kiss her again, and again, and again. I want her. I want to hold her tight and never let her go, because in her arms, everything will be okay. I want. I—

My mouth settles over hers again, and she licks into my mouth, taking, taking. I have no idea what I'm doing. I let her take control, and she smiles against my lips.

"Miles!"

Groaning, I pull away and rest my forehead on hers. "Was that—"

"Your mom? Yeah." She grins. "You okay there, big guy?"

"No."

Her gloved thumb brushes over my cheek. "You will be." She presses a chaste kiss to my lips and then pulls away, releasing her hold on me.

"Miles, honey!"

I force a smile on my face and turn to greet my family.

"Hi, Mom. Dad. Mack, Ash. Aunt Sue. Uncle Bobby. Aunt Carol. Uncle Tommy."

"Aren't you going to introduce us, son?" Uncle Bobby says.

"Everyone, this is Sam," I say, setting my hand on her shoulder. "Sam, this is... everyone."

She's flushed pink, her lips swollen from my kiss. I love it.

"Hey, y'all," she says, giving a little wave. She wraps her arms around me and burrows her face into my chest. "This is embarrassing," she says to me.

"Do you not want me to…?"

She tightens her grip on me. "No, I do. It's just… I'm interrupting your family time. You probably have to get back on the bus soon. I should… I should go."

I swallow the lump in my throat. "If you want to."

"I'll see you tonight?"

"We'll be back on campus in about two hours." My chest feels hollow. I don't want to let her go.

"Perfect. I'll come by the house," she tells me. She reaches up onto her toes and kisses my cheek. "Have fun with your family."

"Sam…" There is so much I want to say to her. So much I don't know.

She slowly disentangles from me. "I'll see you later."

twenty-four

. . .

Sam

TAMAR GASPS at the sight of me. "Where the hell have you been?"

"It's only been twenty minutes."

"Yeah, and you've been making out with someone. Your lipstick is all smeared."

Shit. I rub at my mouth with the back of my hand. "No, I haven't."

"You totally have." She rolls her eyes and settles back in the booth. "Come on, tell us everything."

"There's nothing to tell."

Except inside I'm squealing like a stuck pig. He kissed me! *He* kissed *me*! In front of all of his friends and family, the person he wanted to see most after his terrible game was me.

The person who got him benched from the game. Yeah, I forgot about that little tidbit.

I'm not sure which anonymous internet stranger sent me the video. I don't know how they got my number, how they knew I was there. I'm a little scared, to be honest. That's some grade A internet sleuthing. What's next, doxxing? I'm more concerned about the video on his social media profile. Both he and

O'Rourke were tagged, and it was clearly not taken by one of the volleyball teammates. Someone all the way across the dining hall decided it was their right to film and their obligation to post it.

My sisters are all looking at me expectantly. I want to tell them. I should tell them.

But I also want to keep that moment wrapped up tight, keep it close to myself for just a little while longer. He wants me. He wants to kiss me! He isn't as uninterested as he's made it seem.

I hope.

I don't know where we stand. I'm going to see him in a few hours. That will have to be enough for now. I can't obsess over it. Time will pass, whether I want it to or not.

We settle into the booth and conversation turns, like usual, to the formal coming up in a few weeks. Kiersten is on the decorating committee. Haleigh has to babysit the freshmen. I've been manipulated into helping clean up after the event, which means I get to miss the after-party that will continue into the wee hours of the morning. Not my scene. I'd call that a success in my book. I don't have to corral crunk people, I only need to clean up after them.

Tamar nudges me. "Will we see you at the Delta party?"

She's giving me an out. "Why wouldn't I be there?"

"I don't know. You might have plans with the person who smeared your lipstick." She gives me a triumphant grin. Yeah, she hasn't forgotten about that.

"I think I'm going to skip the party tonight." I say, a little too loud. Stretching my arms over my head, I yawn theatrically. "I'm beat. Practice today was rough. I think I'm just going to chill and watch a movie."

"Have fun," Kiersten says.

"We'll miss you," Haleigh says.

It's nice to be out and about with my sisters. We don't spend nearly enough time together, what with my softball commitments and their everyday lives. They have stuff going on, too.

Kiersten drives us back across town to campus. It's bitterly cold out, that kind of cold that seeps into your bones and lingers. I want to curl up under a pile of blankets with a certain dark-haired, dark-eyed someone and leech his body heat. I want to do a lot more than that.

As much as I want the cozy couple-y things we've been doing, I want more. I want to map the curves of his body, the strength of his muscles. I want to feel the crush of his weight on top of me, pinning me down as he thrusts inside of me. I want to feel his breath on my lips, his smile on my mouth. I want to—

It's been a long time since I've had good sex, the kind you can't stop thinking about and want to replay in your mind over and over again. College boys are great at mediocre sex, the kind you kind of regret in the aftermath, the kind where it's up to you to get yourself off because they don't know how to make that happen. I'm done with mediocre.

I don't think Miles is mediocre in any respect. The way he kissed me...

It's been nearly three hours since I saw him. It's like there's an itch beneath my skin I can't scratch. I want to see him. I *need* to see him. I need to know where we stand. Are we kissing friends now? Was it a fluke? Was he simply so hopped up on emotion, it poured out? Does he regret it?

I hope he doesn't. I don't.

Knocking on the door to the linebacker house, the door is yanked open almost before I can pull my hand away. Miles stands in the doorway, wearing a pair of Newton sweats and an NSC Football sweatshirt.

"Hey," I manage.

He steps outside in his dingy white socks, shutting the door behind him. He must be freezing.

"Hi." He swallows thickly. "Listen, about earlier..."

He regrets it. He wishes it didn't happen. I was reading too much into it. He was being nice—he doesn't actually like me. My chest aches. I've got this all wrong.

"I should go," I say. There's still enough time. I can go to the Delta party and get drunk and forget this day ever happened.

He catches my hand. Tugging sharply, he pulls me into him. I stumble into him, and he wraps his arms around me.

"Don't go," he says, before he lowers his head and kisses me thoroughly. So thoroughly I see stars behind my eyes.

Miles pulls back and licks his lips. "So, yeah."

Something deep within me spurs me into action. I slide my hands up to his chest, mapping the strong contours of his muscles. He tenses beneath my touch before he lets out a gusty sigh, relaxing. His warm breath drifts over my face, minty fresh.

I clear my throat. "Is there a reason we're outside?"

His face tints pink, but he meets my eye. "I want to make sure we're on the same page."

Oh. Maybe I skipped a few steps and just assumed we wanted the same things. I start to disentangle myself from him. He ducks his head and kisses my cheek this time, first one, then the other. That knot in the pit of my stomach lessens its grip on my intestines.

So maybe he's not great at the delivery. Maybe my mind keeps going to the dark place of its own accord. That doesn't mean he's in the dark place with me.

I run my gloved thumb over his cheekbone. "What page is that?"

He swallows thickly, clears his throat. "Look, I like you, Sam."

"I like you, too." In case all of the kissing wasn't making that obvious.

"I want to be with you."

"Hey, I want to be with you, too." My attempt at humor

falls flat. He swallows again, and I relent. "I'm interested in seeing where this could go."

He maps my cheek with his thumb. "Yeah?"

I nod dumbly. He dips his head, like he wants to kiss me again, but pulls back at the last second. His eyes flash with an emotion I can't identify.

"My roommates are all inside."

"Do you… not want them to know?"

"No, that's not…" He clears his throat. "I don't have any expectations for tonight. For us. We can just watch a movie. We don't have to… you know." His face flushes.

Sex. He's not presuming we're going to rush to the finish line. I like him, yeah, but maybe we should talk a little before we hop right into bed. I'm not opposed to a one night stand; I just want more than one night with him. It won't be nearly enough.

I tighten my arms around him. "I like the idea of a movie."

Cuddling on the couch again? Maybe some light making out? Sign me up, baby, I'm all in.

His smile takes my breath away.

"Come on, you must be freezing." I can feel the chill on the fabric of his sweatshirt. "Let's go inside."

He offers me his hand, and I take it. It feels right, my hand in his.

Inside the house, none of his roommates so much as look up when we enter. Wes is in the corner with a book. Barrett, Tucker, and Amir are on the couch playing a video game. Greg is in the armchair, watching the action.

There's only one open seat.

Miles swallows. "We can…"

I push him toward the armchair. His eyes are locked on mine as he takes the seat. Shedding my winter outerwear, I perch on his knee, balancing my weight over his thigh.

He sighs contentedly, pulling me into him. I'm not small by any means. Thick, some people might call it. Muscular. He balances my legs over his legs, spreading his thighs to more easily distribute my weight. His arms come up to wrap around me, pulling me into his chest. He presses a kiss to my temple.

"So this is a thing," Wes says blandly, turning a page in his book.

"Yeah, it's a thing," I tell him. "You okay with that?"

He grunts, as if that's an answer. And maybe for him it is.

"Good job, man," Greg says with a broad smile. He reaches over and claps Miles on the shoulder. "Happy for you two."

"Thank you." I like Greg. He's fun and jokes a lot but he knows when to be serious. I love his long hair. Not many guys are confident enough to pull off a man bun and caveman beard combo.

My head on his shoulder, we watch as the guys play their game. Miles runs his hand up and down my spine, as if he's memorizing each and every one of my vertebrae. It's peaceful, sitting here with him. He smells like IcyHot and classic Old Spice and something else, something uniquely Miles. I love it.

After about half an hour, the guys agree to turn on a movie. It's another superhero movie, this one featuring a female spy and her ragtag group of computer geeks turned secret agents. I've seen it before, but it never gets old.

I visit the bathroom—surprisingly clean, considering it's shared by six college guys—and come back to find Miles has made a nest on the floor with the couch pillows and a blanket. Amir and Barrett are on the sofa. Tucker has moved over to our armchair. Greg's armchair is empty, the sound of popping popcorn the telltale indicator of his absence.

"C'mere," Miles says, patting the floor beside him. Taking a seat, he shifts until he's leaning against the gap between Amir and Barrett's legs. He tugs me into his chest again, pressing a kiss to my temple. I don't hate it, not one bit.

I love how physically demonstrative he is. For such a reserved person, I thought any sort of PDA would be like squeezing toothpaste from a rock, impossible and futile. I tip my chin up and meet him for a soft kiss. He makes a noise deep in his throat and cups the back of my head, his thick fingers threading through my hair.

"All right, lovebirds, break it up," Greg says.

He's towering over us. There's a bowl of popcorn for us and another for the guys on the couch, plus separate bowls for Wes in his corner and one more for Greg and Tucker to share. These guys go through popcorn like other people go through water.

"We know you like each other," he teases. "Save it for when we don't have to see it."

Miles's face goes red, but I laugh and grin up at him. "Close your eyes, then."

Greg snorts out a laugh and takes his seat. Amir presses play.

twenty-five

• • •

Miles

I CAN'T CONCENTRATE on the movie. Not with Sam in my arms.

She smells like vanilla and cherry. Not that fake cherry body mist so many girls use. She smells like actual cherries and warm vanilla and something else that's uniquely Sam. I can't get enough. I drag my nose along the shell of her ear and she sighs, melting into me.

The guys are going to give me shit for this. I just know it. I can't bring myself to care. I like her. She seems to like me. She wants to kiss me.

Sometimes that's enough.

Shit. I should probably take her on a date. I have no idea what college kids do on dates. Isn't date just a euphemism for sex? Sure, I want sex with Sam, I'm not going to lie—but I want more than that, too. I want to walk through campus with her hand in mine. I want to walk her to her classes and kiss her in the hallways. I want to go to sleep with her in my bed, and wake up to her in my arms, and spend all day together just because we can't get enough of each other. I want dinners together in the dining hall—with and without the guys—and lazy Sunday afternoons on the couch. I want it all.

I want to make her happy, and for her to be happy when I'm around. I want her to *want* to hang out with me.

She falls asleep halfway through the movie. I'm exhausted. Today was pretty miserable, interspersed with some pretty fantastic moments, but I can't sleep. Every fiber in my body is alive and humming at the feel of her pressed against me.

Her hand slips down from where it's curled on my collarbone to my stomach. I tense, holding my breath. She shifts in her sleep, her arm wrapped around my belly. It's like she's hugging me.

I've never been hugged in a romantic sense. My mom, sure. My aunts. Maybe my sisters. I'm not a physically demonstrative person. I don't like being touched. My dad contents himself with fist bumps or a clap to my shoulder.

On the football field, it's different. They're not touching me; they're trying to get past me, and I won't let them.

With Sam, though… I want to touch her. Not even in a sexual manner. I want to hold her hand, and hug her, and run my fingers through her hair, and just… indulge in the profound simplicity of her touch.

I don't know if I'm ever going to have football again. I was filmed breaking the code of conduct, a pretty flagrant violation of the rules. It doesn't matter that I was provoked: I made the decision to make my point with my fists instead of my words.

O'Rourke is a piece of shit. He's slimy. He's going to get off with a slap on the back of the wrist. I'm the one that's going to feel the effects of this. He might have a broken nose, but I could lose my scholarship. I could lose football. I could lose everything.

Glancing down at Sam, asleep on my chest, I can't imagine that night going any other way. I can't say I'd do it again in a heartbeat, but I'd certainly consider it. She doesn't deserve to be talked about in that way. Nobody does.

But I'm sacrificing a hell of a lot for a girl I barely know.

That's why I'm going to take her out on a date, so we can get to know each other better. Every time she's around me, my mind goes blank, and my tongue gets tied. I can't talk, can't think. Hopefully with repeated exposure I'll be able to keep my wits about me. She won't like me if all I ever contribute is grunts and monosyllables. I'm better than that.

"So you really like her," Amir says, his voice low and his eyes on her.

Like doesn't begin to cover it.

"Yeah."

"Good for you," he says. "She's way out of your league."

"Tell me about it."

She's gorgeous, she's fun to be around, she's popular. Everyone likes her—except for O'Rourke, who doesn't like anyone. She's a fucking catch, and she wants to be with me. With *me*. With the tubby loser who can't seem to talk in her general vicinity, the guy who stands out in a crowd no matter how much I want to blend in.

She stirs, making a noise deep in her throat, and it goes straight to my cock. She adjusts the angle of her head on my chest and tightens her grip around me. She likes this.

I don't know how the movie ends. I've seen it a few times before. I'm watching the best thing there is: Sam's face as she sleeps.

Is that weird? It's weird.

A deep and overwhelming affection for her threatens to overtake me. There's a lump in my throat I can't clear. She feels safe with me, comfortable enough to fall asleep on top of me. She can't be repulsed by me if she's snuggling with me.

I shake her shoulder.

"Sam."

She sighs and burrows into me.

"Baby, it's time to get up."

"Don't wanna."

"We need to go to sleep. In a bed and not on the floor."

She lifts her head a fraction of an inch. "Floor?"

"That's right, baby, we're on the floor." I brush some loose strands of hair out of her face. "Let's get you to bed."

"Mm. Okay." She plops her head back down on my chest.

"Sam."

She doesn't wake.

Greg and Tucker are laughing.

"You okay over there, big guy?" Barrett asks. He's heard her nickname for me.

"Fuck you. All of you."

Gently disentangling my limbs from hers, I struggle to my feet and rearrange the blanket over her. In a movement that isn't nearly as graceful as I'd like it to be, I scoop her into my arms, cradling her to my chest. I can lift more than double my considerable body weight. She weighs practically nothing in my arms.

Amir tucks the blanket in around her. I nod at him, and he laughs. Fucker. All of them. I hate them all.

Lumbering slowly up the stairs, I make my way to my room. Luckily, it's not too messy. My bed isn't made—it never is—but I change my sheets religiously every Friday night so I can crash into a clean bed after a brutal game.

Sam stirs when I set her down on the bed. I wait with baited breath as she settles again. I go to take off her boots and she thrashes awake.

"Wha's goin' on?"

"It's just me."

"Miles?" She struggles to sit up. "Where am—oh."

"We're going to go to bed," I tell her. "I was just taking your shoes off."

She blinks the sleep out of her eyes. "I can stay?"

"As long as you want, baby."

She melts into the pillows with a smile on her face. "We can have our slumber party."

"That's right."

Sam manages to take off her boots, kicking them to the floor. "Can I... never mind."

"What's wrong?"

"I want to sleep in your shirt."

Bam. My cock reacts instantly to the mental image of her in my clothes. I have to work to swallow the lump in my throat. How am I supposed to *just* sleep beside her tonight?

"Anything you want."

Her smile makes my stomach lurch.

Withdrawing a shirt from my dresser, I hand it over to her and point her in the direction of the Jack and Jill bathroom I share with Greg.

All of the houses in Athlete's Village are laid out the same. Two bedrooms and a bathroom downstairs, four more rooms and two bathrooms upstairs. Small galley kitchen, bigger living room. Virtually no yard. Pre-furnished. They're comfortable enough. I have no complaints.

Greg keeps spare toothbrushes handy for his infrequent overnight guests. I snag one for her, and we brush our teeth side by side. It's oddly intimate. I kind of dig it.

My shirt hangs down to her knees, the neckline gaping open to expose her bare shoulder. Her fuzzy neon blue socks come halfway up her shins, leaving a solid six inch gap of leg on display. I can see the pointy pebbles of her nipples through the thin fabric of the shirt.

I hold out my hand and she takes it, scurrying to my side. Sam wraps her arms low around my waist and tilts her head up for a kiss.

I can't get enough of her. It's like there's an itch under my skin I can't quite scratch. I'm not sure I want to.

We crawl beneath the covers, and she gets all up in my

personal space bubble. Her socked feet tangle with my legs. She takes my favorite pillow and I let her.

"You good?" My voice is scratchy. I clear my throat. "You keep passing out on me."

"Sorry," she says, giving me an impish grin, not sorry in the least.

"Don't be. I kind of like it."

Sam shifts so we're facing each other. She grabs my arm and situates it across her hip. She moves my other arm to use as a pillow. Her knees kiss mine.

"I kind of like you," she confesses, and my heart gives a painful tug.

"Good. I'm glad."

She lets out a massive yawn. "I really am sorry I fell asleep."

"Don't be. You didn't miss much."

"I'll make it up to you," she promises.

"You don't have to—"

"I will." She presses a feather-soft kiss to my lips. I want to deepen it, want to roll over and press her beneath me, want to feel the length of her body pressed against mine. I do none of that. Now isn't the time. Instead I leave a kiss on her forehead and pull the blankets up around her.

"Go to sleep, baby."

She falls asleep with a smile on her face.

twenty-six

. . .

Sam

I WAKE up to a thick steel pipe pressing against my ass. Rolling over, I'm confronted by Miles's sleep-slack face. His palm is under his cheek as he breathes rhythmically in and out. He looks younger like this. Peaceful. He's so fucking gorgeous, I want to wrap him up in my arms and never let him go. How has nobody else snatched this guy up?

Trying not to wake him up, I attempt to slip out of his arms. He makes a noise and pulls me deeper into him, molding my body to his.

"Miles."

He makes a sleepy questioning noise.

"I need to get up."

"No. 'S too early," he says, not opening his eyes.

"I need to pee."

He whines deep in his throat and releases me. I use the bathroom and crawl back into bed. He wastes no time in tugging me into him. My back aligns perfectly to his front. It's like we were made to fit together.

"Good morning," he sighs, his breath ruffling against my hair.

"Morning."

"Go back to sleep."

We doze for—a few hours? I'm not really quite sure. I'm wrapped up in the warm embrace of his arms. Just being with him is relaxing. Curled up in bed, snuggling together... it doesn't get any better than this.

Noise in the house wakes me up a little after nine. His roommates thunder down the stairs as they go about their day. Miles whines and tucks my head under his chin. His massive hand travels from my hip to my stomach, his thumb brushing the underside of my breast.

Instantly I'm awake. Parts of me that have long gone dormant perk right back up.

Arching my back brings me into direct contact with his erection. Miles lets out a low groan. His hips flex up, pressing into my backside.

"We can't," he murmurs.

"Why?"

He grinds into me. "I haven't taken you out on a date yet. I want to do this right."

I move away, and he grunts his disapproval. Once I have enough space to maneuver, I try ineffectually to push him onto his back. He rolls over, and I crawl on top of him, straddling him. This brings us into intimate contact, and we both make a noise of approval.

My borrowed t-shirt has ridden up my thighs. He hesitates before setting his hands on my legs. I move his hands higher still, beneath the fabric barrier.

"We don't need to wait for an arbitrary number of dates. I like you, you like me. This isn't rocket science." I run my fingers up his chest, covered by the thick fabric of his sweatshirt.

His fingers flex into my thighs. "You deserve a date. A nice date."

"So we'll go on a date," I tell him. "But don't make me wait."

The first kiss is a little timid. His morning breath is sleep sour. I don't care. I lick into his mouth, and he responds to me eagerly. His cock twitches beneath me, sending a rush of blood to my clit. I want to learn the ridges and veins of his cock with my tongue. I want to know what that thick length will feel like inside of me. I want it all.

He doesn't make any move to touch me. He doesn't try to get my panties off. It's like he's content to stay here and make out. It's surprisingly refreshing. Most college guys are just trying to rush to the finish line. Instead he's savoring this.

I break the kiss, and he makes a noise of disappointment. He perks right back up when I pull the shirt over my head, leaving me straddling him in just a thin pair of panties.

He stares at me, his mouth open. "Sam, you're…"

A little thick. Chunky. Curvy. I know I've got a lot going on. I'm never going to be some twig.

"You're perfect," he says, a muscle twitching in his jaw as he stares at me with open-eyed wonder. "Can I…?"

He reaches out towards me. I take his hand and place it on my breast, his thumb over my nipple. He groans, and his cock twitches beneath me again.

"You have to show me what you like. I haven't… I've never done this before."

"You've never had sex before?" I work to keep the incredulity out of my voice. He's so gorgeous and has such a great personality. How has nobody else scooped this guy up yet?

"I've had sex," he says, a little self-consciously. "I wouldn't say I have a lot of experience. We never really did any foreplay. It was just straight to bing bang boom."

"Miles…"

"Look, I'm not proud of it," he snaps. His frustration is such a turn on. "It just happened that way. I want to learn. I want to know how to get you off. I want to be able to get you off, so that you enjoy it as much as I do. But I need your help for that."

My hand covers his. "Okay. So we'll explore together."

He gulps, his eyes wide. His thumb strokes over my nipple, tentative.

"Sex is about more than you sticking your dick in me a few times. There's a rhythm to it. We'll start slow," I promise.

I show him how I like to be touched. He's a quick study. When I slip my underwear off and lay naked in his bed, he goes tense when he should be getting more relaxed. There's a naked, willing woman in his bed. This isn't complicated.

"Sam…"

"Hmm?"

His kiss is soft, sweet, like he's afraid to hurt me.

Taking his hand, I show him where to touch me, how much pressure to use. His eyes are wide with sublime wonder as he rubs my clit the vigorous way I need him to.

Fisting my hands in his sweatshirt, I kiss him, deepening the kiss almost immediately. My nerves are alight with glorious pleasure. I can feel the pressure building, that rubber band inside of me pulled taut as he explores me. His rhythm falters.

His fingers slip low, playing with my wetness. Slowly, impossibly slowly, I feel the tip of his thick finger breach me, tentative. I widen my legs for him, and he groans low in his throat.

"You feel…" He presses his forehead to mine.

"Just wait until your cock is inside of me."

He bites his lip, sweat beading on his hairline. "I don't think I can wait."

"You're twenty-one. You're good for a couple of rounds."

His cheeks flame red. I love the way he flushes, the way his skin glows.

I kiss him, again and again, as he moves his finger inside of me and strokes my clit with his thumb. His touch is a little clumsy, a little unsure. I like that about him. I know what I like, what I need. He takes direction well. We work well together.

Planting my feet into the mattress, I tilt my hips and take as much as I can bear. Everything inside of me is on fire.

I pull him on top of me. He tries to prop himself up and I tug him to me.

"I'm going to crush you."

"I know what I can handle. And right now I want you on top of me." I wrap my arms around his neck, touching as much of him as I can. I map the strong muscles of his shoulders, the curve of his biceps.

He touches me with reverence, like I'm a glass doll about to break. I'm not that fragile.

Swiveling my hips, I take what I need from him. It doesn't take long before that elastic band inside of me snaps under the pressure. Waves of pleasure ricochet through me.

"Holy... wow," Miles breathes. He pulls his finger out of me with a wet squelching noise.

That's all it takes. We're both laughing now. I can hardly catch my breath as aftershocks run through me. My stomach aches from the force of my amusement.

Wrapping my legs around his waist, I bring our lower bodies into direct intimate contact. His laughter dies out in an instant. I can feel the hard, thick length of him, the rigid line of his cock pressed against my center.

"I want to touch you. Can I?"

I've never seen him without his trademarked hoodies. It's nearly winter, so he's always wearing long pants. Baggy clothes. The only time I ever see him in anything form fitting is on the football field, and even then, he wears a long shirt beneath his jersey.

His face is beet red. Rolling over, he sits up and pulls off his enormous hoodie. The fabric drags the hem of his shirt north, exposing several inches of his stomach.

"Shirt, too."

I move to help him, and he flinches away from me.

I want to see him naked. I want him bare to me as I'm bare to him. I want to map the contours of his muscles. I want him to want me as badly as I want him, to be secure enough in his own skin that he isn't afraid of me.

His hand shakes as he lifts the hem of his shirt a few inches.

"It's just me," I tell him quietly. "This is just us."

This time, when I move to help him, he doesn't flinch. Together we lift the hem of his shirt up, up, up. My hand slides over the curve of his belly, appreciating the smooth expanse of skin he's revealing. His broad chest is covered with a smattering of dark hair fanning out towards his nipples. It travels south in a thin, wispy line over his belly, where it thickens into the waistband of his sweatpants that do a poor job in hiding his interest.

He hesitates.

"We don't have to do anything you don't want to do. We can go as slow as you want."

"I want this. I want you," he says, like he's trying to convince himself.

My finger dances along the edge of his sweatpants. Sweat breaks out along his hairline. When I slip my hand into his pants, he hisses. I wrap my hand around the thick length of his cock, and he groans out loud.

He feels like velvet wrapped around steel, satiny smooth. I can barely get my hand around him, he's so thick.

Miles moves, and then he's inching his sweatpants down off his hips. I help him with the thick fabric, and he sighs. He kicks off the pants and then takes my hand, moving it back to his cock.

He's thick, the head an angry red, and weeping with pre-come. Slowly, impossibly slowly, I stroke him, learning what makes him sigh and what makes him groan, what has him flexing his hips into my touch. He wraps his fingers around mine, tightening my grip around him. I love the feeling of both of us working to get him off.

He initiates another kiss, all tongue and wet and delicious. For someone with so-called limited experience, I can hardly tell. He has no issues with taking what he wants from me.

He comes with a shout, hot come covering both of our hands. He's breathing hard, the flush spreading down his neck to his chest. I press a kiss to his nipple, scraping lightly with my teeth, and he gives a feeble moan.

When he can breathe again, he reaches over me for the box of tissues on the bedside table. He cleans off my hands before he mops himself up.

I run my hands over his chest, my thumbs brushing lightly over his nipples. Miles groans again—I love how vocal he is—and pushes me onto my back. He climbs on top of me and wraps my legs around his waist again, pulling the blankets up around him to surround us in a cocoon of warmth. He's up on his knees, so I don't get the intense crush of his weight on me, no matter how much I want it. Need it.

There's a little less urgency now. We kiss slowly, enjoying the moment. The thick length of his cock presses against my center, hot and a little wet, sending delicious zings of friction through my core. He grinds against me. He learns the shape of my body, the curve of my breast. His fingers close around my nipple, gently squeezing. I arch my back and try to get more friction. The head of his cock slips a little low, the tip pressing into me, and we both freeze.

"Condom," I tell him, and he nods without hesitation. He reaches over and digs through his bedside table. It takes him a full minute and twelve seconds to find the unopened box of foil squares.

I take the strip from him, tearing off a square. He scoots back a little, and I mourn the loss of intimate contact.

"You're sure you want to?" He meets my eyes. "I do want to take you out. You deserve—"

"I want that, too," I tell him. "Right now I want you to fuck me."

Without delay, he takes the condom from my hand and rips it open. He rolls the protection down his length and fists his cock a few times.

"I've never done it in this position before," he admits, guiding his cock to my entrance.

My eyes fall closed, and I flex my hips as he slides into me. He's still too far away. He sinks in another inch or two. He's breathing hard, his broad chest rising and falling. His round belly brushes against mine in the best possible way.

"Miles…" I arch my back, bearing down as he slides deeper into me, until he's buried balls deep.

He falls forward, propping himself up on his hands. My hand on his cheek guides him back to me for a messy kiss, all tongues and teeth. I can't breathe. I don't need to breathe. I just need more of this.

He pulls back a little and thrusts back in. His hair falls into his face, and I brush it away. He leans his cheek into the contact.

I lose myself in the rhythm, in the push and pull of it. We're both active participants. He feels so good inside of me, surrounding me.

Sliding my hand between our bodies, I rub at my clit. Miles lets out a growl and eases back so he can work a hand between us.

"I want to—" He's panting, breathing hard. Sweat covers his forehead and chest. "I want to be the one."

"It takes teamwork." Taking his hand, I show him where to touch me and how much pressure to use. I need a different kind of touch than before. He picks it up quickly.

Between the intense friction and the feel of him inside me, surrounding me, it doesn't take long for me to fall to pieces.

He thrusts inside of me two, three times, and then he comes with a shout that I muffle with a kiss.

He sags on top of me, his belly pressing into mine. I let out a soft grunt as I take the brunt of his weight. It feels delicious, his immense bulk pinning me down. His cock twitches inside of me, and we both groan.

He's breathing hard and sweating. "I didn't know it could be like that."

"Like what?"

He kisses me softly, like he's memorizing the moment.

"Perfect."

twenty-seven

. . .

Miles

I **MEET** with Coach first thing Monday morning. Not even the threat of getting kicked out of school can bring me down today. Sam and I spent all day in bed yesterday, only leaving to get food, and then quickly returning to get naked again.

It wasn't all an endless sex fest. We spent a lot of time curled up in my bed, talking and getting to know one another. She told me about her softball teammates and her sorority sisters and growing up in the suburbs in Mississippi. Haltingly, I talked about growing up with two younger sisters, about living in the city across the street from my cousins, about anything that popped into my head. She didn't get frustrated with me. She didn't try to jump in and dominate the conversation. She just listened, like my words were important to her.

I've never had that before. Sure, my parents always asked about my day at school and how practice went, but they asked that of all of us. They were too busy taking care of my sisters and with their own lives to sit down and *talk*. Talk about nothing, talk about everything. I know they care about me. I know they love me. That doesn't mean they don't have their own lives to worry about.

Sam doesn't make me feel like I'm wasting her time. She doesn't try to hurry me along when I can't find the words. She's there for me, whenever I'm ready. And eventually, I'll be ready.

She makes me feel like there's more to me than just football. Like I can have more in my life. I can be more than another dumb jock trying to string two sentences together. I can have anything I want.

I want her.

I also don't want to get kicked out of school. I want to keep playing football. Sure, I'll do my time. I'll serve whatever punishment they assign. But I don't want this to be the end for me and Newton.

I punched a guy. Yes, I was provoked, but that doesn't matter. I was the one that made the decision to break his face. I felt the crack of cartilage beneath my fist, and I didn't stop. I saw the stream of blood pouring out of his face, and I didn't stop. If they hadn't pulled me off of him, I'd still be punching him. Nobody talks about women that way. Nobody talks about Sam that way.

I fucking hate O'Rourke, but I hate what he said more. I hate that he thinks it's okay to talk about people like that, that it's okay to target people and pick on their insecurities and spew blatant lies about them. I hate him. I hate everything about him.

Coach isn't optimistic. "You broke the honor code, son, and you were filmed doing it."

"I understand." I fold my hands in my lap and stare at my feet.

"I don't care what he said about your momma or your girlfriend, fighting is never the answer."

Swallowing thickly, I nod. "I know that now."

Coach sighs. "I have no choice but to suspend you until the case is resolved. My hands are tied, son."

"Yes, sir."

All of the fight leeches out of me. I'm tired. I'm so fucking tired. I don't want to give up Newton. I don't want to give up football. Sure, my parents could scrape together enough money to pay for my tuition next year or help me cosign for a loan, but they shouldn't have to. They have enough to worry about with Mack's three sports and Ash's expensive cheer schedule. Money is stretched tight enough as it is. I'm doing my part by getting a partial athletic scholarship and making up the rest in grants. I can kiss all of those goodbye. Nobody's going to want to give me free money when I get kicked off the football team.

"You'll still attend practice, but you'll be in your suit on the sidelines come game day."

I work to control my frustration. It's not his fault. It's mine.

"How many?"

"I don't know. Until the hearing, at the very least. They're scheduling it for next Wednesday. You'll be out this week. Possibly longer."

Shutting my eyes against the tears pinpricking there, I swallow my exasperation and square my shoulders. "Yes, sir. I understand."

"You're a good kid. You've got a good head on your shoulders, Cavanaugh," Coach says. "In all the years I've known you, you've never gotten into a fight. Never heard so much as a raised voice. What gives?"

"He deserved it." My hands clench into fists, and I take a deep breath. "The things he was saying… It doesn't make it right, I know that, but he needed to learn his lesson."

"It wasn't your job to do that," he says gently. "Not when you've got so much on the line."

"He can't keep going on like that." If he starts in on Sam again, I'll do more than break his nose.

"You're lucky he didn't press assault charges, son. He's well within his right to do so."

"I—I—"

"The committee is going to look for remorse," he tells me seriously. "You can't fake it. If you can't prove you regret what you did, they might not let you come back. They might not let you back anyways. I can't coach you on what to say. All I'm saying is, this is out of character for you. Think long and hard about what you're going to say in your defense."

That's the problem: I don't regret what I did. That I got caught? Yes, absolutely. I can take whatever poison he says about me. That's not my concern. What I can't take is his deliberate targeting of an innocent bystander caught in my crossfire.

How am I supposed to show remorse when he deserved what he got, and should have tenfold more?

That's the thing. I'd defend her again, and again, and again. Not because of how I feel about her, but because she is worthy of respect. She doesn't deserve to be talked about that way. Nobody does.

twenty-eight

. . .

Sam

ON A RARE DRY and relatively warm day, the team heads outside for batting practice. I'm one of the best batters on the team, and if I'm going to be playing this season, I have to be up to snuff. I can't be unprepared for the challenges of the upcoming season. Interpersonal problems are the least of my worries.

Being a student athlete is all-consuming. We're a commodity for the university, a bargaining chip they've bought and paid for with the promise of heavily discounted tuition. In exchange, it's up to us to give our best athletic performance every day, every practice, every game. And once the season starts, they own us. Hell, even before the season starts, they own us.

In the off season, we have practice a casual four days a week and have weightlifting sessions four more times a week. Every Monday night we have a team meeting, and every Friday we have dinner together. For the most part, the team is tightly knit. There's always an adjustment period when new freshmen join the team and graduating seniors leave. That's life, though. People move on, and new ones come to take their place.

I step up to the plate and take a practice swing. My shoulders are tight. I might need to visit the team's assigned physical therapist for a stretching session. My elbow twinges as I extend my arms for the followthrough. Yeah, something is definitely not right.

Softball is work. It's hard work, physical labor and physically intense. I'm putting in the work now for a future payoff some time once the season starts. I almost feel guilty for not enjoying the routine of practice when other people have had their sports ripped away from them.

Miles.

Miles has had football taken away from him.

And it's all my fault.

Okay, it's not my fault. It's because of his actions.

Which he took in defense of me.

That I didn't ask him to take.

But he stepped up. He refused to let O'Rourke spew his hateful bullshit.

I should feel grateful. I should feel appreciative. I should feel—

There are no rules about how I should be feeling. It's okay that I'm conflicted. I can be thankful for his defense and also resent his actions at the same time. Physical violence is unattractive. There's no right way to feel about my new friend bashing in the bully's face.

Are we friends? Are we more? He likes me, and I like him, and we've had sex, so I have to think there is some implication of possession there. I'm not ready to start going around calling him my boyfriend, but if he wants to be exclusive... yeah, I'm okay with that. I don't want some other woman getting her claws in him. I want him all to myself.

I don't think what O'Rourke said was particularly heinous. He's done worse things than call me a cheap whore to my face, and I'm sure behind my back as well. I'm certain he's behind all of the poisonous gossip about me online. Just looking at him makes me feel slimy, like I need a good shower. Josh Sinclair and I aren't friends, more acquaintances than anything else; I have no idea how he tolerates hanging out with O'Rourke on a daily basis.

Aleesha lobs a ball at me, and I swing low, my bat missing the ball by millimeters. She gets ready to reset, and I settle into my stance, balancing, preparing. On the second try, I connect, the ball soaring into the midfield. The third pitch is a pop fly directly to our shortstop. The fourth ball? That beauty hits the back wall. One more inch and it would have been out of the park.

Coach gives me a high five as I retake my place in the dugout, chugging my water. The last few days, I've had an unquenchable thirst for grape Gatorade. I can't imagine why.

I haven't seen Miles since I crawled out of his bed somewhere around two o'clock in the afternoon on Sunday, when both of our stomachs started growling. After I went home and showered the scent of sex off of me, my roommates and I hit up the ASC, but he was nowhere to be found. It didn't feel right to knock on his door like he did mine last weekend. He probably needs some space to figure everything out, and me barging in on him and demanding more of his time isn't fair. He needs time to process everything. Truth be told, so do I.

I started this semester knowing that I don't have time for fuckboys. Not that I think Miles is a fuckboy. I don't have time for *distractions*. And Miles is definitely a distraction. A very welcome one, the place between my thighs reminds me. It's been awhile since I last got laid, and even longer since it was any good. He was attentive and effective, and if he fumbled around a bit, it was only in his eagerness to prove himself. I certainly enjoyed myself. I have no complaints.

Well, maybe one. I don't know what we are. Then again, it's equally my responsibility to question what we are. I don't think he's a "hit it and quit it" type of dude. His interest isn't going to up and vanish now that he's scored. I can give him some time to figure everything out on his own before I start pushing to define the relationship.

Do I want a relationship?

I don't have time for one. I don't have time for anything that isn't school or softball or the sorority.

For Miles… I'll make time.

Maybe.

I don't know.

I like him. He's cute and he's funny and he's kind and he's just so—so—*I like him.* And he likes me. Isn't that enough? Can't that be enough?

There's no easy answer. Mulling it over in the shower, on the walk to the ASC, during the team meeting, on my way to the sorority house… I still don't have an answer.

There is a cluster of Gamma brothers on the front porch. They've been hanging over at our place ever since the president of the frat started dating Wendy, our sorority president. I nod hello and go to open the door when it swings open.

"Sam. Hi." Jake blinks at me, like he's not sure what I'm doing there.

"Hi?" This is my sorority house, not his. Hell, I have even *more* of a right to be here than he does.

"We missed you at the party on Saturday," he says.

"I had plans."

"Oh?"

My face flushes against my will at the memory of Miles's body pressed to mine, his thick length pressed between my legs.

"Yeah. It was… I'll be there next week."

Jake nods, his smile a bit distant. "Cool."

We have never been anything but friends. We met at a frat party freshman year, when we were both rushing. I'm the one who introduced him to Stacey, who was in my rush class and ended up pledging Theta. We've been friends ever since. He's a self-proclaimed geek, a computer science major and political science minor who wants to go into the FBI and prevent terrorism. He loves to talk conspiracy theories and serial killers.

He's also on the clean-up committee for the Kappa formal, so if nothing else, I'll be entertained while I pick up trash and clean up after drunk people.

"Haven't seen you in awhile, girl."

"You know how this time of year gets," I tell him. "Midterms are hell."

"I feel that." He meets my fist with a bump. "We'll have to plan something one of these days."

I've been so focused on Miles, I've barely been spending time with my friends. I have to do better. I will do better.

"For sure."

"Cool."

"It's a plan, Stan."

One of the other brothers, listening in, raises his eyebrows. "What exactly just went down?"

"What do you mean?"

"Was this a drug deal or a secret sex plan?"

I laugh. "Not everything is about sex."

Except when it is.

"We're just friends," Jake says, rolling his eyes. I know this isn't the first time he's had to correct his brothers on the status of our friendship. "Besides, I have a girlfriend."

"How is Stacey? I haven't talked to her in a while."

He goes red and coughs. "I need a beer."

"It's, like, four o'clock."

"Perfect beer drinking time," another brother says.

"Who's down to hit up McRory's?" Jake asks.

"Oh. I was hoping I could talk to you for a second."

"About?"

I glance at the accumulated brothers desperate for gossip.

"Don't worry about it. I'll figure it out."

"Sam—"

"Enjoy your day drinking, boys." I force out a laugh and waggle my fingers. "See you around."

twenty-nine

. . .

Miles

WE HAVE A ROUTINE NOW. Nothing has changed since Sam and I got together. She still sits with the guys for breakfast and dinner. We still walk home hand in hand. I get to kiss her goodbye when I drop her off at her house. On Tuesday night, she joins us for our Wheel of Fortune and Jeopardy! episodes, and then when the rest of the guys are watching a movie, we sneak up to my room and have sex again. It's as brilliant the second go-around as the first time was.

She spends the night in my bed, and she doesn't even complain when I have to get up at six for weights. She burrows into my covers, and I debate calling out sick and staying in bed with her. I'm not playing this week anyway. What does it matter if I miss a training session?

No. I've got to prove to Coach that I want this, that I deserve to stay on the team. There are a half dozen second string guys dying to take my place. I have to prove that the starting position is mine.

Sam meets us in the dining hall at eight-thirty. She's wearing leggings and—my cock jerks—she's wearing one of my hoodies. It's way too big on her, falling nearly down to her knees like a tent of fabric, and she's had to push the sleeves up over her wrists, but there's no denying that's my Newton Football sweatshirt with my number on the back.

Crossing the dining hall, I drop my tray on the table and wrap her up in my arms.

"Good morning," she manages, before I kiss the ever-loving daylights out of her. She laughs and wraps her arms around my neck. "What's that for?"

"Never take this off," I tell her seriously. I kiss her again, and she opens for me readily.

"Get a room," Greg says, rudely interrupting us.

"Go to hell."

"Already there," he says, and Sam frowns.

"Honey…"

But she's not talking to me; she's talking to him.

"I'm fine. It's fine," he says, even though it's clearly not. "Can we not do this now?"

She untangles herself from me to pat his shoulder. "What-ever you need."

"Thanks."

He tucks into his breakfast, and Sam watches him for a few moments before she turns back to me.

"So you like me wearing your sweatshirt?"

"I'm having some thoughts that are very not appropriate for the dining hall," I confess, dipping my head to kiss her again.

Sam laughs, and it's like waking up early and seeing the sunrise, pale gold turning the world a brilliant bright white. Everything is a little bit magical.

My stomach growls, shattering the moment. She kisses me one last time and then gently shoves me away.

"Breakfast first," she tells me. We take our usual seats opposite one another.

"What do you have on the agenda today?"

She sighs. "Class, more class, studying for my poli sci

midterm, practice, and then our study session." She meets my eyes. "We're still on for seven?"

"Why don't we have dinner first and then study at my place?"

Sam laughs. "Because we would never study. We would be too busy getting busy."

My face heats up. Barrett coughs, reminding me our conversation is far more public than I'd like it to be. "We can study. We'll sit at the kitchen table."

"If you think we won't get distracted," she concedes.

I'm offended by the insinuation that I can't manage to multitask around her. Although some days it certainly feels that way when she's nearby, I don't actually have a one-track mind. I'm perfectly capable of maintaining rational thought around her. I want her for more than sex.

Although the sex is pretty damn fantastic. It's never been like this before. There's an itch under my skin I can't quite scratch. My cock kicks in my jeans just thinking about last night and my face goes red.

The few girls I've been with were never interested in me. They were hooking up with a football player; they didn't care whose name was on the jersey, just that I wore one. Their enthusiasm was clearly forced. Some of them didn't manage to get off, and the ones who did, did it all on their own.

Not only did Sam let me help, she enjoys it, if the sounds she makes are any indication. As much as I love being inside her, I enjoy getting her off more. I'll do whatever it takes to help her get off as many times as she can physically manage.

Tonight I want to go down on her. We haven't gotten to that step yet. It's been on my bucket list—yes, I have a sex bucket list.

I never imagined it could be like this. Having someone who wants me, who wants to be with me... I know it's only been a few days, we're definitely still in the honeymoon period, but I don't care. I want to be with her. I'll do whatever it takes.

Even if that means giving up football. Giving up my scholarship. Nobody deserves to be talked about in the way she was. Nobody deserves to be treated that way. I'd do it again, and again, and again.

I don't think they'll kick me out of the school. Not for one fight. I'll take out student loans, find a part-time job, whatever it takes. My education is more important than a girl who wouldn't even look at me a few weeks ago.

Right?

thirty

. . .

Sam

I SHOULD ASK Miles to the sorority formal. I need to do it. He's the only one I want to go with. He's the only guy I want to be with.

So why is this so hard?

I just need to come right out and ask him.

There never seems to be a good time. I don't want to ask him in front of all the guys. I don't want to put him on the spot. And I can't ask him while we're studying. He's right that studying at his place is rife with distractions. Mainly me. I can't stop derailing the conversation.

The other guys troop in and out of the room on the way to the small galley kitchen, making popcorn (Amir) or tea (Wes) or a peanut butter sandwich (Tucker, Greg, Tucker, and Tucker again). If I didn't know better, I'd say they were doing it on purpose, except I know Tucker is studying hardcore for his media ethics midterm, and Amir and Greg are just oblivious.

I want to suggest we take our studying upstairs, except we'll get even less work done if we're locked away in his room. I'd get him naked in less than sixty seconds. I'll have to wait an hour until we're done with statistics, the most boring and uninteresting subject on the planet, even when my tutor is a hot and intelligent man who knows what he's talking about.

Miles is in the middle of explaining today's lecture when the words burst out of me.

"There's a formal coming up in two weeks," I tell him.

He breaks off in the middle of his sentence about mean and mode. "Okay?"

"A sorority event. I want to—we should go. Together."

"You want me to go with you to your sorority event?" His eyebrows knit together.

"Yes. It will be awful—bad alcohol, bad food, bad music. We'll get dressed up and dance and—" I cut off. He doesn't dance. I can still feel the sting of his rejection at that frat party. I thought us getting together would wipe away that hurt. It hasn't. "It'll be fun."

He's still frowning. "Is it, like, frat party dancing?"

"Yeah. Are you okay with that?"

"I don't dance. I'm not—" He coughs. "My body doesn't work that way."

"I'm sure you're a great dancer."

His face is pink. "I'm really not." He sighs. "I want to tell you to take someone else so you don't have to go alone, but I don't like the idea of you taking anyone else. I want to be there with you. For you. So, yes, if you want me to, I'll go to the formal."

"It'll be awful, but we'll be together, so it won't be too bad," I tell him. "You'll like Kiersten and Haleigh. And you already know Tamar."

His lips tighten into a firm line. "I do, yeah."

He's not a fan. Some days, I'm really not sure if I am, either. I thought we were best friends. Ride or die, there for each other through thick and thin. I never would have imagined her to make the kind of mean, fat-phobic comments she's made. I thought she was more compassionate than that.

She's working on it. She's trying to be better. But I need her to *be* better, not just put on a show.

"It's the weekend after next. Saturday night. You guys have a game at noon that day, I already checked, so the game will be over, and you can still visit with your parents before we need to meet." I've thought this all out. There's a way for him to have his cake and eat it, too. "The food there will probably be awful, so it's good if you eat before the event. But there will be an open bar and—"

"I don't drink," he says.

Oh. I didn't know that. I could have sworn I saw him with a beer in his hand last week at the frat party.

"I mean, I drink alcohol on occasion, I just don't drink to get drunk," he says haltingly. "It takes so much alcohol for me to feel even a slight buzz, it's not worth it."

"It only takes me, like, two or three drinks, and I'm flat out," I admit. "I try not to have more than one or two. The formal will be a shitshow. Everyone will be super drunk and obnoxious."

He forces a half-smile. "Sounds like fun."

"No, it doesn't. It's okay. I don't really like going, either. Attendance is mandatory, so we do what we have to do." I shrug. For the most part, I like being part of the sorority. I've made friends. Sisters. We have fun together.

So if I need to, I can put on the fancy dress and high heels and wear the makeup. I can actually brush my hair for once. I'll put in the effort for one night.

Maybe with Miles by my side, it will be different. True, we haven't exactly gone on a date yet—he's promised that's coming soon—but we've spent enough time together that I know we'll have a good time. I like spending time with him, both naked and fully clothed.

And thinking of getting naked…

"Do you want to head upstairs?"

His face goes pink. "We should study a little bit longer."

Oh. Does he not want to…?

"Let's get this done, then we can enjoy ourselves a little," he says. He glances over his shoulder and lowers his voice. "I want to show you how much I like you in my hoodie."

My stomach gives a little flip of anticipation at the glint in his eye.

"Maybe I should wear your hoodie more often."

"Never take it off," he says seriously.

"That can be arranged."

He meets my eye and gives me a private smile that promises loads of dirty things to follow.

We work for another hour or so. At least, Miles works, and I try to follow along with the complicated ideas he's explaining. I'm only moderately successful.

Barrett and Greg are in the living room, playing a video game. Wes is in his usual corner with a book.

"Have fun, you two," Greg says as we head towards the stairs. "Use protection!"

"Thanks, we will!" I tell him brightly.

Miles's face is bright red. When he kisses me outside his room, it's hard and eager. Gone is the shy, sweet guy I got on Saturday night.

"Inside," he says, swatting me lightly on the ass.

"Soon enough." I give him my best lascivious smirk.

He growls and scoops me up, throwing me over his shoulder. He palms my ass with one hand as he opens the door and throws me onto his bed.

"Take your pants off," he demands, locking the door behind him.

I prop myself up onto my elbows. "Excuse me?" I'm not some sex toy that opens my legs on command. That's not how this works.

"Please," he says thickly. "Please take your pants off so I can eat your pussy."

A shiver of heat runs through me.

My hands are shaky as I work at my boots. Miles makes a noise of frustration and kneels down in front of me, unzipping and pulling off my shoes one by one. I slip my leggings down my legs, and he's there to help, pulling the fabric down my thick thighs. He presses a kiss to the inside of my knee.

Anticipation crackles along every nerve. I can hardly breathe.

He kisses his way up the inside of my thighs. His hands stroke my ankles, my shins, my knees, as he works his way up. I spread my legs, and he noses at my center, rubbing his cheek against me.

"You're okay if these come off?" He fingers the strap of my thong, his voice thick and husky.

"Please…"

He tugs at the fabric, and I lift my hips to help him.

"I've never done this before," he admits, before he presses a kiss to the top of my mound. "You have to tell me if you don't like it."

He's been excellent at everything we've tried so far, and more than that, he's eager to learn. I thread my hand through his hair. "I'm going to enjoy the fuck out of this."

thirty-one

. . .

Miles

IT WAS a mistake bringing the guys with me. People are staring. They can't stop staring.

Greg and Barrett are 6'4" and both over three hundred pounds. Wes is as big as a pissed off grizzly bear. Tucker and Amir are like children in a candy store, throwing everything into our cart.

We came here with one simple task: find date night food. To me, that's something I can easily cook and won't result in me burning down the house. I'm a passable cook. I can make eggs. I can make chicken. I can make a handful of dishes. I just don't do it often. It's easier to walk the mile and a half across campus in the snow to the ASC and the dining hall than it is to make enough food that will satisfy me. And if I want to cook for my roommates? Forget about it. I'd be standing at the stove all night.

"So what's the game plan?" Amir asks. "What do you want to do?"

We usually use our kitchen for making popcorn, sandwiches, and the occasional frozen burrito. Wes has a very exacting preference as to how he makes his tea. The rest of us will drink hot cocoa when there's a chill in the air. I make Sam a cup every night she's over... which is most nights now.

"What about steak?" Greg suggests. He's pushing the cart with the weariness of a haggard stay at home mother of five. Which, to be fair, is not far off.

"And mashed potatoes," Barrett adds. "That's easy enough to do."

Amir tosses some broccoli into the cart. "Fiber," he says, like that's an explanation.

"Not broccoli," Wes says. "No cruciferous vegetables. Too gassy."

Oh, good call. I didn't even think of that.

"What's your idea then, Mr. Chef?" Amir fires back.

"Green beans or—"

"How about a nice kale salad," Tucker jumps in. "That's easy enough you can't fuck it up."

"Thanks, asshole," I tell him. A mom with two little kids in her cart a few feet away glares at us and pushes her delicate little offspring away from our terrible influence.

We make our way through the store. The guys throw anything and everything into the cart. Even though we get the bulk of our food on campus in the dining halls and the grab and go nutrition stations, sometimes it's nice to have snacks at home. Especially when the weather starts getting colder and wetter and it starts getting dark at, like, three o'clock in the afternoon, and we don't want to walk the mile and a half to the dining hall in the snow and wet.

Fuck, I hate winter. It's only October. I'm not ready yet.

"Maybe you should light a fire," Tucker suggests. "Get all nice and cozy on the couch."

"Not the couch," Barrett and Amir say together.

"No fire," Wes adds.

"We're not going to hook up on the couch," I tell them, a little self-consciously. "We've been trying to keep it on the down low."

"Yeah, except we can hear her through the walls," Greg says. "She certainly sounds like she's enjoying herself."

"Fuck you."

"That's her job," he grins, clapping me on the back. "You seem happier lately."

I grunt my agreement. "She makes me happy."

"Well, I'm happy for you two. It's about time you have someone in your life."

"What about you? You haven't brought any girls home in a while."

Greg grimaces. "It's complicated. Haven't been in the mood."

Wes doesn't date—he barely leaves the house. Barrett will sometimes bring a girl home after a party. Amir has this on and off thing with his girl, though that's been off for most of the semester as far as I'm aware. Tucker is more interested in his phone than anything else.

It's weird being the only guy seeing someone. The only guy getting laid on the regular. I've never had a girlfriend before. I haven't hooked up with anyone since freshman year. It just hasn't been on my radar. Girls don't go for guys like me.

Except Sam. She likes me. She wants to be with me. With *me*. She could have any guy on campus, and she chose me. She wants to go to the sorority formal with me. I still can't quite believe it.

thirty-two

. . .

Miles

WITH SOME CONVINCING, the guys clear out of the house on Thursday night. I don't ask where they're going and they don't tell me. Wes grunts as he leaves not to burn the house down.

Asshole.

Sam has spent the last two nights in my bed. It's a dream come true, waking up to her in my arms every morning. I never want to sleep alone again.

Now I know why people made a big deal about dating and relationships. This is why guys are always chasing hookups. It's like I'm on a constant adrenaline high just from being around her—without the crash. My heart beats a little bit faster when she's around. My tongue feels thick in my mouth, and I can't get my words out. Not that that's all that different from usual. But the brain fog when I catch the scent of her perfume is new. My nerves go haywire when she touches me, when she lets me hold her hand on the way to class, or when she hugs me goodbye.

It's not just the sex. Don't get me wrong, I love sex. Now. I love sex with Sam. She's fucking fantastic in bed and out of it. Her skin smells like heaven. She tastes like honey.

I never want to give her up. Never, ever, ever.

But in order to keep her, I have to prove that I'm worthy of her. I have to show her how I feel about her. I don't have a lot of money; I can't take her out to a fancy restaurant. I can barely afford $10 movie tickets for two. My football schedule means I can't swing a part-time job and still go to school full-time. My parents kindly donate money to my bank account every so often. I have to budget it wisely.

Splurging on a night with Sam isn't a hardship. Taking the guys to the grocery store with me might have been a mistake.

There is a knock on my door at five past six. Shit. I was supposed to go pick her up. I wipe my hands on my pants—jeans, not sweats, in honor of the occasion—and open the door.

She looks drop dead gorgeous. She's wearing a puffy coat that goes down to her knees and a forest green scarf wrapped around her neck. Her hair is tied back in an elaborate braid, falling neatly to the middle of her back. She's wearing makeup, more than usual, emphasizing her dark eyes and her pouty mouth.

"Hey," she says, breaking into a wide smile, and my heart tries to beat its way out of my chest.

Tugging her inside, I wrap her into my arms and kiss her thoroughly. She responds to me eagerly.

"Mm. What's that for?"

"Missed you." I tug at the zipper of her coat, hanging it up beside mine on the rack. "Haven't seen you since breakfast."

"It's been far too long," she agrees seriously, winding her arms around my neck to kiss me again. I push her back against the door and take my fill, my tongue slipping into her mouth to tangle with hers. I can't get enough. I can never have enough of her.

She presses her body against mine, bringing us flush together. Her breasts brush against my chest, and I can't resist the urge to touch her. There are too many clothes in the way. I want her naked. Now. Now, now, now.

I kiss her one last time and pull away. I'm gratified to hear her whine of disappointment.

"Dinner first," I announce, taking her hand. I lead her into the small dining room, where the table is set for two. Amir went all out with the candles; there are at least five different shapes and sizes lit around the table. Tucker couldn't decide between the different bouquets of flowers so he picked four. I hand one to her. "For you."

She dips her head to smell the sunflowers. "Mm. Thank you."

Wes contributed the dessert, a chocolate cream pie—she's mentioned it's her favorite whenever it's served in the dining hall. Tonight's menu definitely doesn't fit in with our diet plan. I'm not playing on Saturday, which still rankles; she's in her off-season. We can have a cheat meal or three.

"Dinner will be ready in just a minute."

"Can I do anything to help?"

"I've got it covered." I lean down and kiss her cheek. She smells so good, like vanilla and cherries and something else uniquely Sam. I love it. "How was your day? Your poli sci paper went okay?"

She sighs. "It's over, at the very least."

"That good?"

"Yeah. No. I don't know." She worries the hem of her shirt, a boxy black thing that only serves to emphasize her curves. "I did the best I could. If I pass, I'm happy."

"I feel that."

"This semester kind of sucks," she admits. Her mouth drops open in horror as she realizes what she's said. "Not us. That's not what I mean. School-wise, academically, this semester isn't great for me. If I don't pass the stats test next week, I'm facing down academic probation."

My stomach flips. "You'll ace the test. You know the material backwards and forwards by now."

"I have a good tutor." She bats her eyelashes at me. "Maybe you know him?"

"Hm, I might." I set the salad plates down on the table. Tucker was right; kale salad was a good choice. I don't think I managed to screw it up too badly.

"You cooked?" She looks up at me in wonder.

"I dabble." Greg made the steaks—he didn't trust me not to fuck it up, he said—and Amir made the asparagus and mashed potatoes. I put together the salad. It wasn't that complicated.

Sam leans over and kisses me. "I love it. Thank you."

"Anything for you."

She has my heart in her hands. She has control over me in every possible way. I would do pretty much anything she asked, including going toe to toe with O'Rourke again.

We talk all through dinner, her hand in mine. We chat regularly, yes, but it's not the same as having an intimate one on one conversation. There's no distractions, no other guys to jump in and steal her attention. I love my boys, and I'm glad she likes them and fits in well with them, but sometimes it's nice to have her all to myself.

I serve the steaks and sides. Her eyes go wide.

"This is perfect. This entire night is… thank you."

"All for you." I drop a kiss to the top of her head, and she sighs with contentment. "I'm sorry I can't take you out on the town the way you deserve. You should be wined and dined and I—I can't—I—"

"I love this," she says. Her hand covers mine, and she squeezes gently. "This is perfect for us. I don't need some fancy night out. All I need is you."

I work to swallow the lump in my throat.

She deserves so much more than I can offer her. I don't have a job. I still get an allowance from my parents. She deserves a real man, someone who will treat her like the princess she is.

"Okay, so first thing, I want to eat this awesome dinner that you cooked," she says. "And then while we have the house to ourselves, I'm going to give you the best damn blowjob you've ever had."

My cock perks up.

"Sam…"

"So that's my plan for the evening," she says casually, as if she's talking about the weather. "Do you have something else in mind?"

I clear my throat. "I'm good with that, sure."

The smile she gives me is positively wicked.

thirty-three

• • •

Miles

MY COCK IS in her mouth. Holy fuck, my cock is in her mouth. This is not a drill.

Sam looks up at me from between my knees, her eyes bright. Her hand is wrapped around the base of my cock as she sucks on the head like there's no other place in the world she would rather be.

"Baby..." I touch her face, her hair, anything I can. Her skin is satiny smooth. She's too far away. I want her everywhere.

She swallows around me, and I briefly see stars. She leans forward and takes more of my cock into her mouth.

I've had a few very unenthusiastic blowjobs before, mostly from girls who liked to hang out with the football team. At seventeen, eighteen, I was a horny idiot who thought the hot girl actually wanted me. She didn't. When I saw her at the mall two weeks after our... interlude beneath the football bleachers, hanging out with her friends, I thought maybe it would finally be my chance to ask her out. She acted like she didn't even recognize me. She might not have seeing as I was in regular clothes instead of a football jersey. She cut me down in two quick flicks of her eyelashes and laughed at me in front of the crowd of people.

I haven't asked out anyone since. It was easier to stick to the football groupies if I really needed to hook up with someone. Which was rare to begin with. It's simply easier to take care of any *needs* on my own than involve anyone else.

Until Sam waltzed into my life. No, she didn't waltz. She crashed into me and set my life on fire.

This is what I've been missing all these years. This is why people write sappy love songs, why people fly to Paris to propose to people they barely know. Why people constantly consume books and TV shows and movies about falling in love, finding love.

This is it.

She makes me feel alive in a way I've never felt before. I notice every breath my lungs take. I wake up every day with her in my arms, and I've never been so glad to be alive. I don't notice my aches and pains, the tight hips and sore knees and bruises leftover from a brutal practice. It's not that they're not there—I definitely feel them—but I can't care how much it hurts when she's moaning for me to fuck her harder, please, right there, oh yeah.

Sam on her knees for me is almost too much. I have to close my eyes, and I'm subject to an onslaught of fantasies that can't possibly compete with my reality. My imagination can't compare to what's going on in front of me.

"Baby, I'm…"

She rocks forward, taking more of me deeper into her mouth. Her berry-red lips are stretched wide around my cock. Her hands stroke the parts of me she can't fit. My balls draw up tight, full and aching.

She sucks—hard. And then I can't control it anymore. I lift my hips, and she groans around my length as even more of me slides in, fucking her mouth. She takes it, she takes it all. A few thrusts and I'm coming, the relief spasming through me.

She takes it all.

I'm breathing hard, a little bit sweaty, my stomach rising and falling with every breath I take.

She touches me with reverence, all of me.

"Come here, baby." I pull her to her feet and on top of me. Her weight is like a warm weighted blanket, heavy enough for me to notice and be comforted by it, not enough to pin me down. She's fully dressed, and I have my pants around my ankles.

She kisses me, soft and sweet, and I tug her close and deepen the kiss. She tastes like me. I think I'm not supposed to like it based on what I've heard other guys say in the locker room. I don't care. How can I not kiss her when she willingly went down and took responsibility for my pleasure? She might have been the one on her knees, but she's the one with all the power here.

When I've caught my breath, I run my hand over her hair carefully. I can count on one hand the times I've seen her do something with it aside from throwing it up in a grubby top knot; I'm not going to mess it up for her now.

"What's wrong?" she says, her brows knitting together. I press a kiss to the furrow in her forehead.

"Nothing's wrong."

I should tell her. I need to tell her. It's bubbling up inside of me, a pot threatening to boil over.

I love her. I love her. I love her.

And not because she just rocked my world. Because of who she is. Because she's kind and caring, but knows when to take a step back and let someone sort out their own problems. And because she sees me for who I am, the kind of man I want to be.

I love everything about her.

Sam pulls off of me, and I let out a whine of disappointment. She grins at me and pulls her shirt over her head, leaving her in a green lace bra and her jeans. I've only seen her in jeans a few times before, and never in bed.

"Come here, big guy," she says, her hands at her waistband.

Surging forward, I trap her beneath me and kiss the ever-loving daylights out of her. My hands work at the button and fly of her jeans, sliding the fabric down her legs. I press a kiss to the inside of her knee, and she sighs.

"You're good at this," she says, threading her fingers through my hair. She directs me to that spot that makes her curl her toes and moan.

I lap at her pussy like a man stumbling through the desert drinks from a well. I'm parched, and she's the source. Her thighs tighten around my ears.

She tells me what she needs. I slip a finger into her tight, wet heat, and she clenches down around me. I can only imagine the supreme bliss of sliding my cock inside her. Later, I remind myself. There will be plenty of time for that later.

Sam arches her back and sighs as I go to work. She tastes like honey, like heaven. Eagerly I lap up the pearlescent evidence of her desire. She's so responsive, I love it. She isn't afraid to tell me if I don't get it right. I'm doing this for her; of course I want to make it good for her.

I can't believe more guys aren't interested in doing this. From what I've heard in the locker room, guys rarely initiate going down, though they seem more than happy to receive. They're crazy, selfish idiots who don't know what they're missing. There's nothing quite like a beautiful girl with her legs clenched tight around my ears, coming on my tongue.

We're the only ones in the house, so we don't need to worry about being quiet, and Sam doesn't hold back. The sounds she makes, the way she tightens around my fingers, has me ready to go right this fucking minute.

She sags against the pillows, tugging ineffectually on my collar. I hover over her, and she pulls me down on top of her.

"Mm. Thank you."

"Nothing to thank me for," I tell her, wrapping her into my arms and holding her close. She likes to cuddle immediately after, and I'm here for that. "Just doing my job."

She grins tiredly up at me. "Your job?"

"Yeah, as your boyfriend."

Sam blinks.

Shit. What if she's not ready? What if I'm jumping the gun? I've never had a girlfriend before. Do we need to—

"I like the sound of that," she says, running her thumb over my cheek.

My heart spasms in my chest. "You do?"

"Yeah." She kisses me softly, sweetly. "I like the idea of you being my boyfriend."

I roll over, bringing her with me so she's sprawled across my chest. She sits up, straddling me, and I briefly see stars when her bare pussy rubs against my cock.

"I know it's soon, tonight is only our first date, and—"

She silences me with another kiss. Her hands dip to my shirt, slowly undoing the straining buttons. Whereas before I would have been embarrassed for her to see me with my shirt off, now I'm moderately more comfortable—enough to let her do it, enough to keep the lights on, enough to be naked with her.

"I don't know how many times I have to tell you, but I'll keep repeating it until you believe me," she says quietly, seriously. "I like you. I want to be with you. This isn't some trick. Being with you makes me happy. It doesn't need to be any more complicated than that."

Pulling her into my arms, I kiss her, telling her all the things I can't say out loud. The fear, the insecurity. The way I feel about her. I tell her everything in that kiss.

"I know," she says, running her thumb over my cheek. "Me, too."

thirty-four

. . .

Sam

"WELL, aren't you a sight for sore eyes," Lex says when I sneak into the house a little after six o'clock in the morning.

"Shit!" I jump and knock two coats off the rack.

She laughs. "Someone's up early. Or did you never go to bed?"

My hair is coming out of last night's braid. I never took off my makeup. I'm definitely doing the walk of shame. Except I have not one single ounce of shame over what happened last night. Strut of pride, maybe.

"He had to leave for the gym," I explain. "I wasn't about to stay at his place without him there. I'm not some football groupie."

Except I have the feeling that he would enjoy it pretty spectacularly if I was still naked in his bed when he came home from weight-lifting. And by that, I mean I would enjoy the benefits.

"So when are we going to meet this guy?" Lex says. "For real meet, not from across the cafeteria."

"He leaves in a few hours for an away game. He won't be back until late tomorrow night."

Even though he can't dress for the game, he's still required

180

to be sitting on the sidelines with the rest of the team. I know it's killing him that he can't play. He's dying to get back out there with the boys.

It's all my fault. O'Rourke targeted me. I just wish I knew why. I've never talked to him. I've had classes with his team-mates, but aside from that, he might as well not be on my radar. He's a total non-entity as far as I'm concerned.

"Will he be back in time for the Delta party?" Lex asks.

"He's not big on the party scene." I wince. It sounds like a total cop out. I'm not purposefully trying to hide him from my friends. "I'll see if he wants to come."

"We've barely seen you this week," Lex says. "We should do a girls' night tonight."

My stomach flips. For this crowd, that usually means getting dressed up and hitting up any party we can find. I'm not in the partying mood.

"Leesh wants to go to the Gamma party," she adds. "Or there's a party with the swim team."

"Yeah, how's that going? Make any progress with Lover Boy?"

Lex has a crush on one of the swimmers. He's cute, he's fit, and he's not an asshole, which is like the holy trifecta of college boys.

"He knows I exist," she says, and she doesn't sound happy about it. She punches the button on the blender with far more force than is necessary. I'm treated to the whir of the blender blades as she pulverizes her smoothie.

"Going that well?"

She sighs. "I'm in hell. This is fine. Everything is fine."

"Maybe we should do a girls' night in," I suggest carefully. "We haven't spent time, just us, in a while. We can break into that bottle of vodka and watch 90's movies. I'll even let you paint my nails."

I hate having my nails painted. The smell of the polish gives me a headache, and when it starts chipping ten minutes later, I have the urge to pick all of it off. But I know she loves it, and more than that, she loves giving other people manicures. For her, I can tolerate it for a few hours.

Lex considers. "And then go to the swim party?"

I laugh. "Yeah, and then I'll wingwoman for you at the party."

She beams at me. "Thanks, Sam. It's a plan."

I crawl into my cold bed. It feels so empty without Miles' warm body beside me. It's been nice, staying with him the last few nights. I definitely didn't anticipate everything unfolding this way, but I have no regrets. I like him. He makes me happy. Sometimes that's all that matters.

Even though it's Friday and I have nowhere to be until practice at noon, I get up at eight and arrive at the dining hall by eight-thirty to have breakfast with the guys.

I like eating with them. I like spending time with them, all of them, including Wes and his book and Tucker and his phone and Greg and his moods. Barrett and Amir are all right; they don't talk much.

Miles greets me with a kiss like we've been separated for two weeks instead of two hours. I love his enthusiasm. For a guy that claims to have no experience, he's really nailing this dating thing. That homemade dinner was the nicest thing a guy has ever done for me. Especially a college guy.

Greg steals a slice of bacon off my plate, even though he has at least three slices on his. Jerk.

"You going to be okay tonight?"

I blink at him. "Why wouldn't I be?"

"Without your teddy bear there?"

Greg nods to Miles, who flushes on cue, but looks inordinately pleased with himself at the same time.

"You're such an asshole," I tell him. "It's one night. I've slept alone before, I do it almost every night. I think I'll survive."

"Don't think I'll be taking your place." He nods to Miles. "We're roommates. I won't cuddle with him, though."

"Fuck you," Miles says, and I laugh. He doesn't drop f-bombs left and right, so when he does, it matters. They're usually reserved for his buddies when they're being idiots. "It's just one night."

That reminds me...

"How do you feel about going to the Delta party tomorrow when you get back?" He can't quite hide his expression fast enough. "I know, you don't drink and don't like parties. Just for a little bit. I want you to meet my friends."

He musters up a smile, clearly forcing it. "Yeah, sounds like fun."

No, it doesn't, but I appreciate him for agreeing to it all the same. We can't spend all of our time holed up with his roommates. I have a life outside of the football team. It's time for him to spend time on my side of the world.

thirty-five

. . .

Sam

GIRLS' Night starts with a shot of vodka, because why not?

We're all exhausted after a tough practice. My hamstrings are so tight I can hardly walk. I need a session with the team physical therapist, stat.

It's an hour and a half drive to UNH, longer with traffic. Miles hasn't texted. I know he's with the guys, I know he needs to focus, but I also know he's going through some shit right now. I've never been benched before, not for outside misconduct. The few times I've sat on the sidelines have been due to my poor play the day before at practice—or during the middle of the game.

I feel for him, I really do. I don't know what O'Rourke said that set him off. He spews the same disgusting bullshit towards everyone who's not part of his special little circle of friends. He really seemed to target Miles. He doesn't deserve that, nobody does.

Lex, Aleesha, Tamar, and I haven't hung out in a group since the football game a few weeks ago. Admittedly, my life has gotten a lot busier in the last week. Although I don't regret Miles, I do wish I was able to balance spending time with him and my friends a little better.

I'll work harder at it. I'll get better at it. I'm out of practice; I haven't had a boyfriend since that frat boy freshman year, and I wouldn't call that six week dalliance a particularly successful relationship. Mostly we just had sex in my dorm room, and he ignored me in public. Yeah, he was a real winner.

Miles has the rare quality of wanting to hang out with me fully dressed as much as he wants to get me naked. And we do indulge in some quality naked time. But sometimes it's nice to just walk through campus hand in hand or curl up under a blanket and watch Jeopardy! together.

I'll do better. I'll be a better friend.

Aleesha turns on Clueless and we drink our way through the movie. We've all memorized it, of course. It's a classic.

Lex paints all of our toes, even though it's winter and we're not taking off our socks for anyone. We do face masks and eat popcorn and just hang out.

It's nice. I didn't know how much I needed time with my girls.

Around ten, we get dressed up to head to the swim team's party. Well, they get dressed up. I wear leggings and a t-shirt I pilfered from Miles' closet. It has his name and number on it. It's so big, it's nearly a dress on me, which suits me just fine.

I like the feeling of being wrapped up in his clothes. It's the second best thing to being wrapped up in his hug. If I can't have him here in person, I can have the scent of him enveloping me in an embrace of Old Spice and something else uniquely Miles.

Tamar and I take a few selfies, and I pick out the best ones to send him. His shirt is blatantly on display. I have no interest in any of the guys who will be at this party, and I want him *and* them to recognize that.

Lex's swimmer crush is a tall, broad, tanned dude with a goatee and overly plucked eyebrows that make him look constantly surprised. He gives her a nod when she walks in and goes back to his conversation with Josh Sinclair.

Shit.

Josh is on the volleyball team with O'Rourke. Does that mean O'Rourke is loitering about here?

Tamar and I make drinks in the cramped galley kitchen. The house is laid out inverse to ours, with the kitchen on the left instead of the right. Everything is a little bit backwards. I feel off balance, off kilter.

"Hey, Sam," Josh says, propping his arm on the cabinet above me. He's tall, nearly as tall as Miles, and lanky like a piece of taffy that's been stretched a few times. "Haven't seen you around lately."

"Why would you?"

Josh and I aren't friends. We had a class together. We've never really spoken. There's never been a need to.

He nods to my shirt. "So you and Cavanaugh…"

"What about it?"

"You're a thing?"

"Yeah, we're a thing," I confirm, taking a sip of my drink. Tamar was a little heavy on the vodka, light on the orange juice. Oh well. I take another greedy sip.

"O'Rourke's going to be pissed," he says.

"Why should I care?"

"Because he's had a thing for you for, like, ever," he says.

My eyebrows go up. "That's news to me."

"Why do you think he pulls your pigtails?"

My eyes narrow. "What are you talking about?"

I think I've talked to O'Rourke twice in the two and a half years I've been on campus. We've never had any classes together. We don't have any friends in common. He's a jerk to everyone. He doesn't pull my pigtails—he deliberately targets me. He targets everyone, finding those little fissures of insecurities that turn into enormous caverns of doubt.

"He's always trying to get your attention."

"Well, he's going about it all wrong. I'm not interested. I never have been."

Even if I didn't have Miles in my life, I would have absolutely no interest in O'Rourke. He's a mean bully with no redeeming qualities. Sure, he's good-looking, but that's all the more reason to stay away from him. Pretty men who are used to having the world handed to them don't react well in the face of rejection.

"If he would have just come up to me and asked me out, I would have turned him down," I tell Josh. "It never would have worked out for him."

Josh sighs. "Yeah. I don't want to tell him that, though."

"So, what, you're his minion? Doing his dirty work for him?"

He laughs. "Nah, man, I'm just here at this party and chilling, making conversation."

"Good luck with that."

I duck beneath his arm and escape into the party. Lex is making doe eyes at her swimmer, who is pretending she doesn't exist. Ouch. Aleesha is pouting—she wanted to go to the Gamma party. Tamar is talking to a well-built guy I recognize as being on the men's gymnastics team.

As much as I thrive being around people, tonight I just want to be curled up in my bed. Preferably with Miles. My hips are tight and my back aches, a telltale sign I'm going to get my period in a few days. I just have to get through tomorrow night's frat party, and then I can relax all day on Sunday. Hopefully with Miles to join me. I hear orgasms can help alleviate menstrual cramps. I look forward to experimenting with that.

Lex draws me into her arms. "You okay, baby?"

"I'm good."

"You miss your boo." She's a little tipsy, listing to one side. "Don't worry. You'll see him again soon. It's good for you to have a night out. A night with the girls."

I force a smile. "Yeah, totally."

I would have been happy staying in and watching a few more 90's movies. We didn't have to go out. We could have chilled on the couch together.

Like the guys do. Amir, Barrett, Greg, Tucker, and Wes are happy enough staying in every night. They don't need to go out and get shit-faced to have a good time. They're secure enough in who they are that they don't feel the need to pretend to be someone else.

Tonight I'm definitely pretending. In my mind, I'm this confident, secure woman who doesn't need a man by her side. In reality, I miss Miles. It's only been a week, but we've been doing this dance around one another for considerably longer, and at the end of the day, he makes me happy. With his support I feel like I can do anything, whether that's survive through an intense softball practice or pass a statistics test. He believes I can do it, so I feel like I can, too.

Maybe that's not the healthiest behavior. I don't want to be some fragile, delicate little flower that can't do anything without her man. That's not me. I'm perfectly capable of doing things on my own, of going to parties and making small talk and studying for crazy hard tests that might kill me.

Josh is watching me from across the party. I don't see O'Rourke here anywhere. Maybe he didn't show up. Maybe he's biding his time until I'm alone and—

No, O'Rourke is not some serial killer. He's not an incel. He's just some pretty boy who's had the world handed to him and doesn't know what boundaries are. He's not evil; he's just an asshole.

thirty-six

. . .

Miles

LAYING on my uncomfortable hotel bed, I flick through social media and try not to pout. Sam is at a party. She sent me a few selfies and there are plenty of pictures of her at some party, talking with Josh fucking Sinclair, O'Rourke's best friend.

As much as I hate being around drunk people, I want to be where she is. I want to go to the stupid frat parties with her. I want to be with her, period, even if that means putting up with idiots who don't know when to shut up.

If she wants me to meet her stupid friends who treat her like crap, I'll gladly show up and keep my mouth shut. I can't fight her battles for her. She says they're decent people; I have to give them the benefit of the doubt.

But if they hurt her again...

Greg is snoring. He fell asleep with no issues, the bastard. He's my best friend. I hate him so much.

Tomorrow I have to put on my game day suit and sit on the sidelines as my teammates take on our conference rivals. I have to sit on the sidelines and watch as my brothers battle it out without me. My hands itch to touch the shitty astroturf and tear down any guy who gets in my way. My heart hammers in my chest like I'm on the field, ready to attack anyone who dares to get past me.

Except I'm in this dinky hotel two blocks off campus of the university with the roommate from hell and an itch in my veins I can't scratch. I'm benched. I made the decision to beat the shit out of O'Rourke, and I got caught doing it. It's time to suffer the consequences.

Okay, so maybe Greg's not so bad. He lets me take the first shower instead of using up all the hot water. He doesn't bring girls back to our shared room. He sits there with his books and gets his homework done during our quiet study time. There are a lot worse roommates to be had on the road.

At least my parents won't be there to see me sitting out the game. Since it's an away game—and I'm not playing—I told them not to travel. Ash has a cheer competition they should be at. They've always done a good job at not picking between us, not prioritizing one kid's athletics over another, but my sisters tend to get the short end of the stick. I can't help that my games are nationally televised and the cameras usually pan to the family section.

They shouldn't have to choose this week. I made it so they didn't have to.

I roll over and mourn my cold, empty bed. I've gotten used to sleeping with Sam. It's only been a few days, but already, I feel the absence of her presence here beside me. I like being able to hold her as she falls asleep, that she feels safe enough and comfortable enough with me to close her eyes and drift off to sleep.

I fall asleep some time before dawn. I'm woken up by Greg doing his pregame yoga in the tiny space between our beds.

"Good morning, sunshine," he chirps. His hair is coming out of his bun, wild and loose about his face.

"Fuck you."

"Breakfast is in an hour," he reports. "You going to join us?"

I roll over and crawl out of bed. My head feels achy, and my mouth is as dry as cotton. I probably only slept for two, maybe three hours. If I don't sleep tonight, I don't know what I'm going to do. Maybe I can convince Sam to stay over again —no sex, just cuddling. I like cuddling with her.

Okay, maybe a little sex. Sex and cuddling and early to bed.

Shit. No. We have that stupid frat party to go to. Damn it.

I know it's important that I meet her friends, that they like me and approve of me. I wouldn't want to date someone my friends outright hated. I trust their opinions; I have to trust hers, too.

"You should come with us to the frat party tonight," I tell Greg when I get out of the shower. He's still doing his yoga, getting his body limber for the game.

"Yeah, we'll see," he says.

"I'm sure Sam knows someone who would—"

"Thanks, but I'm not interested," he says. "I'm bored. I need something to shake it up. No amount of slutty college girls are going to do it for me."

"So, what, you're just going to abstain for the next year and a half?"

He's going into the NFL for sure—he's a legacy, and more than that, he's the best player on the team. He's destined for more.

He considers this. "No. I need a break. A few weeks, maybe a month or two. I just need to get my head on straight."

"You do you, man. Whatever you need." I pull my clothes out of the closet. My dress shirt is already wrinkled. Oh well. It's not like I'm a quarterback or a receiver. Nobody cares about me. ESPN probably won't even report on me sitting out. In the grand scheme of things, I'm not important. I'm nobody.

And that's just the way I like it.

thirty-seven

. . .

Miles

WE GET off the bus at eight-thirty. It's been a long fucking day, my knees and hips ache, and I didn't even play today. I'm not in the mood to go to a party tonight. All I want to do is take a shower, put on my sweatpants, and crawl into bed, preferably with Sam beside me.

But I don't get to have what I want. Not tonight.

"Miles! Honey!"

My parents are waiting outside the practice facility with a bunch of other parents and family members. I thought they weren't coming today. I thought we were skipping our weekly dinner.

"Hey, Mom." I let her dote on me, and my dad claps me on the shoulder.

"We thought we'd surprise you," she says, straightening my scarf.

"You certainly did."

"Where's your little friend?"

"Who?"

She looks at me like she can't believe how stupid I am. "Your friend. The one you kissed last week in front of your entire family. Did you know that Aunt Carol asked me how long you've been together, and I didn't have anything to tell her?"

"Oh." My cheeks heat up. "Sam is around. I'm going to see her later for a party."

"You should invite her to dinner," she tells me.

"Maybe another time," I suggest. Or maybe never.

"We should head out. I'm sure you're hungry," Dad says.

We had a quick dinner after the game and snacks on the road, but it's not the same as sitting down to a full evening meal. Travel days are always rough on my schedule.

The drive to the pub is short and sweet. My parents don't mention the game at all. Ashley's at a sleepover with a bunch of her cheer teammates, and Mack is at home, studying for a history test on Monday.

"She's just so swamped this time of year, the poor duck," Mom says. "She'll be at the game next week."

"Oh, she doesn't need to come. Actually, nobody needs to," I say, and they blink at me. "I'm not playing."

"I thought it was just today? A problem with your lower back again," Mom says.

"No…" I look at my dad, who shrugs. He didn't tell her. "I had a… disciplinary issue off the field. I'm resolving it, but I'm benched for a few weeks. Until they straighten everything out."

Mom's eyes are sharp. "What kind of disciplinary issue?"

"I might have, um…" I fiddle with my menu. "I punched a guy."

"That's it? You punched someone?"

"Another athlete. Not someone on my team. But, well, we were on campus, and I was wearing a Newton shirt, so now the school is involved…"

She can't believe it. I've gotten into plenty of scraps, not-so-friendly tussles with the neighborhood boys, but I've never gotten into a fight before. I'm not the fighting type of person. I prefer to let the cruel words roll off my back than take action to confront it. I've heard it all before. Bullies are a dime a dozen in my hometown, little kids thinking they've got big britches. Being twice their size didn't keep them from running their mouths about me. If I did anything about it, I would be fingered as the aggressor because of my size. It's a lose-lose situation.

"I broke his nose," I admit. "He deserved it and more, I stand by what I did, but I got caught, so until we have a hearing, I'm on the sidelines. So you don't need to come to the game next week."

"We come to see you, honey," Mom says.

"Yeah, well…"

"Bring your friend to dinner next week," she says, flicking open her menu, even though we come here every week and she always orders the same thing.

"I'll ask her," I finally agree.

"Have you been dating long?" Mom asks casually.

"A week. We had our first date on Thursday. I cooked dinner for her." I clear my throat. "I know it's soon, but I really like her. I wasn't trying to hide anything. I just don't want to spring the entire family on her all at once. There hasn't been anything to write home about until recently."

"Understandable," Dad says, clapping me on the shoulder. "She makes you happy?"

I nod.

"Then I'm happy for you, son. Treat her well."

"I intend to."

Our waiter takes our orders—I only order one entree instead of two, since I didn't play, and sure enough, Mom orders her usual chicken curry pot pie—and we relax into silence.

It's comfortable and familiar, being with my parents. I never went through a rebellious teenage phase. We get along well. We're all pretty even-keeled.

"Mack is taking her SAT in two weeks," Mom reports. "I was thinking you might take her out to celebrate after."

"Yeah, I can do that." Mackenzie and I aren't super tight, but she's still my sister. "Maybe she'll want to spend the weekend here."

We have Parents' Weekend coming up. We'll have to get through that first.

"In a smelly college house?" Dad wrinkles his nose.

"I mean, if she wants to. She'll be here next year." I'll take her to a college party, let her see for herself how awful they are. Maybe that way some of the allure will fade away before next fall.

I don't care if she drinks. I don't care if she parties. She's seventeen, going to be eighteen in two more months; she can handle herself.

And it will be good for her to see the school in a different light. It's not all sunshine and roses like the recruiting people tell us. It's late nights studying and early morning practice and partying so much you end up puking at practice. It's staying up late with the guys watching scary movies and going to the diner at three o'clock in the morning. It's drunk people everywhere, at all times of the day. It's people who wouldn't look at you twice in street clothes who decide to be your new best friend after a good game. It's the best people you'll ever meet in your life, and the worst.

thirty-eight

. . .

Miles

AS WE AGREED, I meet Sam at her sorority house at ten. She answers the door wearing skintight jeans and a boxy green shirt that hangs off one shoulder. She looks fucking fantastic.

"You made it!" she chirps, throwing herself at me. I catch her and set my hands on her hips. Her eyes are a little glassy. I can smell the alcohol on her breath.

"Got a head start?" I remember she mentioned she's a lightweight. How much has she had? Is this just one drink, or has she had more?

"We're pre-gaming," she announces.

This is going to be fun.

She tugs me into the house. "Guys, this is Miles. Miles, this is... everyone."

I recognize Tamar, her so-called best friend and softball teammate. Kiersten is a short, curvy woman of Asian descent with her hair braided back into two pigtails. Haleigh is tall, thin, and Black, her natural hair falling in tight corkscrew spirals.

Both are done up with a full face of makeup. They're all wearing short, tight dresses and heels, which seems inappropriate for early November. It snowed two days ago. Aren't their toes going to freeze off?

"Do you want a drink?" Haleigh asks, shaking a bottle of vodka in my direction.

"I'm fine, thank you." I set my hands on Sam's hips, pulling her back against my front. "How was your night out with the girls?"

She spins in the circle of my arms, winding her arms around my neck. "I missed you," she admits.

One of the girls coos.

"Missed you, too." I touch my lips to hers, and it's like the first good thaw of spring, relief seeping through me as ice melts. She deepens the kiss, and I bring my hand up to cup her cheek, relishing the feeling of her skin against mine.

"Last night kind of sucked," she says.

"My night sucked, too." I tighten my arms around her. "Want to just stay in and watch a movie?"

Sam laughs. "You're not getting out of this that easily."

Damn.

There are a half dozen other girls that she introduces me to. Wendy, the sorority president. Makayla. Jun. Sarita. Amanda. Jenn. They're all perfectly nice to me, if not a little curious as to what I'm doing there. There aren't any other guys around.

We set off for the frat house, Sam's hand in mine. The girls link their arms and cheer as we walk the half mile or so to the Gamma house.

It's a giant brick monstrosity on a corner lot. People spill out of the house and onto the lawn. There's a line to get in— an actual line, like this is some exclusive club and not a dirty, smelly frat party. There's a guy with a clipboard checking IDs at the front.

Wendy leads us up the walk, bypassing the line of people clamoring to get in. The guy nods to her and casually inspects the girls. He must like what he sees because he grins and moves aside so we can pass.

"Hold up, big guy," he says to me, and I don't like that he's using Sam's special nickname for me. "I need to see some ID. You over twenty-one?"

Fishing my wallet out of my pocket, I prove I'm of legal drinking age and he nods again, letting me pass.

Sam takes my hand again and pulls me into the house. It's opulent as fuck. There's a crystal chandelier high above us, glittering and sending beams of light throughout the party. My ears are assaulted by the bass from the hip-hop music that's turned up about five decibels too loud. It's just past ten, but already the room is thick with the stale stench of body odor.

The living room is packed full of people getting their freak on. Sam tugs me through the house to the kitchen, where a few kegs are set out alongside a wide range of hard liquor.

"Do you want a drink?" she asks me.

I'll take one to be sociable. It will keep people from asking me why I'm going through the party without one.

"Sure." I pour a cup that's mainly Coke, a tiny splash of rum. "What're you having?"

She considers. "I can only have one more drink before I get flat-out trashed."

"I'll carry you home if I have to," I joke. She doesn't react. "You don't have to drink if you don't want to. Don't ever feel like I'm pressuring you into doing something you don't want to do."

She fills a cup with Coke. "Nobody has to know there's no alcohol in it."

I tap my plastic cup against hers. "Exactly."

She smiles slowly at me. Her eyes are still a little foggy, the alcohol winding its way through her system.

"I'm glad you're here," she admits, then takes a quick sip of her drink. "Thank you for coming with me."

"This is your life. These people are important to you," I tell her seriously. "I want to get to know them."

Even if I don't trust them. Not yet. These aren't the same catty bitches who gave her shit for being friends with me. I don't know a lot of sorority girls, but from what I've seen in books and movies, they're nearly as vicious as the cheerleaders my sister competes with.

Hand in hand, we wind our way through the party. Like the Delta party, there's a game room full of brothers playing video games. There's a movie playing on a big screen TV that couples are ignoring as they make out. From the way one guy's hand is moving under a blanket, I'm pretty sure they're doing more than making out.

In the dining room, there are two separate games of beer pong being played. There are clusters of people watching the games, drinking, laughing, having a good time.

Sam's fingers tighten around mine as she leads me to a pocket of sorority sisters. There's Jun and Sarita, who I recognize from the walk over, plus a few others I haven't met yet.

"So you're on the football team," Jun says slowly, looking me over. "I never would have guessed."

"I'm a linebacker."

"Cool. I don't really know what that means," she says, and I chuckle as I explain the basic duties of the position.

Sarita smiles kindly at me. "I'm sure it must be hard, balancing school and football. Sam said you're a math major? What do you plan on doing with that?"

"I haven't decided yet," I admit. "Maybe grad school. Maybe a teaching degree. There are a couple of career paths open."

"That's good," she says, approval in her eyes. "That you have options."

"I'm never going to be a professional football player," I say with a shrug. "After graduation, I have to go into the real world whether I want to or not."

Jun is an electrical engineering major. Sarita is studying physics. They tell me that Amanda is also a math major, though she has her eye on grad school and being a university professor. Jenn is in the aerospace engineering program. Makayla is pre-law and had an internship last summer with Ashby and Ashby, one of the largest law firms in the state. Wendy, the sorority president, is pre-med and has already been accepted to her top choice Ivy League program.

The Kappa sisters are nothing like what I pictured them to be. They're all intelligent, driven young women with ambitions. They like to get dressed up and go to parties, yes, but they also know when it's time to settle down and get serious. They volunteer in the community. They raise money for important causes.

And they also know when to kick back and have fun.

I like these women, the sisters Sam has surrounded herself with. The people she chooses to spend time with rather than being stuck to. She may have only joined the Kappas to make her mother happy, but in the process, she seems to have found some true friends, and I'm glad she has them to fall back on. I have my teammates. She has her sisters.

There's a guy in a tight Gamma shirt making his way over to us. He touches Sam's shoulder lightly.

"Hey, girl."

She beams and lets go of my hand to wrap him in a hug. "Jake! Hey!"

He's about a head shorter than me, maybe a hundred pounds lighter, with medium-short brown hair and dark eyes. He works out.

"Miles, this is my friend Jake," she says, reaching blindly for my hand. I find hers, and she squeezes. "Jake, this is Miles. My—my boyfriend."

It's the first time she's said the word. My heart thumps loudly in my chest.

"Nice to meet you, man," he says, clapping my hand in his. "I've heard nothing but good things."

"Thanks." I don't mention that she hasn't mentioned him.

"How's Stacey?" Sam asks.

He makes a face. "We broke up."

Her easy smile falls. "Again?"

"For good this time." He sighs. "Then again, I said that last time, so who knows."

"I'm sorry, honey," she says, touching his shoulder.

"Thanks, girl." His eyes flick between us in silent question. "So this is new."

She beams up at me, and in an instant all of my anxiety bleeds away. She likes me. She wants to be with me. She has friends who are guys, yes, but they're just friends. It's good that she has positive male friendships. She isn't going to leave me for this chump. She isn't trying to hook up with Josh Sinclair. She's just living her best life.

"Yeah, it's new," she admits, moving closer to me. Automatically, I drop a kiss to the top of her head, and his eyes soften a bit at the easy display of affection.

"You guys look good together," he says, tapping his plastic cup against hers. "I'm happy for you, babe."

She laughs. "I'm happy for us, too."

His smile doesn't quite reach his eyes. He excuses himself, pushing his way through the party. I track him into the next room before I lose him in the throng of people.

"You good?" Sam is gazing up at me, her heart in her eyes.

I touch my lips to hers in a light, chaste kiss. "Never better."

thirty-nine

. . .

Sam

MY BACK IS KILLING ME. I'm about ready to saw out my spine with a rusty plastic spork. It's not just my vertebrae. My hips are aching, and my stomach feels tight and bloated at the same time. I'm not due to get my period for another week, I'm right in the sweet spot in my cycle, so I know it's not that. Yesterday's workout wasn't particularly strenuous, and this morning we did a team run around campus, so I'm not overextended.

Still, life doesn't stop for back pain, so I try my best to go about my regular day. Practice. Study group for political science. Work on my Japanese paper. Dinner with my sorority sisters.

Kiersten pulls me aside shortly after I walk into the house. "Girl, you don't look so good."

"Thanks. I didn't put on makeup today."

There are bags under my eyes, and my skin is clammy. I am about five shades paler than usual, and not only because I'm not wearing any foundation or contour. I don't feel well.

"No, I mean… you really don't look good," she says. Her eyes are worried. "Are you okay?"

"Just some back pain."

She nods knowingly. "Period? I get cramps in my back all the time."

It's not that, but it's easier to go along with it than explain the likely cause.

"Yeah. It's not fun."

"Can I get you some ibuprofen?"

A laugh bubbles out of me, radiating pain through my belly and centering low in my abdomen. "I'm already maxed out on ibuprofen, acetaminophen, and Midol. Thanks, though."

Kiersten rubs my shoulder consolingly. "I'm sorry, babe."

I try to make it through dinner. I pick at my food—I have no appetite, which is thoroughly unlike me. This isn't my first go around with an ovarian cyst, or even with one rupturing. I won't know for certain until it either passes or I nearly pass out from the debilitating pain.

It's fun. I'm having fun.

"Are we going to talk about it?" Haleigh asks the table at large.

"Talk about what?" Tamar says.

"Sam has a new boyfriend."

My eyebrows go up and heads swivel in my direction. "And?"

Wendy looks at me impatiently. "And he's hot! This is new? When did this happen?"

"Recently."

She rolls her eyes. "No shit. You weren't together two weeks ago, you didn't show up to the Delta party last week, and then you bring him to a Gamma party? How did it happen?"

"He's so sweet," Sarita adds. "I just want to hug him. He looks like a teddy bear."

Ducking my head, I hide my smile. "Me, too."

"How'd you meet?" Jun asks.

"We're in the same statistics class. We study together."

"He's a math major," Amanda mentions. "We've had a couple of classes together. He destroys the curve, like, every time."

"Yeah. I've asked him not to do that," I admit. "He politely declined to agree."

"I thought you didn't have time for a boyfriend," Makayla says.

"I don't," I say honestly. "He's worth it."

"Aww." Two of the sisters sigh and sag against each other.

"I want that," says Megan, a sophomore and a Newton cheerleader. I'm amazed at how well she balances the sorority life with her cheer schedule.

"I have no idea how I'm going to make it work during softball season. I'm already stretched thin enough as it is. All I know is being with him makes me happy, and we all need to do the things that make us happy more often."

"Agreed," Wendy says. She lifts up her drink. "To us, and to being happy."

All of the sisters raise their glasses in toast.

We have a pleasant evening planned. It's nice being surrounded by my friends, my sisters. After being around the testosterone of my new breakfast and dinner table, it's kind of nice to be in the embrace of the comforting femininity of the sorority.

I never thought I would be the type of woman who enjoyed being in a sorority. I don't like getting dressed up in fancy dresses or high heels, I don't wear a lot of makeup, I don't like the color pink, I don't like stereotypically feminine interests. That doesn't make me wrong or anti-feminist.

There is merit to wearing dresses and high heels, just like there is merit to wearing oversized overalls and combat boots. Liking one or both or neither isn't wrong or right. I'm "not like other girls" in that I'm me, not because of how feminine or tomboyish I am. I'm exactly like other girls in that I am, in fact, a girl.

The good thing about being in a sorority is that I'm surrounded by women: women who are like me, women who are different than me. I'm exposed to a variety of people and I've been forced to expand my horizons beyond the limits of the softball team. I've stretched my wings and made friends, especially with people I never thought in a million years I'd be friends with. The best thing I've done since coming to Newton is join the Kappas.

Okay, second best thing. The best would probably be joining the softball team and getting a scholarship. That can't be discounted.

Between the team and the sorority, I've met so many interesting people. Beyond the confines of the athletic department, I've met people in my majors and people in the Greek system, and I've made friends—real, true friends. I've found a community of people. I've made Newton my home. I have a life beyond the team, beyond the sorority, beyond the day to day monotony of school work. I've made myself a home.

forty

. . .

Sam

MY PHONE VIBRATES on the nightstand where it's plugged into the charger. I don't have the energy to roll over and check it. It's been buzzing all afternoon.

Fitfully, I doze on and off. Everything hurts. I might be dying. My back seizes up with spasms every time I so much as think of moving. My stomach feels like it's being stabbed by a thousand dull rusty knives. I'm just going to lay here on my side with a heating pad and slowly die.

There's a knock on my door. I moan weakly.

"Leave me alone. I'm dying."

"Sam?"

It's Miles.

"Hey," I croak out. I try to roll over and my back lights up with fireworks. I might groan out loud.

"You okay, baby? I didn't see you in class today."

"You can come in. I'm not contagious."

I crane my neck as he cracks the door open. He's fresh from football practice, his hair damp and his cheeks flushed from being outside in the cold. His backpack is slung over his shoulder.

"What's wrong?" He doesn't make any attempt to cross the threshold.

"I think I'm dying."

He frowns, his eyes softening. "You weren't sick yesterday at breakfast."

"It came on in the afternoon. I spent the morning at the student health center." A skeptical nurse and an ultrasound confirmed what I knew to be true: an ovarian cyst ruptured. Not my first. Most likely won't be my last. That's the fun of polycystic ovary syndrome. There's always another cyst just waiting to go kaput and rupture. "You can't catch it."

He sets a bagged container on my dresser. "Lex said you weren't feeling well. I brought you soup."

"Thank you. That's so nice of you."

Miles sighs, scrubbing a hand over his face. He looks tired. Haggard.

"I don't like seeing you like this."

"I don't like feeling like this, either."

"Is there anything I can do to help?"

I moan pitifully. "Can you hold me?"

He lets out a ragged breath. "Yeah, baby, I can do that."

He toes off his shoes and lifts the blankets. Sliding in behind me, he molds his front to my back, his arm coming up to wrap around me. He makes a puzzled noise at the discovery of the heating pad practically glued to my stomach. I need all the help I can get.

"Bad cramps?"

"Cyst ruptured." I feel more than hear his sudden intake of breath. I grab his hand, bringing it up to my chest, over my heart. "Everything hurts."

He doesn't try to feel me up. I'm almost a little disappointed by that. Maybe he can tell how not into it I am. He's not weirded out by the idea that I have a working uterus. Well, semi-functional at best. His hand strokes over my hip and IT band, rubbing at the tense muscles there.

He kisses the top of my head. "I'm sorry to hear that."

"Yeah, it's not a lot of fun."

"You didn't miss anything interesting in class today," he comments idly. "I'll leave you my notes."

"Thank you." I rest my head against his strong chest. "Thanks for laying here with me."

His arm tightens around me. "Any time."

We doze. I don't know how long I sleep, if I actually sleep at all. Mostly I'm just aware of his presence behind me in the bed, curled around me. He keeps me warm.

I wake up around three to the bed jostling behind me. I turn over as best as I can. My back isn't on fire anymore. My stomach still aches, but it's the dull ache that tells me the pain medicine is finally starting to kick in.

"Where're you goin'?" My speech is sleep-slurred.

The mattress dips as he places a knee on the bed. "I'll be right back." He leans over and kisses my temple.

I crawl over into the warm spot left by his body heat and sigh happily. It's so warm.

He pulls the covers up over me and slips out of my room.

I finally have a chance to check my text messages. He texted me at the start of class and again once it was over, checking in on me. Messages from Lex and Aleesha, letting me know I have a guest. Texts from Kiersten and Haleigh, letting me know how much they enjoyed meeting him the other night. Jake, trying to schedule a study date. Josh Sinclair with an ambiguous *hey*.

There's a knock on my door, and then Miles is back, his hands laden with a plate I recognize as being from his kitchen two doors down.

"I made you a sandwich," he says, setting the plate down on the dresser. He's also brought an apple, a pear, a small bag of chips, and a chocolate swirl pudding cup probably pilfered from the dining hall. "How's your appetite?"

I assess. The pain meds are working.

"I could eat."

He helps me sit up and props the pillows up behind me. It's a little easier sitting upright. I don't require the heating pad nearly as desperately as I did before.

"Do you want to take a bath? Do you think that may help?"

I stare at him. "Who are you?"

Miles goes red and chews his cheek. "My sisters, when they have bad cramps, they like to take bubble baths. They say the hot water helps. I figure a cyst rupturing is like mega cramps turned up to ten?"

"Up to eleven."

He gives a little chuckle. "Let me go draw you a bath."

The turkey sandwich is simple but satiating. I haven't eaten all day. I'm halfway through the pear when my stomach tells me it's had enough.

Miles is in the bathroom I share with Tamar, kneeling on the tile as he tests the temperature of the water. He's filled the tub with my cherry pomegranate soap, making it froth and bubble.

My heart melts.

Padding over to him, I slip off my cozy socks. He lumbers to his feet. He towers over me, surrounding me with his presence.

"Feeling a bit better?"

I wrap my arms around him and burrow into his chest. "Thank you."

"For what?"

"For doing this for me. For making me a snack. For holding me. For being you."

He chuckles, drawing me into his hug. "That's just basic human kindness, baby. I like spending time with you, and whether you're conscious or delirious in pain, I want to be here with you."

"Still. I appreciate it."

He palms the back of my head with his enormous paw. "Take your bath. I'll be here when you're done."

"Sit with me?"

"I'll give you some privacy." He closes the bathroom door behind him.

Discarding my clothes, I slide into the warm bath and sigh with delight. The hot heat of the water seeps into my bones, soothing my bruised and battered muscles.

Miles cracks the door open. He's acting like he's never seen me naked before. "You all situated?" He clears his throat, keeping his eyes above my chest. The bubbles can't hide everything. Not that I have anything to hide from him. He's seen everything, the good, the bad, and now the ugly. "Can I bring you anything?"

"I'm good, thank you." I splash in the bubbles a bit. It's oddly relaxing.

He sits back against the bathroom cabinets, his eyes drifting closed.

"How was practice?"

He sighs. "They have me working out with the third string guys."

The guys who don't get any playing time unless something goes terribly, desperately wrong.

"I'm sorry. That's rough."

Miles shrugs. "It is what it is. After the honor code meets on Wednesday, I'll know more. I just want it to be over and done with already. I want to know my fate."

I want to wrap him in a hug, to reassure him that it will work out. But I don't know that it will.

He's a first time offender. A model student, a great athlete. Will they show leniency? Or will they throw the book at him?

He clears his throat, clearly done with that conversation. "Are you feeling better?"

"A lot. The sandwich helped. The bath… it's not making things worse."

The soft smile he gives me is devastating. My knees go weak. It's a good thing I'm already sitting down.

"Good. I'm glad."

forty-one

· · ·

Miles

I'M MINDING my own business in the library when I hear it.

"Tubby! Hey, Tubby!"

O'Rourke.

He's flanked by Josh Sinclair and another guy I recognize as being on the volleyball team. They're towering over my study table, glaring down at me.

I ignore them and flip a page in my linear algebra textbook. Nothing good will come from getting involved with them.

He's never been a kind person, he's never had a good thing to say about anyone, but the last few weeks, he's really stepped up the taunting. I don't know what I did to catch his ire. Just exist, I guess. The broken nose probably didn't help matters.

I have my honor code review panel tomorrow afternoon. I have to keep my head down and toe the line.

"Come on, Tubby, you a pussy all of a sudden?" O'Rourke smirks down at me. "You get laid for the first time and lose your balls?"

Clenching my fists, I slowly breathe in and out. He won't get to me. I won't let him get to me. I face down three hundred plus pound guys on the football field every week, guys who say all sorts of nasty shit trying to get under my skin.

He means nothing. He's meaningless. He's a mean-spirited bully with nothing good to say.

Punching him out won't make me feel better. Sure, it might feel good for a minute, but I'm already dealing with the consequences of punching him the first time; it won't look good to the honor code if I'm busted doing it again.

I can handle guys insulting me. I can handle the mockery. It's nothing I haven't heard all my life. I'm a big guy. Some people take that as a personal offense. I'm not sure why. It has nothing to do with them. People think that because I'm big, I have to be dumb. They don't like when it turns out I actually have some brain cells in the squishy space between my ears.

I'm not trying to be anyone but myself. If I had my way, I'd stick to the shadows, lurking about beneath people's notice. I can't help that I'm big and tall and stick out like a sore thumb. The thing that gets me revered on the football field makes me an easy target everywhere else. It's like people can't possibly stand to let me be healthy and happy in my own skin.

O'Rourke is one of those guys. I don't know why he decided to target me or why he's decided to ramp up the ante in the last few weeks.

What I can't tolerate is him badmouthing Sam. That's a hard limit for me.

"You got any brain cells left, Tubby, or have they all been knocked out by football?" he taunts. One of his sidekicks snickers.

O'Rourke plants his hands on the table and looms over me.

"What's the deal with you and Samantha Burke?"

My heart skitters to a stop. "She's my girlfriend."

Every time I say the words, it's like it's the first time all

over again. My stomach lurches, and I get these fluttery feelings in my chest. She likes me. She wants to be with me. It's
not a trick; she really is my girlfriend.

"Not for long," he says.

"What's that supposed to mean?"

His eyes narrow. "Stay the fuck away from her."

"Or what?"

"Or you won't like what happens next," he sneers.

"Who are you to tell me who I can or can't date?" I
demand.

"Just stay away from her."

Scoffing, I roll my eyes. "Yeah, like I'm going to listen to
you."

"You should," he says.

"Why should I care what you say?"

"If you want to play football again, you're going to listen
to me." He glowers at me.

A glimmer of fear runs up my spine. I push it back, stomp
it down, bury it deep in the back of my mind.

Who the fuck is this guy to threaten me?

I shove my chair back and stand up. We're the same
height, though I outweigh him by a good hundred pounds.

"Go ahead," I tell him with a bravado I don't recognize.
"Try it. See what happens."

We stand toe to toe, breathing down each other's necks.

There are footsteps approaching us. He breaks first,
glancing at the person standing there. He takes a step back.

"Samantha," he says, and I turn.

Sam shoves her phone into her pocket. "O'Rourke."

"Hey, baby," I tell her with forced lightness in my voice. "I
didn't realize it was already two o'clock. You ready?"

Her smile is tight as her eyes dart between us. "Am I interrupting something?"

"Not at all." His voice is silky smooth. He has what other

people might describe as a charming smile plastered on his face. To me it just looks sleazy.

She grimaces and turns to me. "You ready to go?"

Shoving my books into my bag, I throw all of my things together. She offers her hand, and I take it, threading our fingers together.

She leans in, and I meet her halfway for a chaste kiss. She melts into me, deepening the kiss. She doesn't care that we're in public, that we're in the middle of the library. She doesn't care that O'Rourke is watching.

"I missed you," she says, leaning into me.

I can't shake off O'Rourke's eyes on us. "Missed you, too," I mumble, dropping a kiss to the top of her head. I nudge her forward, and we make our way through the library.

She waits until we're out of the building before she turns to me.

"Are you going to tell me what that was all about?"

"Just O'Rourke being O'Rourke."

Her eyes narrow. "Really? Because it sounded to me like he was bullying you. He was trying to threaten you."

There's a lump in my throat the size of Rhode Island. "It's fine. I'm handling it."

"It doesn't seem like you are. It seems like you're avoiding it."

How does she see through me so easily?

"I got him," she says.

"Got what?" My heart is in my throat.

"I filmed it, him threatening you. We can use that in the hearing tomorrow."

What we? There is no we. There's just me, alone, facing down the giant threat of being kicked off the football team for something I don't regret in the slightest.

"Delete it," I tell her.

Her forehead wrinkles. "But it will help you win."

"I don't care about winning. I just want football back."

"And winning is what gets you football again," she says slowly. "He's targeting you. He's threatening you."

"I'm not scared of him."

Even if maybe I should be.

O'Rourke may be a mean-spirited bully, but I'm not a victim. I won't let him relegate me to some weak peon. I'm not a favorable choice in this fight. I'm taller than him and outweigh him by a considerable amount. Nobody will believe it. They're going to take one look at me and presume that I'm the one wreaking havoc and threatening people left, right, and center.

"He has a thing for me," Sam blurts, and my world crashes to a stop. I turn to face her. "Josh Sinclair told me the other day. That's why he's ramping up his attacks on you. He's trying to get to me."

"Do you…" I clear my throat. "Are you interested in—"

"No," she says immediately, reaching for my hand. "No, no, not at all. He's an asshole. Just because he has a thing for me doesn't mean I want anything to do with him."

"If you wanted to…"

"I don't," she tells me. "I have absolutely no interest in him. I just wish he would leave you alone. I wish he wasn't targeting you because of me."

"I can handle it." I can handle him. We just have to get through tomorrow.

"Then what's your game plan?" she pushes. "What are you going to say?"

"I'll figure it out."

"Miles…" She reaches out for my arm.

"I don't want to talk about it, not with you, not right now."

She frowns.

"I just need some space. I'll catch you later, babe." I lean down and kiss her temple. I can't be around her right now. I can't do anything right now.

forty-two

. . .

Sam

RIVER STARES at me disapprovingly from over their tortoiseshell glasses. "You didn't."

I sigh. "I did."

"Sam…"

"I know. I *know*," I tell them. "It's not like I set out deliberately to defy your advice. It just kind of… happened."

"It happened," they repeat. "You tripped and fell into a relationship with your statistics tutor."

"We're still studying?"

"Studying statistics? Or studying biology?"

My cheeks flush. I can't deny that we've definitely spent some time studying one another…

"I feel confident about my test this morning," I say instead. "I think I've got this."

"No," River says. "I *know* you've got this."

"I do. I know the material backwards and mostly forwards. I'm confident. No last minute cramming, no frantic studying… we've reviewed everything until I know what I'm doing."

"Good. That's exactly what I want for you."

The real test will be this afternoon, at Miles's honor code board hearing. I hope the work I've done will be enough.

I can't tell River about that, though; I know they will be less than supportive. Technically I shouldn't be involved at all. Really I shouldn't know anything about the details. In reality, Miles has told me pretty much everything—except how he plans on defending himself. He's said it himself, he's not sorry he did it; he's sorry he got caught. He's not a fighter... except when he is.

And today, he needs to fight. He might not be willing to stand up for himself, so it will fall to me to stand up for him. He's being stubborn. I have video proof of O'Rourke threatening him. That has to be enough to get him off the hook. Right?

But the altercation with O'Rourke happened before Miles and I ever got together. He's been targeting Miles for ages. Whatever his issue with me is, it can't be what's driving this.

O'Rourke is just an asshole. He's slimy. He goes after anyone he perceives to be weak enough to tolerate his bullshit. I know he's made comments to Greg and Tucker. He's gone after some of the baseball guys. He doesn't discriminate in who he discriminates against. He's an equal opportunity bully.

Jake and I might not have gotten to the bottom of this new weirdness between us, but he was happy enough to help me out. He knows how important this is to me. He knows how important Miles is to me.

We've only been dating for a few weeks. We've been friends scarcely longer. There's something about him, something that makes him different than any other guy I know. He's not an alpha male asshole, and he's not a beta roll over and show his belly kind of dude. He just... he's calm and confident and composed, except when something triggers him. And only one thing seems to trigger him.

One person, rather.

I can't believe he thinks I would actually be interested in O'Rourke. He's slimy and sleazy and just all around awful. And even if he didn't go out of his way to harass me... he's not my kind of guy.

I like Miles.

His quiet strength. His steely spine. His unyielding kindness. His soft heart.

His kisses. His hugs. His touch. His cock.

Yeah, somehow it always comes back to sex. It's more than just sex between us, though. He makes me happy. We haven't been together long, but I have absolutely no complaints about dating Miles.

Okay, maybe I have one. I want him to stand up for himself like he stood up for me. Only without the suspension and disciplinary review this time.

River gives me some last words of advice and sends me on my way. I grab a bagel from the snack cart outside the math building, healthy brain food to keep my stomach from growling. When I get stressed, I forget to eat, which isn't good. I need to fuel myself like I'm getting ready for a softball game. This isn't a physical exercise: it's a mental one, and my brain needs all the help it can get right about now.

Miles is already sitting at his desk at the front of the room. I hand over the purple Gatorade I acquired for him before my appointment and he smiles wanly.

"You okay?"

"I will be," he says. Exhaustion lines his face.

"How did you sleep?"

We spent a needed night apart. If we'd been together, we would have spent more time having sex than studying and preparing for the exam. Not that there isn't a time and a place for sexy times. But the night before a midterm that I absolutely cannot fail? I went to bed early, got a good night's sleep, and ate a healthy breakfast before my first class of the day.

Professor Cassidy breezes into the room like nothing important is happening today. Without a word, he starts distributing the exam packet.

I can do this. I've got this.

Cracking my knuckles, I flip over the test and take a deep breath. This is totally doable. I'm a strong, capable, mostly confident woman. I've been studying for weeks. Miles and I have drilled these concepts until I know them backwards and forwards. I know this. I can do this.

The first question is something that we talked about just last night. I solve the problem quickly. The second question? Easy peasy.

I take my time going through the test. The nervous jitters fade away as I answer three questions in a row. I've got this.

My athletic eligibility depends on me passing this test. I'm reasonably confident I know the material. Miles and I have been drilling for weeks. I know this. I can do this.

forty-three

. . .

Miles

I'M NOT sure what I expected the honor code review board meeting to be. Something huge and imposing, with a judge in a robe on a podium gaveling judgement. Maybe I've been watching too many courtroom dramas.

We're in one of the conference rooms at the ASC. There's a staffer from the athletic department there to take notes. My judges are three people from the Council of Athletic Representatives, students elected by their teams to be judge and jury on disciplinary matters. Today they're a woman from the tennis team, a woman from the basketball team, and a guy I vaguely recognize as being part of the track and field squad.

Good. I was worried. I thought for sure there would be a guy from the volleyball team on my panel, a biased insider who would automatically vote in O'Rourke's favor. He has plenty of minions to do his bidding; he doesn't need any more.

Now, I might actually have a chance.

I don't know what kind of outcome I'm hoping for here. I want football back. I don't want to be kicked off the team. I don't want to lose my scholarship. But I'm not sorry for what

I did, and I can't force remorse that isn't there. O'Rourke is a dick, and he needed to be put in his place.

"Why don't you tell us what happened," the athletic department staffer says kindly. "Walk us through the night of October 9th."

My mouth is inexplicably dry. I wish longingly for one of my grape Gatorades. Anything to quench this impossible thirst.

"I was in the dining hall," I say, and then stop.

There's nothing I can say to defend myself. I beat on a seemingly defenseless dude until his nose broke, and then I kept punching him.

The tennis player waves at me. "Go on."

"I was minding my own business, returning the trays."

My sweatshirt feels impossibly tight. Did it shrink in the wash? No, it couldn't have. It fit perfectly fine this morning. My stomach gives a little lurch, and my lunch tries to decide if it wants to make an appearance.

"And then I punched him."

Track and field dude frowns at me. "Out of nowhere?"

"He was running his mouth. He said something—you know, fighting words? Something so grave, it has to be dealt with physically? Honor was on the line."

I sit back in my seat, breathing hard like I've just run fifty yards in full gear. I can't do this. I can't relive this, not again.

"What did he say?"

"I won't repeat it. It wasn't about me."

Basketball frowns. "Then what was it about?"

"He—" I stop, swallow. "I'm not a tattle tale."

"Help us help you," the staffer says. "From all accounts, you're an honorable guy. Good GPA. Good attitude. Your coach says you're a standout player with not one single disciplinary issue in the last two and a half years. So why now? Why this guy?"

"Was it about a girl?" the track and field dude asks. He

gives me a knowing look. "You and O'Rourke go after the same girl?"

I don't want to bring Sam into this. She doesn't deserve to have that kind of disgusting nonsense spread about her.

"He doesn't like me. He's never liked me."

"So you decided to beat his face in," the basketball chick says, full of doubt. "Got it."

The door bursts open. Sam pushes her way into the room, clutching her laptop.

"Excuse me, you can't be in here," the tennis player says. "This is a closed meeting."

Sam's eyes dart to mine before she squares her shoulders and approaches the conference room table. "I have information relevant to the subject of this hearing."

The track and field dude rolls his eyes. "This isn't some courtroom drama."

"I have a video of what happened," she says, standing her ground. "The entire conversation leading up to the punches. I can prove he was provoked."

Tennis player's eyes widen. "Let's see it."

"That's not relevant," I tell them weakly. I don't want them to see this. I don't want the entire fucking school to know how big of a tubby loser I am, to hear that kind of disgusting nonsense spread around about a girl who deserves the world. It starts here, and then the video will go viral. I can't handle that. Even if it would plead my case, I don't want that. I will never survive the whole world knowing exactly how pathetic I am.

"I think we'll decide what's relevant, Mr. Cavanaugh," the athletic department staffer says. "Play the video."

Sam sets up her laptop and plugs in a USB drive.

But the image on the screen isn't me punching Cavanaugh. Instead she plays several short clips, each one full of O'Rourke taunting me in the dining hall. Different days. I have no idea how she got the footage. I don't want to hear it. It's bad enough I hear his poisonous bullshit in my head every night when I go to sleep. Now I have it on video to replay whenever the memories get fuzzy. Now it's going to go viral, and the internet will never be scrubbed clean of the evidence. I'll never be able to move past this and forget.

"This isn't the fight," the athletic department staffer says sternly. "Don't make me kick you out. This is a closed hearing."

"We're getting to that. I didn't edit the videos together."

She's not really contrite, she's just acting like she is. I wish I knew what was going on in her head. What on earth made her think this is okay? I don't want her help, and I certainly don't need it. She's making a nuisance of herself inserting herself into something that has absolutely nothing to do with her. I would have reacted the same way no matter who he was talking about; he's heinous, and just because he was spewing poison about the woman I have feelings for doesn't mean I wouldn't stand up to defend an innocent bystander.

It just feels worse because he was targeting her, same as he was targeting me. That rock in the pit of my stomach sits heavy, bringing the nausea into full force. I can't believe she's inserting herself into something that has nothing to do with her. How could she? I told her to leave it alone; I told her I didn't want her help.

"You shouldn't be here," I tell her weakly. "I've got this."

"No, you don't," she tells me firmly. "You won't speak up in your own defense, so I'm going to do it for you. We're a team. You stuck up for me. The least I can do is stand by your side."

Track and field dude frowns. "He stuck up for you? This is all because of you?"

"O'Rourke has been targeting him for weeks. He finally snapped under the pressure," Sam says, standing her ground. "He threatened him in the library yesterday. I have video of that, too, if you want to see it."

The basketball chick and tennis woman exchange a look I can't read.

"We'll need to talk about this," the athletic department staffer says.

Sam clears her throat. "I also have proof that someone in the men's volleyball house is posting stuff about the two of us online. Rumors, insults, you name it. I wasn't able to confirm which player is behind it, just that it's coming from their house. O'Rourke has been targeting Miles for weeks. It's not one isolated incident. It goes back weeks before the punching incident. Another player on the volleyball team said that O'Rourke was bragging about it."

"How—" My throat doesn't want to cooperate. "How do you know it was them?"

"Jake is a computer science major. He tracked the IP address of the worst social media profiles back to their house. Either it's O'Rourke or one of his buddies that's been bullying you." She looks smug, overconfident.

And there it is. The word I've been hiding from all this time: bully.

I'm not a victim. I'm not helpless. I can fight back; I *did* fight back.

And that's why I'm here now. I retaliated. I stood up for myself, for her, and I'm the one who gets punished for it.

"I didn't know she was going to do this," I say quickly. "I don't have any comments to add."

I'm not about to cry out that O'Rourke is bullying me. I'm not trying to throw him under the bus to save myself, not because of who he is, but because I'm not a weakling about to crack under the pressure. I can handle some whiny little punk talking shit about me. Grown men pull apart my game play every week and whine about what a little bitch I am. I can handle this. He's a jerk, and one time I let it get to me. I won't let that happen again. I'll find the mental fortitude to push past his disgusting comments and let it go.

He won't be able to control me any more. He won't be able to have any influence over me anymore. I refuse to let him.

The panel whispers quietly amongst themselves.

"We'll have to take this under further review," the administrative staffer says. "You're free to go."

I stare blankly at them. "What does that mean?"

"It means you can go, dude," the basketball player says.

"I mean… can I play again? Am I going to get expelled?"

The three student athletes whisper amongst themselves again.

"You will serve a one-game suspension for punching another student athlete, in addition to the games you've already sat out," the tennis player says. "Any further disciplinary action will be communicated via email and your coach. You're free to go."

I don't feel free: I feel trapped.

forty-four

. . .

Sam

MILES DOESN'T LOOK HAPPY. He should be elated right now—a one-game suspension? That's practically nothing. It's a slap on the wrist. He gets to play again. He isn't at risk of losing his scholarship and getting kicked out of school. He has to sit out one more game, and only one more. His coach has already promised his starting line position back.

So why doesn't he look happy?

I follow him out of the ASC. He pulls on his gloves without looking at me. He makes no attempt to hold my hand. Normally he can't wait to touch me. Today it's like he doesn't know what to do with himself. He looks lost. Bereft.

"You won," I tell him gently. "Miles, you beat this thing."

"Yeah, let's talk about that," he says, bitterness choking his voice. He turns to face me. His eyes are hard. I feel like he's staring me down like he would an opponent on the football field. "How could you?"

I blink. "How could I what? Stand up for you? Prove you were provoked?"

"You barged in there! You had no right!" He's breathing hard, his face red. His hands clench into fists at his side. "I was handling it. I had it covered."

"Except you didn't," I tell him. "They were going to throw the book at you."

"I was fine!"

"We have proof that someone in the volleyball house is starting shit about you online," I remind him. "That's not nothing. O'Rourke has been targeting you for weeks."

"It's fine. I can deal with it."

"But you shouldn't have to." I reach for him, and he flinches back. "We're in this thing together. You stood up for me. Why won't you let me stand up for you, too?"

"We're not," he says, taking a step back.

"We're not what?"

"We're not in this together. It's just me," he says. "I'm by myself in this. It's my ass on the line here, Sam, not yours."

"Miles. This is how a relationship works. We lean on one another."

His eyes are sad. He looks broken down. Defeated.

"Then maybe we should be in a relationship anymore."

Um, what? What the actual fuck is this about?

He turns and walks away.

"Miles!" I chase after him, stopping him in his tracks. "We need to talk about this."

"There's nothing to talk about," he says firmly. Resigned. "I don't want to do this with you."

Flabbergasted, I stare at him. We've been on the same page every step of the way, and all of a sudden, he's ripping pages out of the book.

"What's that supposed to mean?"

He sighs. His eyes cloud with remorse. "It means I'm done."

forty-five

. . .

Sam

TAMAR COMES home to find me sitting on the couch in my pajamas, crying into a pint of ice cream.

"Oh, honey," she says, taking a seat beside me. "What happened?"

"He—he—" I can't get the words out. I break off into tears again.

"Yeah, she's been like this for a few hours," Lex says from the armchair, where she's been watching over me like a protective hawk. "I don't know what happened, either."

Saying the words will make it real. And I don't want it to be real.

I thought I was doing the right thing. I was helping him. And he seems to think that I betrayed him instead.

"Let's turn on Legally Blonde," Tamar says in her soothing voice. "That will make everything better."

She settles in beside me on the couch. Lex joins us and the three of us huddle together under a blanket as Elle Woods's douchebag boyfriend breaks up with her.

It just makes me cry harder.

He broke up with me. I keep replaying it over and over

again in my head. The sadness on his face. The resignation in his voice.

I just don't know why.

I thought we were good. We were a team, a partnership. Us against the world. I thought we were happy.

Never in a million years did I think he would dump me. And for trying to help him!

"So you really like this guy," Tamar says idly, and I glare at her.

"I don't want to talk about him."

"Okay, but didn't you say he had a big hearing today, for punching that volleyball asshole?"

I shove another chunk of ice cream into my mouth.

"Oh, honey. No. Tell me he didn't get expelled," she says quickly.

"He didn't. One-game suspension. Barely a slap on the wrist."

"And we're upset about this?"

"I don't want to talk about it."

"Sam…"

"My life revolves around more than a stupid guy who doesn't understand that I was only trying to help him." My chest aches, and I sigh. "He's not stupid. He's just being really stubborn."

"And you like him?"

Slowly I nod. "Until today, I thought we were solid. Until today, I thought we had something special."

"And now?"

I blow out a breath. "And now my boyfriend suddenly hates me, and I'm second guessing my statistics exam, and I might get kicked off the team and drop out of school, and—"

"Woah, there," Tamar interrupts. "You might get kicked off the team?"

"If I didn't get a good enough grade on that stats test," I

explain. "I'm teetering the line of academic ineligibility. Miles —he was tutoring me. We studied together."

"And did it help?"

"I thought it was." I sigh. "But now that I've had some space from the test, I know I could have done more. I didn't study near enough as I could have. I prioritized helping Miles over studying."

"Forget about that," she says. "What's done is done. How do you feel about your performance? Do you think it was enough?"

"I don't know." Pitifully, I eye the ice cream melting in my hand. "I really don't know."

"Why would you have to drop out of school?" Lex pushes. "You can take out a loan and—"

"I can't. I won't qualify, and my parents won't co-sign for me," I tell her. "It's more than I can afford, it's more than my parents can afford even if they agreed to it. If I don't pass this class, I'm academically ineligible, and I lose my scholarship for next semester. I don't have the kind of cash I'd need to make it work. And I can't raise my GPA without taking more classes, but I can't take more classes without the scholarship."

"Shit," Tamar says. "It's that bad?"

There's a lump in my throat. "Yeah," I whisper. "It's that bad."

"Oh, honey…" She rubs my back. "We'll figure it out. You'll pass this class and stay eligible, and you'll be back at second base next semester like nothing ever happened."

"I hope so. I really hope so," I admit.

"Why didn't you tell us?" Lex asks.

"I didn't know how. I don't want to be a burden on you guys. Things were already so tense, I didn't want to add to the fire. I thought if I studied my ass off, it would be enough. But now I'm second-guessing everything. Nothing I do is right. Maybe that was the wrong choice, too."

"Sam, we're friends," Tamar says gently. "Even if we're

going through a rough patch, we're still here for you. We'll always be here for you."

I inhale sharply and turn my head away, trying to hide the tears welling in my eyes.

"Then why were you such a bitch about Miles?" I can't say his name without the tears starting to fall. Angrily I swipe at my eyes. "He's done nothing to you. He doesn't deserve that."

"I didn't think you were serious about him," she says, like that's an answer.

"I was. I am."

"Even now?"

"Even now," I confirm. "We'll calm down, and we'll figure it out. We have a good thing going. He just needs to wake up and realize I was trying to help him."

Tamar blows out a breath. "We'll figure this out, too. We have a good thing going."

My smile doesn't reach my eyes, but it's a start. "I'm sorry I didn't tell you guys how serious it was."

"I'm sorry I was mean about him," Tamar says. "You're right, he didn't deserve that. I was jealous."

"Of what?"

"I didn't want you to find a new best friend." She looks away. "It's petty and childish, but—"

"Tamar, I have other friends. You're my best friend," I tell her flatly.

She swallows.

"Just because I have a boyfriend... had a boyfriend? Fuck if I know," I say. "Whatever is going on with me and Miles, that doesn't mean I don't have room in my life for you, too. You satisfy very different needs for me. I lo-love him, and I love you, in very different ways."

This makes the tears start up again. I love him, and he acted like I betrayed him by helping him! What on earth is going through his head right now? I really have no idea.

Plaintively, Tamar looks at me. "Are we going to be okay?"

I give her the benefit of an honest answer.

"It's not going to be fixed overnight, but I think with time we can get there."

Lex rubs my back and Tamar pulls the blanket up over us. I lean against my friends, and let their comforting presence soothe some of the ache deep inside of me.

All I want is him. His warm hugs and his devastating smile and his perpetual good mood. The way he'd run his hand over my spine, memorizing each and every one of my vertebrae. The way he held my hand without hesitation, the way he kissed me in front of his entire family without a care in the world. The way he went to bat for me, time after time, and refused to let me do the same.

The stubborn set to his jaw. The obstinate way he held his ground. His refusal to let his guard down. The way he haltingly revealed bits and pieces of his life, never giving me the whole picture.

I've got my friends by my side. Who does he have?

Sure, he has his teammates, but they're not close. He's all alone. He's always alone. He prefers to be on his own.

My heart physically aches for him. I miss him. It's only been a few hours but already I feel the absence of his calming presence, the void in my life.

I don't need a boyfriend to be happy. I don't need a man to feel whole. What I wanted was a partner, someone I could lean on when the going gets tough and in turn lets me support them when they need a little extra help.

And he won't let me. He refuses to accept my help.

And, yes, maybe I shouldn't have barged into the middle of his hearing. I could have submitted my findings to the panel without turning it into some big production.

I wanted to protect him, to stand up for him like he stood up for me. And instead all I did was hurt him.

Elle Woods is a badass. She applies to Harvard Law School to win back her ex-boyfriend—and she gets in.

I don't have a way to win back Miles. I can't magically win a position on the men's football team. I can't make him see reason.

I've been single before. I'll probably be single again. I didn't expect Miles and I to last forever. But I rather thought we'd make it more than two and a half weeks before it ended. I thought we were happy. I thought we were in a good place. It turns out I don't know nearly as much as I thought I did.

forty-six

. . .

Miles

GREG TELLS me I'm being a dick. I don't fucking care.

She crossed the line. She's the one who did the unforgivable.

It's been three days since my hearing. Three days since I ended things with Sam. I can't sleep. I don't want to eat. I can't focus on anything, not my linear algebra test or my English paper, not the TV or the video games my roommates want me to play. All I can think about is her.

Her, barging into a meeting she had no business being part of.

Her, with the devastating smiles and the innocent laughter.

Her, with the video that condemns me to a lifetime of hell.

Her, with the easy acceptance of me, the good and the bad and the ugly.

Her, with the knife in my back.

Her, with the beautiful body and the gorgeous pussy I want to bury myself in, again and again and again.

Her, with the meddlesome need to always be right.

And then at night, when I lay awake in my bed mourning

her absence beside me, I'm treated to the greatest hits of O'Rourke's best taunts. Tubby. Fatso. Loser. Pussy. Weak.

I hate this. I hate him. I hate her.

I don't hate her. I love her.

But she hurt me. She betrayed me. She had no business interfering in my private disciplinary matter.

A one-game suspension is practically nothing. It's a slap on the wrist. I'm a first time offender with a stellar record, and they have video proof that O'Rourke started it. It's not a difficult decision—for them or for me.

It sucks that the game I have to sit out is Parents' Weekend. Then again, nearly every weekend is parents' weekend for me. My family is set on coming to the game whether or not I'm playing. They're going to take me to dinner after, and it'll be like nothing is wrong.

They don't need a tour of campus; they both went here. Besides, they'll be back the next weekend, when Mack is spending the weekend with me. And they'll be back the weekend after that, for the Veterans Day game. Then we have an away game, and I'm sure they'll travel to that, too.

They're there for me. They support me unconditionally.

And I know that's what Sam was trying to do. She wanted to support me. But I don't need her support. I don't want to be weak in front of her. I want to prove to her that I'm strong, that I can handle it.

Even if I can't.

Because it's Parents' Weekend, I convince Coach to allow me to sit up in the stands with my family. It's not like I'm much use sitting on the sidelines in my suit. I can't call plays or hand out water—all I can do is sit there. So I might as well sit with my family.

Ash talks my ear off about her cheer competition and her newest girlfriend, a girl who's on the team at the rival high school. Ash is always finding new girlfriends, dating them for a few weeks, and then dumping them.

I guess we have that in common now.

"Where's your friend, honey?" Mom asks, smoothing out a wrinkle in my scarf.

"Not here."

"I'm sorry. Your girlfriend." She makes a face. "I'll do better."

"You don't have to do better. It's over."

"Oh, baby, I'm so sorry." Her hand slips down to mine and she squeezes my fingers.

Ash perks up. "Do we hate her? We hate her."

"I can beat her up," Mack offers, cracking her knuckles.

"We don't hate her," I tell the overly violent women in my life. "I'm the one who—who ended it."

Mom's eyes are wide with surprise. "But you like this woman."

"She did something that I can't forgive."

"She cheated on you?" Mack practically yells. "That's it. Where is she? I'm going to beat her up."

"She didn't cheat on me. She did something that I don't appreciate." I rub at my forehead. "It's complicated."

"So uncomplicate it," Mom says. "I was making plans to invite her over for Thanksgiving."

"Wow, that's a little much." I can't hide the sting of hurt. Sam and I won't have holidays together. We won't have a future together. We're nothing now.

I haven't seen her. She's eating in the dining hall at different times. We haven't had a stats class since our test, since everything went down. She lives two doors down from me, and I haven't seen her.

I wonder if she's avoiding me like I'm avoiding her, both of us going out of our way to hide away. I don't want to see her. If I do, the ache inside of me will open up and swallow me whole. I hate her.

I love her.

And people who love one another don't pull stunts like this. They don't throw a knife into one another's back. They support each other.

That's what she was doing, a voice says in the back of my head. She was trying to support me. She had good intentions, even if the delivery was off.

I didn't need her support. I didn't need her to rescue me. I was doing fine on my own.

It's hard to feign remorse when you don't feel any. I don't regret punching O'Rourke. I don't regret standing up for her.

"You're being an idiot," Mack tells me.

"Thanks, brat." I punch her lightly in the shoulder. She slaps at my hand. We tussle like we're children again.

"That's enough," Dad declares, and we settle onto the uncomfortable stadium seats. How do people sit on these things all the time? "Miles, apologize to your sister."

"Sorry, Mack."

"Mackenzie, apologize to your brother."

"I'm not sorry," she says resolutely. "He needs to get over himself and go get his girl back."

"I don't want to get her back."

She rolls her eyes. "She hurt you. Boo fucking hoo. Get over it."

"Language," Mom chides.

"I've never seen you as happy as when you kissed her in front of the entire family," Mack says. "You didn't even care that Aunt Carol was there. Aunt Carol! And the last few weeks, it's like you're lighter, like there's a heaviness to your shoulders that's gone away. Now there's a rain cloud over your head. You miss her."

"You don't know anything about the situation."

"I'm guessing it has something to do with your disciplinary hearing."

I gape at her. "How—"

"You're not very smart," she says.

"Mackenzie," Dad warns.

"You're not good at hiding your thoughts," she amends. "It's been hanging over you for weeks. You finally have your hearing, and then you dump her? You're an idiot. She's the best fucking thing that's happened to you in years."

"Of course she is," I snap. "She's amazing."

"Then why the hell did you dump her?"

"She… she…" I'm at a loss for words.

Sam doesn't care if I'm weak. She doesn't care if I'm benched or playing—she likes me all the same. She wanted to support me, and she did the only thing she knew how. What does it matter if her fraternity friend compiled those videos? Apparently they're all readily accessible online anyway. They haven't gone viral yet. Maybe they won't. Maybe there isn't a ticking timeline over my head.

She's heard all of the poisonous bullshit O'Rourke has spewed—and she doesn't care. She knows better than to believe it.

I should have given her the benefit of the doubt.

Shame strikes me like lightning. I should have heard her out. I should have opened up to her instead of shutting down. I should have talked about my feelings instead of abruptly ending it. I should have—I should have—

I should have told her I love her when she was more receptive to hearing it. She's never going to want me back now. She's not going to welcome me back with open arms. I'll be lucky to get a second of her time. All of her smiles? Those won't be mine. Not anymore. I don't deserve them. I don't deserve her forgiveness.

"Try to make it up to her," Mack says gently. "Apologize. Prove how much of an idiot you were. If she knows you the way you claim she does, she'll know this is what you do. You're a quitter."

"I'm not a quitter," I say, quietly but firmly. I straighten my spine and square my shoulders. "I'm *not* a quitter."

"Then go get your girl back, big guy," she says, clapping me on the back.

I scowl. "You don't get to call me that. Only she gets to call me that."

forty-seven

. . .

Sam

WHETHER I WANT to go or not, formal is going to happen. I have a dress. Tamar curled my hair. Lex did my makeup. My nails are freshly painted and my legs freshly shaved. I don't think Jake and I will be getting busy, tonight or any other night.

I don't want to go to formal with Jake. I don't want to go to the big dance, period. He was a last resort escort, and he knows it. He doesn't care. He's still too broken up over the breakup with Stacey to date for real. I'm okay with that. We're friends; we're only ever going to be friends.

I'm nearly ready to go when there's a knock on the door. It's probably Jake, ready to walk me over to the Kappa house.

I open the door to find not Jake but Miles on the other side, wearing a suit and tie.

I haven't seen him in three long days. I've been avoiding the dining hall at our regular meal times. I take the long way through Athlete's Village to get to campus. I do everything I can to disrupt my normal predictable habits.

And a lot of crying on the couch. My teammates are good at cheering me up. They just keep shoving pints of ice cream into my hand. I'm not complaining. My dress zipper might protest it, but my soul has been soothed. I can't cry any more tears over him. I refuse to allow it.

"What are you doing here?"

I have to resist the urge to fling myself at him.

"I told you I'd be here." He thrusts a bouquet of flowers at me. Sunflowers. My favorite. "For you."

I don't know what to think, how to react. He's here. He's seeking me out. After three days of avoiding him, I'm confronted by the reality of the situation: I don't want to avoid him.

But I don't know that I'm ready to forgive him quite yet. He can't sweep this under the rug.

"Miles…"

"I fucked up," he says. "I was thinking about me when I should have been thinking about you, about us. I'm sorry, Sam, I'm so sorry. I just… I couldn't do it. You were trying to support me, and I wouldn't let you."

I stand in the protection of the doorway, not letting him enter the house. He must be freezing. I'm freezing.

"You hurt me."

"I'm not used to needing to care about other people's feelings," he says, then winces. "That sounds wrong. I'm not used to letting other people help me. It'll take some time for me to… accept everything."

I swallow. "Everything?"

"Like the fact that I'm in love with you. That's pretty new. And it's terrifying," he says.

My heart skips a beat. "You—you love me?"

He nods. "I do. I think I have for a while now."

"Miles…"

"You don't have to say it back," he says immediately. "It's enough for me that you know. I was an idiot. I was selfish. I want to do better. I'm going to do better."

"I—I need to go."

"To the formal. Right." He pushes the flowers into my hand again. "For you."

"I have a date," I say.

And I watch as his heart breaks right in front of me. His eyes shutter first. His easy smile falls. He shuts down. He squares his shoulders and nods, like he's about to face down a fearsome opponent on the football field.

"I shouldn't keep you," he says, turning to go. "Take care."

"Wait." The words blurts out of me before I can stop it. "Let me call Jake. He'll understand."

He gapes at me. "You—you want to—"

"I never wanted to go with him," I tell him. "I've only ever wanted to go with you."

He crosses the porch in two giant steps. Before I can so much as blink, he sweeps me into his arms and bestows upon me the lightest, gentlest kiss in the history of the world.

"I love you," he says. "I don't deserve you, but I'm going to spend every day trying to be worthy of you."

I trail my finger across his cleanly shaven cheek. "You already are."

He kisses me again, his lips hard and demanding. His hand slips down to my hip, and he pulls us flush together.

"I'm crazy about you, Samantha Burke."

I run my hand through his hair. "I'm pretty taken by you, too, Miles Cavanaugh."

He coils a finger around one of my curls. "You look amazing, Sam. Like, I can't even... you..."

Laughing, I kiss him again, and again, and again.

He loves me. He wants to be with me. This was just a blip. We'll be back on track. He will—

I take a step back. I'm not the type of girl who falls to pieces over a guy. I don't like that that's what he turned me into. He can't magically heal the bruise on my heart with a well timed I love you and some sweet kisses.

"You don't get to unilaterally decide we're over again," I tell him. "You're supposed to lean on me like I've leaned on you. We're a team. We're in this together."

"I'm working on it," he says. "I was wrong to just shut down like that. I should have talked to you about what I was feeling. I was all caught up in how *he* made me feel, I couldn't process how I felt about it myself."

O'Rourke.

"I hear they're investigating him," I mention casually. "He's been bullying other people. It's not just you. He's—"

There's an angry slash of red coloring his cheeks.

"Don't use that word," he says quietly.

"What word?"

He swallows thickly. "That's not—he wasn't—it's—"

He's still processing. He can't admit that's what happened to him. O'Rourke's targeting of him was bullying, plain and simple.

And now O'Rourke is going to get what's coming to him. If the school can pinpoint that the online harassment is originating from his phone... well, he won't just be kicked off the volleyball team, he'll likely be expelled from the university. The school takes their bullying policy seriously.

"Okay," I tell Miles, running my thumb over his lower lip. "Okay."

He kisses my finger, swirling his tongue around the digit. "How serious are you about going to this formal thing?"

I laugh. "You're not getting out of it that easily."

forty-eight

* * *

Sam

THE BALLROOM at the Walton Hotel is decked out in Kappa turquoise and white. The decorating committee did a kickass job in setting everything up. Miles and I arrive a little late—we missed the hour of taking pictures, thankfully—and hand in hand. I'm not letting him go that easily.

Wendy has a few sharp words for my tardiness. She lets the lecture fall when she sees the smile on my face. I haven't been smiling lately. My sisters have helped to pick me up, but I haven't been myself.

I don't like that I fell to pieces over some guy—any guy. That's not me. Once I've had some distance from the last few days, I'm going to need some serious time to reflect.

Being with Miles makes me happy. It's as simple as that. We work well together. He's strong, physically and mentally, and if he needs me to pick up the slack emotionally, well, I'm happy to do so. Time will tell if he will really let me support him the way he needs to. A relationship is all about give and take. Right now, I'll give a little more if that's what it takes.

I can't keep my hands off of him. We sit down to dinner, and my hand lands on his thigh. He wraps his arm around

246

the back of my chair, drawing me into his side. I meet him for a chaste kiss that quickly becomes much less chaste.

"Jeez, get a room," Tamar says. She's grinning, her eyes bright. She's not poking fun; it actually seems like she's happy for me. For us.

"How about it, big guy," I tease, rubbing my nose against his cheek in what I hope is an alluring seduction. "Want to get a room for tonight?"

He swallows. "Here?"

"Or your place. Or my place. I'm not picky." My hand slides ever so slightly higher. He gulps. "As long as there's a bed, I'm happy."

He covers my hand with his and drags it back down towards his knee. "I'll go wherever you are." His voice lowers and his eyes soften. "I've missed you, baby. I'm sorry I was—"

"I know." I cuddle into his side. "I've missed you, too."

Dinner is adequate. Roasted chicken, some vegetables, potatoes. It's an average size portion for me. Poor Miles is left starving after he eats his tiny portion. His stomach growls and his face flushes a brilliant red.

"I haven't been eating so much the last few days," he admits. "I haven't had an appetite."

"I've been eating all the things," I admit. "My dress nearly didn't fit."

His eyes roam over my curves with a predatory glint. "You look great to me."

"Thank you." I meet him for a chaste kiss, mindful of the dozens of people in the room. If this escalates the way I want it to, I'll be pulling off his clothes within an hour. And I spent way too long on doing my hair and makeup for it all to be over so soon.

As dinner winds to a close, the dance floor gets more and more packed with people. Couples gyrate on the crowded dance floor. The tables empty out as everyone gets busy getting busy.

I place my hand high on Miles's thigh. "Would you like to dance?"

He gulps, his cheeks flushing a deep, velvety red. His eyes dart to the grinding couples and then back to me.

"I don't... my body doesn't move like that."

"We don't have to dance like they do," I tell him quietly. "I just want you to hold me."

He swallows. "Yeah, I can do that."

Offering my hand, he takes it and threads our fingers together. With the help of my heels, my head can rest on his strong shoulder. He pulls me close and slides his arm around my back, supporting me, grounding me. I twine my arms around him. He smells like Old Spice and something else uniquely Miles, enticing and familiar and so, so good.

The excessively loud hip-hop has people grinding and gyrating around us. We revolve slowly in a circle. His chin settles on top of my head.

This is all I wanted, to be held by him and to relax in the comforting circle of his embrace. A sense of calm washes over me. He soothes my aches and comforts my hurts. He doesn't magically make my life better. I'm not a better person or more whole because I have a boyfriend. I'm still me.

But now I have someone who loves me—and lets me love them in return. It's still early days. We have a lot of road to cover. We're going to have blips. We're going to fight. Life is hard. Relationships are hard.

I'm confident we can get through it together.

"My sister is coming to visit next weekend," Miles says, his arms tightening around me. "How do you feel about going to the Delta party?"

I lift my head to goggle at him. "You want to go to a frat party?"

"Not really," he admits. His thumb brushes over my

cheek. "I'm fairly certain you're going to want to go, and if you're going, I'm there."

"Yeah, it's part of the plan."

"So we're going." He gazes down at me, warmth in his eyes. "And you're okay if Mack crashes the party? We have to watch out for her."

"I'm cool with that." I want to get to know his sisters. I want to get to know his family.

"And my mom wants to know what you're doing for Thanksgiving. I know we still have a few weeks. Are you going home to Mississippi?"

"I haven't decided yet." My parents and I talked about it last week. It's a long, expensive trip for a quick weekend. I miss my family. I want to see them. But sometimes it's easier not to go home.

"She wants to invite you. If you're okay with that."

There's a lump in my throat the size of Rhode Island. "That would be... I..."

"Don't feel like we're forcing you into it," he says quickly. "The guys will all be there. If you want to go home or just don't want to deal with my giant crazy family—"

"I want to be with you. Wherever you are," I assure him. "Let me work everything out with my family. If I don't go home, I would love to join you."

He bestows a soft, sweet kiss upon my lips. "I love you," he says, brushing his nose against mine. He kisses me again, and again, and again.

forty-nine

. . .

Miles

THE FORMAL ISN'T NEARLY AS terrible as I was anticipating. Yeah, the food is mediocre, and the music is downright terrible, but I have Sam back in my arms where she belongs. Nothing could possibly compare.

She doesn't hate me. She still wants to be with me.

She's right that it's a shitshow. The party is full of sorority girls drunk off their asses and frat dudes drunk as skunks. I have one drink and nurse it for two hours. I'm not interested in alcohol like that.

Sam is pleasantly buzzed. Her hands are all over me. She can't stop touching me, like she's half afraid I'm going to up and disappear on her again. I'm not going anywhere, not without her by my side.

As the party dwindles down, we begin the laborious process of cleaning up after a hundred drunk college kids. The decorations are easy enough to take down. The people puking in the bushes, not so much.

Around one thirty in the morning, Sam drops into the empty chair beside me and groans.

"You okay, baby?"

"I'm so tired," she says. She rubs at her forehead. "Can we just go home?"

"Of course." I hand over her coat, helping her shrug into it. My fingers linger over the neckline. She shivers.

I offer my hand, and she takes it, threading our fingers together. We head to the portico, where we hail the first cab we see.

She doesn't waste time, snuggling up to me. I can hardly get my seatbelt on before she's curling up against my side, her arm slung around my waist. She rests her head on my shoulder, and I drop a kiss on the top of her head. She tilts her face up, and I give her a light kiss.

Sam deepens the kiss immediately, slipping her tongue into my mouth to tangle with mine. I can't hold back my groan. I thread my fingers through her hair, pulling her close.

"Hey, now," the cab driver says. "Not in the car."

Once the cab reaches campus, we have a half mile trek through Athlete's Village to get home. I don't care about the bitterly cold wind or the light rain sprinkling down on us, not when I have Sam's hand in mine.

She pauses when we reach her house. "Your place or mine?"

I shrug. "It's all the same to me."

With a coy smile, she leads me up the stairs to her house. Her room is on the second floor, first door on the right. Her window overlooks the limited expanse of the side yard.

It's only the second time I've been here. The first and only time I was here, she wasn't feeling well. I'm glad she's doing better now.

Sam strips out of her coat and scarf, leaving her in the thin little scrap of lace she calls a dress. She pulls her hair over her shoulder and looks up at me from beneath her lashes.

"Can you help me with my zipper?"

I cross the room in two strides to get to her. I pull her into my arms, pinning her back to my front. My hands trace the curve of her hips.

The first kiss lands on the side of her neck. The second is just below her ear. Sam sighs and sags against me. She moves my hand from her hip to her breast.

My cock kicks in my suit pants. I nose my way around the shell of her ear, breathing in her warm vanilla and sweet cherry scent. She smells good enough to eat.

My clumsy fingers find the tiny tab of her zipper. I inch the zip down, down, down, exposing more and more of her sweet flesh.

She steps out of the dress, letting it crumple to the floor.

Sam stands before me in her matching bra and panties and her sky high heels. She looks up at me from beneath her lashes.

"How you doing, big guy?"

My hands work at my tie, pulling it loose. Shrugging out of my coat and jacket, I slowly unbutton my shirt. She wants to see me, all of me. She doesn't care what I look like.

"Could be better," I say lightly, and she raises her eyebrows in silent question. I pull my belt through the loops. "Could be inside you."

She grins. "That can be arranged."

"Wear the shoes," I tell her, before I shuck my pants and stalk back over to her. I kiss her, threading my hands through her curls and pulling her flush against me. Her chest brushes against mine, her belly brushes against mine. I can't get enough of her curves. I can't stop touching her.

Limbs tangle as we fall onto the bed. She kicks the blankets down out of our way.

I break the kiss to make my way down her body. Pressing a kiss to her fabric-covered mound, she sighs and tilts her hips up. I nose aside her sodden underwear, and I wrap my lips around her clit and suck. Hard.

Sam moans, arching her back off the bed. Her breath is coming in short, rapid bursts.

I pin the fabric out of my way as I lick up her slit, gathering the evidence of her desire. She tastes like honey and sex. I can't get enough. I could do this all day. Her fingers thread through my hair. This time she doesn't direct me. She lets me go to work. I slip a finger inside her tight, wet heat, and her walls clamp down around me.

Laving my tongue over her clit, I suckle the sensitive bud as her moans increase in pitch and her hands scrabble at the sheets. The sky high stilettos dig into my back, scraping my skin in a delicious burn that's sure to leave a mark. I don't care. Her walls flutter around me and she throws her head back, letting out a long, loud groan. A burst of wetness coats my already slick fingers.

"Miles…" She can hardly breathe. There's a pleasant pink flush spreading over her cheeks, down her neck, and across her chest. "I need you."

Something inside of me breaks. My willpower is completely shattered.

Sam grabs the condom from her nightstand drawer. I roll the protection over my shaft and give myself a stroke.

I love her. I *love* her. I love *her*.

"Fuck me," the lady says, and I happily oblige.

Every time we do this, we get better and better. I know her rhythm now, what she likes and what makes her moan. She can't stop touching me, her hands tracing the contours of my shoulders and my chest, her nails digging into my back.

She doesn't care that all of her roommates are home and probably asleep. She's loud and unreserved, and I fucking love it.

Her moans urge me on. Working my hand between us, I rub circles at her clit, and a burst of wetness coats my cock. Her head tips back, and she arches against me.

I kiss the column of her throat, sucking the sensitive skin

there. I'm surrounded by the heady scent of her, vanilla and cherries and something else uniquely Sam.

"I—I—" She comes with a long, loud moan, her walls clamping down around me with a vise grip. Sam's legs tighten around me and then relax, her knees opening her up further for me.

My balls draw up, tight, aching. Pressure mounts in the base of my spine, threatening to overwhelm me.

Sated, her hand runs up and down my back, touching as much of me as she can.

Sweat slicks my chest. It pours down my face. She doesn't care. I pin her down and take, take, take what I need from her. Our lips meet in a hasty, heady kiss, tongues clashing. Sam bites down on my lower lip and that's it. Pleasure courses through me. She holds me through it, grounding me.

Withdrawing from within her, somehow I find the coordination to make my legs work. I clean up in the bathroom and come back with a warm washcloth. I help her clean up, and she falls back against the pillows with a sigh.

"You okay, baby?" I brush some of her hair out her sweaty face.

"Never better." She presses a kiss to my palm. "Come here and hold me."

Chuckling, I crawl into bed beside her. I scoop her into my arms and hold her close. "Your wish is my command."

In her arms I find peace. She likes me for me, for the person I am instead of the person everyone expects me to be. She doesn't care about my shape or my size or how well I perform on the football field. She doesn't care about my brains or lack thereof, or my grades or lack thereof. She likes me for me. She makes me want to be better. And for her, I will be.

epilogue

. . .

Miles

MACKENZIE WILL BE the death of me. My sister is only seventeen, but dressed up in a pair of tight jeans and a t-shirt, her hair and makeup done, she looks old enough to be a college student. I feel like I need to hang a sign around her neck: NOT LEGAL. DO NOT TOUCH.

Next year, I won't care. Next year, she'll be able to do whatever the hell she wants.

But right now, she's an underage high school student getting ready to go to a frat party, and that scares the living daylights out of me. I'll punch anyone who tries to mess with her.

"Now, let's talk about the rules," I say, and she rolls her eyes.

"Yes, *dad*."

"I don't care if you drink, but I don't want you getting trashed."

To my surprise, Mack nods readily. "I'll nurse one beer. I'm not interested in getting wasted."

"No hooking up with guys. Or with girls."

She's never really shown much interest in either sex, unlike Ashley, who's been dating since she was twelve. As far as I know, Mack has never dated anyone. Tonight is not the night for her to start, surrounded by people a few years too old for her.

She scoffs. "Please."

"You're underage. You could ruin someone's life."

"I know better than to go for older guys," she says, rolling her eyes again. "I'm not interested in hooking up with anyone tonight. I'm sleeping on your couch. Trust me, I'm not going to run off and bang some dude in the bathroom."

I cough. "Mackenzie."

"What? Like you and Sam don't totally get it on whenever you can?"

"That's different."

She makes a face. "Because you're in a relationship?"

"No, because we're both over eighteen and can legally consent to it."

"The age of consent in Massachusetts is sixteen," she points out.

"So?"

"You can relax. I'm not going to pursue anything with anyone. I'm going to nurse my one beer and kick back, have a good time. I just want to know what a college party is like."

She's full of bright-eyed wonder. I remember what it was like, being recruited, everyone wanting me, going to college parties with the roster guys trying to show me a good time. I didn't like it much then, either. Maybe parties and I just don't mix. I think I'm okay with that.

"Awful," Wes says from his reading chair.

"Thank you," she says politely.

I goggle at him. He never talks in front of people who aren't part of the football team. He's said a few words to Sam over the last few weeks, here and there. They get along. I like seeing her forging friendships with my friends, assimilating into my life. I don't know that I'll ever like Tamar, but I like Lex and Aleesha, and I get along with her sorority sisters.

Jake is an all right dude, even if he's more of a Call of Duty dude than a World of Warcraft guy. We both care about Sam, which is the most important part.

We start the walk over to the Delta house. As much as I would prefer to go to a Gamma party if we have to go to a frat party; they card everyone who comes in. The Delta douchebags don't care who shows up. On any other night, I should probably care more that they're letting seventeen year old high school kids in. Tonight, though, I don't care. What Mack wants, she gets.

Sam and Tamar link arms with Mack for the walk, chattering away. Sam is great with her, encouraging and friendly without crossing boundaries. I like to see my girlfriend and my sister getting along.

I smile to myself. My girlfriend. Yeah, Sam and I are on the mend. We're not going to be one hundred percent perfect overnight. I'm going to have to work harder to open up, to let her in more. It goes against my natural inclination to bottle everything up inside, but with her help, I'm confident I can get there. Eventually.

Inside the party, I pour three beers from the keg and pass them out. As an afterthought, I grab one for Tamar, too, who gives me a pleasant smile. She knows she's not my favorite person.

The music is already too loud, pulsing at a decibel that others might consider deafening. The place already reeks of body odor and stale pot. People are crammed into the house like sardines. Couples are hooking up in plain view.

And people like this shit?

I keep an eye on Mack as we make our way through the party to the back deck. It's bitterly cold out here even with the help of the space heaters.

Sam laces her fingers through mine. "She's a big girl," she tells me. "She can handle herself."

"I know. I just worry."

She leans up on her tip-toes. I meet her halfway for a kiss that I intend to keep chaste. She deepens the kiss immediately, her tongue slipping into my mouth to tangle with mine. My cock jerks, and I have to remind myself there's a time and a place. I won't let her seduce me to distract me.

"You're a good brother," she tells me.

I brush a loose strand of hair behind her ear. "Thanks?"

She tightens her grip on my hand. "Come on. Let's mingle."

Oh yes, mingling. An important part of partying. She talks to various people she knows, other athletes or fraternity brothers. I vaguely recognize some of them. Others, I have no clue who they are. She doesn't care that I don't have much to contribute. Every once in a while, she turns her head and looks up at me, her heart in her eyes.

And maybe that's enough.

I don't want to be at this party, but Sam does, and I want to be where she is. I'm interested in the things that interest her. Just like she'll sit on the couch watching Jeopardy! or a superhero movie with my roommates, I can make some sacrifices if it means I get to spend more time with her.

It's all about balance. We give and we take, ebbing and flowing like the Charles River. When she has a bad day, I know she wants to dive head first into a pint of mint chocolate chip ice cream, macros be damned, and she knows nothing will cheer me up faster than a bottle of grape Gatorade, lightly chilled.

She knows me, period. Every day we learn more about each other. Every day we grow closer to one another. She makes me want to grow more, to be a better man, to stand up for what's right, for the people who can't stand up for themselves.

Sam breaks off in the middle of her conversation with one of her sorority sisters. She wraps her arm around me and rests her cheek on my chest, staring up at me.

"What?"

She shakes her head, burrowing deeper into me, until we're practically fused together. "Nothing."

"If it's nothing, that means it's something."

"I just really like you," she says.

I have to laugh. "You say that like it's a surprise."

"Not a surprise. A pleasant revelation."

I have to lean down and kiss her. I have to show her how much she means to me. And in the process, she shows me how she feels about me. She hasn't said she loves me yet. I know I jumped the gun. She shows me how she feels with her actions, not her words. And for now, that's all I need. For now, all I need is her.

afterword

Thank you for reading *The Game Plan*. This book is my baby and I absolutely love it to pieces.

You know what would make it even better? A review! Reviews are more important than readers realize. If you liked this book, please leave me a review!

Sam and Miles are forever, and you'll see snippets of them throughout the rest of this series. You can read their extended epilogue here.

Join my newsletter to stay in the loop! Lots of unfunny quips, unsuccessful attempts at wit, and general grouching about the writing process.

xoxo,

Allie

about the author

Allie is a queer and AuDHD writer with a hyper-fixation on inclusivity and representation. She loves the color purple, Michigan football, and the Boston Bruins. When she's not absorbed by a book, she likes to spend time with her nephews.

Born and raised in Southern California, she now calls South Carolina home. She is allergic to the cold, rain, snow, and mosquitos.

also by allie lasky

The story continues with BLITZ, a second chance romance featuring peanut butter sandwich-lover Tucker and the track and field star who broke his heart.

———

Meet the Neurospicy Book Club in THE THOUGHT OF YOU: Falling for my Grumpy Roommate, where Johanna finds out she's autistic… because her happy-go-lucky new roomie (and reformed playboy ex-football player) has to tell her.

www.ingramcontent.com/pod-product-compliance
Lightning Source LLC
Chambersburg PA
CBHW030812210726
48290CB00002B/558